Before she started writing l
in I.T. until she came to hei
journalism and writing. Sh
Health & Fitness magazine:
content and media releases
organisation. In 2011 the fiction bug bit and Helen has
been writing fiction ever since.

Helen J. Rolfe writes uplifting, contemporary fiction
with characters to relate to and fall in love with. The
Magnolia Girls is her ninth novel.

Find out more at www.helenjrolfe.com, and follow her
on Twitter @HJRolfe.

The Magnolia Girls

Helen J. Rolfe

To friends I've made along the way ... no matter how far apart we are the best friendships always go the distance

Chapter One

Carrie looked around at the boxes in her apartment. Instead of facing up to everything that had happened, here she was leaving her life and a flourishing career behind. She wished she could put on a brave face and get through it any other way, but this move seemed to be the only solution.

'You don't need to worry about me,' she reassured Kristy. Her sister had come over to help her pack, but Carrie was finding it hard to convince anyone that she could handle things her way.

'Just don't forget I'm here if you need to talk.' Kristy sounded as though she'd resigned herself to the fact that Carrie wasn't going to spill any more of the details behind this sudden move, and pushed a collection of folded tea towels into the top of a box.

As sisters they didn't look much alike – Carrie took after their mum, Kristy after their dad – but they both had the long, wavy blonde hair that turned heads, and the tanned skin that loved the sunshine. Kristy had been the less confident of the two sisters once upon a time. She was the non-academic of the pair, but she was the one who'd come out on top with a successful marriage, a job she was happy with and a sense of togetherness and calm that Carrie envied and hoped to one day find herself. Their mum always claimed that the kindness of strangers was the biggest and best kindness of all, and as girls they'd been taught to include others, welcome unfamiliar faces, embrace peoples' quirks and differences. But over time Carrie had begun to find it hard to let anyone in to her life. Her family claimed she was too independent and resourceful for her own good, and lately Carrie wondered at what point her strengths had become her weaknesses.

Carrie hadn't told many people about what had happened to trigger this major change. Not that it was a huge secret – her boyfriend, Lachlan, knew, but Carrie had always been a private person intent on processing things her way and so she hadn't shared it with anyone else. Sometimes she wished she could let people in, but somehow she'd missed learning that skill growing up and it seemed to get harder the older you got.

She taped up the last box of her belongings and heaved a sigh of relief. It felt like a start. Her things would go to storage until she sorted out her new house and then surely she'd be able to figure out her next step.

Kristy wound her hair up into a high ponytail. 'It's getting hot in here. Mind if I open the balcony doors?'

'Go ahead.' Carrie had already tied her hair back. It was hard work packing up and cleaning the apartment ready for the off, but relief swept in on the breeze that flowed into the tenth-floor apartment. The Melbourne sun graced the apartment for a good proportion of the day and the blinds would usually be tilted when it was so hot, but on moving day they couldn't afford the luxury. They needed to keep going.

Kristy stood in the path of the fresh air for a moment and then looked over her shoulder at Carrie. 'Promise me that if you need anything...*anything*...you'll call me. I know how hard you worked to get to where you are. I'm so unbelievably proud of you, and always will be.'

Carrie smiled, grateful of the encouragement. 'I just need some time out, that's all. Medical school was full on after my degree, and I haven't stopped since.' As a paediatrician, first it was learning the ropes in the preliminary stages, then all the hard work as a trainee on the job, and even once you'd made it there was the ongoing need for continuous learning and staying abreast of the latest research and advances.

'I know you haven't, but I also know you love it. Not everyone can say that about their job and I'd hate to see you walk away from something so dear to you.'

'I love my career, but I need a break,' Carrie said firmly, as though saying it out loud would be enough to convince herself that was all it was, a break. She'd thrived on her career for so long but she couldn't see a way forward unless she moved away from the norm and tackled something different for a while.

With the packing done, Kristy cleaned the insides of the floor-to-ceiling windows, amusing Carrie every time she moaned at how hot she was. 'It's like being in a greenhouse,' she said, yet again moving into the stream of open air from the balcony doors for a bit of relief.

'I appreciate your help.' Carrie called from the kitchen area where she had her head inside the corner cupboard, wiping down the shelves, the back of the door.

Kristy declared her job finished and asked, 'What time will Lachlan be back?'

'He should be here any minute now.' Lachlan had been transporting her things over to a storage facility since the crack of dawn.

'He's been an absolute star. You're a lucky girl, Carrie.'

Carrie smiled. She was lucky. Sometimes it was easy to forget when Lachlan told her time and time again that this move was ludicrous, that what happened was part of her job and she needed to deal with it head-on. She'd not got much sympathy from him; then again, maybe he was trying to help her see sense and be strong, and in some ways he was right. But it didn't mean she wanted to hear it over and over, a constant reminder of how she couldn't handle a situation that many in her position would've taken in their stride.

From the moment Carrie had introduced her heart-surgeon boyfriend, eight years her senior, to her entire family, they'd been in awe of him and how clever he must be. Carrie's mum was an interior designer, her dad ran a chain of bottle shops in Melbourne's outer suburbs, and Kristy was the only other person in their family who had moved anywhere near to the medical profession, by training as a medical secretary. All of them were floored that this man was so clever, so able with his hands, and, as her dad had told her jokingly one night, 'He's not bad to look at either'.

'I still can't believe you've bought a place so far away.' Kristy handed Carrie a can of Diet Coke from the fridge. 'And a place that needs work doing. This apartment is immaculate – I can't see you living in a mess for too long.'

'I'm not that bad!'

'Oh, come on. When we were growing up you used to tidy out the shoe cupboard for fun! You'd clean when Mum and Dad were out to surprise them when they came home. You're a neat freak, Carrie.'

'I'm sure I'll cope.'

'We'll see.' Her sister looked doubtful. 'But, I'll admit, you've chosen well. I fell in love with Magnolia Creek the first time I went there and I have fond memories of Magnolia House, where I got married.'

Carrie smiled at her sister. 'It was a beautiful day and an amazing wedding. I hope you'll come and see me, visit Magnolia Creek again.'

'Just try and stop me.' Kristy sipped her drink. 'When do you start the new job? Carrie-the-babysitter. I can't imagine it myself.' She shook her head, amused. 'You and babies don't exactly mix unless it's in a medical setting.'

Carrie elbowed her sister as she too hopped up on the edge of the kitchen bench, their legs dangling together in a row like they had back in their younger days, cooling down eating ice-creams by the ocean after school.

'I like babies,' Carrie pointed out. 'That's why I took the job.'

The position she'd taken as a nanny, or babysitter as it could also be referred to, was in Melbourne's Dandenong Ranges, at the edge of Magnolia Creek, a town Carrie was already familiar with. She'd be looking after Maria, a ten-month-old baby girl whose parents, Tess and Stuart, worked full time and were waiting for a place to come up in a childcare facility. When Carrie had applied for the job they'd snapped her up even though she didn't have any first-hand experience in nannying: it was her job as a paediatrician that had clinched the deal.

'Think you can handle the job?' Kristy wanted to know.

'Of course I can. She's ten months old – what could possibly go wrong?' In truth, she wasn't sure how she was going to handle three days a week looking after a baby for seven hours straight. Kristy was right. She did love kids, but she'd never spent that long a time with any of them, especially without any other adult company.

'And what about this other job?' Kristy grinned. 'Yes, Mum let it slip that you had something in the pipeline.'

'I can't keep much from you, can I?' She hadn't mentioned it in case she couldn't go through with a new role that would thrust her back into the hospital environment. She didn't want to admit failure all over again. 'Do you remember Serena?'

'Lachlan's friend with the drawn-on eyebrows?'

Carrie giggled. 'That's the one. She works at a new hospital near Magnolia Creek and Lachlan put us in touch. She's got a pilot project she's desperate to get off the ground and wants me to be involved.'

Kristy stopped sipping from her can. 'A paediatric position?' she asked excitedly.

'She's setting up a baby-cuddling program and wants me to be a part of the set-up and the operations of it.'

'Well it's a start – it'll keep you in the game, so to speak. I don't think you'll want to be out of the job for long.'

Carrie knew her sister was giving her a nudge to tell her more about what had happened, but there were a lot of things Carrie couldn't handle right now and analysing the situation she'd been in was one of them.

Kristy finished her drink and rinsed out the empty can ready for recycling just as a knock at the door signalled Lachlan's arrival.

'Hey gorgeous.' Lachlan hugged Carrie the second she opened the door. He always did, and always kissed her full on the lips no matter who was around, who was watching.

'Hey you. That's the last of them.' She pointed to the boxes stacked by the door waiting for him. He'd been hauling boxes all morning but still had that scent of aftershave and an immaculate appearance. With his olive skin, dark eyes and deep brown hair he was neat, together and, most of all, hot. When Carrie had first met him at the hospital, she'd been barely able to string a sentence together because he was, as she'd overheard somebody say, 'drop-dead gorgeous'.

She stepped over the pile of discarded bubble wrap, dodged the rolls of thick brown tape, and handed him a cold can of drink from the fridge.

'Thanks.' He kissed her again before beaming a smile Kristy's way and, as they launched into a chat, Carrie was reminded that this man would do anything for her. When she'd upped and left for the Gold Coast five months ago without so much as a hint that she was walking away from her job he'd still been here when she came back. She'd half expected him to have moved on but he hadn't, and it was that faith in her that drove home how much he cared and how much he was in this for keeps.

'Are you meeting with the property developer today?' Lachlan put down his can of drink and hoisted a box into his arms. 'Owen, was that his name?'

'That's right.' She had told her boyfriend that she knew Owen from way back, via Kristy. He hadn't asked anything more, and she'd already given Kristy the heads-up, saying it was easier not to go into the real details. Kristy had shrugged nonchalantly and said it didn't affect her, but wondered whether honesty would be a better policy in the long run.

Carrie dated Owen more than a year ago, but they'd never been serious. A nomadic, fun guy who bought and renovated properties for a living, Owen was no more a threat than Neville, the short, rotund, balding man who worked alongside Lachlan at the hospital and ate way too many pies on his lunch break.

Carrie had contacted Owen when she saw the house in Magnolia Creek up for sale, asked for his advice and expertise, but she'd never told Lachlan that he was an ex because Lachlan, the confident, unflappable heart surgeon, had an insecure streak when it came to his girlfriend. When they first started dating he'd been adamant that Carrie could have her pick of men and even though she'd insisted she only wanted him, when other men crossed her path, particularly anyone who made her laugh and smile, he got really uncomfortable and didn't like it. At the time she'd been flattered. Her previous boyfriends had let her be herself, do what she liked, talk with whomever she wanted. It was nice to feel as though her man wanted her close, but lately it was becoming a strain. She needed time to think, time to process, and she wasn't getting that here in the city.

'I'm hoping Owen will be able to come to the house today or tomorrow,' she said, 'so we can go through the changes I'm looking at doing to the property.'

Lachlan winked at her. 'Make sure he doesn't rip you off because you're a gorgeous blonde with long legs and…' His voice trailed off when he caught Kristy's look. 'OK, enough details. Just make sure you shop around for prices, get a good deal.'

'Don't worry, I will.' Carrie grinned. She might be blonde and female, but she knew how to handle people who tried to take advantage.

'Good, and we'll soon have a great weekender we can use whenever we like,' Lachlan declared, 'or even rent out to holidaymakers.'

Carrie smiled because it could be a good idea long-term – but, then again, she hadn't really thought much past its purchase and renovation.

When Lachlan and Kristy disappeared with as many boxes as they could realistically put in the lift at once, Carrie got on with the task of cleaning the wardrobe in the bedroom. She wiped it all down and then used glass cleaner on the mirror. Lachlan had ranted on about how meticulous she needed to be to get her full security deposit back and so she'd been up with the sunshine today, ensuring she left everything shipshape.

And now with all the boxes gone, the entire apartment sparkling clean and ready for the real estate agent to do the final inspection, Carrie stood at the edge of the room and took a final look at the apartment she'd lived in for almost two years.

It was time to start a new chapter in her life. And maybe the only way to move on was to turn one page at a time.

Chapter Two

It was early March and the weather in Melbourne was beautiful as Carrie drove her black Mercedes up to Magnolia Creek. She'd stayed with Lachlan last night, enjoying seafood in a restaurant overlooking the Yarra River, and whilst she'd always loved the city, driving away from it this morning felt like the start of something. Quite what, Carrie wasn't sure, but with every kilometre between her and the life she knew, the life she'd thrown everything at since she decided at the age of sixteen to follow a career in medicine, the more she felt that this was the right thing to do.

Two weeks after returning from her hiatus on the Gold Coast, Carrie had found the nannying job. She was needed within eight weeks, and when she couldn't find a suitable place to rent, she decided it was as good a time as any to take the leap and get on the property ladder. Ever since she'd made up her mind, it had been a whirlwind of house-hunting, bidding at an auction for the first time, a 45-day wait for settlement and, boom, her new life was lined up and waiting for her.

'You should be grovelling for your job back at the hospital,' Lachlan had insisted when she'd told him her plans.

'I don't grovel for anything!'

'You can't give up on a career you've worked so hard for,' he said more kindly. 'I'd hate to see you do that.'

She calmed down too. 'I'm not saying I'm walking away for good. I need a little time. This is only a temporary change and it'll give me a break from the norm.'

'You've just had a break. In the Gold Coast, remember?' So together and composed, this man usually took everything in his stride. His jaw tensed and she knew he was finding it hard that nothing he said seemed to get through to her.

She wrapped her arms around him. 'I promise you I'm not going to fall apart again. Think of this as a shrewd business move, a start in the property world, and once I've had the house renovated, we'll take it from there.' She clasped his hands in hers, feeling less confident than she sounded.

Carrie knew Lachlan wanted more for her. Their lives together had been ideal – both of them moving forwards in their careers, both working hard and putting in the hours – but now they'd veered off course, Carrie had no idea how to get back on track.

The sun had pole position in the sky as she got further away from the city and continued her journey up to Magnolia Creek. Before she'd bought the house, her memories of the town were of Kristy's wedding and Owen's parents' sprawling house with its gardens, pool and air conditioning. This time Magnolia Creek was set to be very different and she giggled out loud as she drove along with her shades pulled down, her mane of blonde hair let loose. The house she'd bought could best be described as a 'hidden beauty'. She'd heard the phrase from Owen back when they were dating. He liked to buy properties and see them achieve their potential, and she hoped she'd manage to do the same with this house that needed so much doing that friends and family thought she'd gone a little insane.

She stopped off at the real estate agent in Fernybrooke, the suburb she needed to pass through on the way to Magnolia Creek, and with the keys to the house on the passenger seat she drove on, followed the bend round to the right. She passed the yellow triangle warning sign with the chunky, black wombat silhouette that signalled to her this wasn't the city anymore, and, beneath the canopy of trees that formed overhead as the road narrowed, she saw the sign reading 'Welcome to Magnolia Creek' in big loopy letters.

The house she'd bought was at the top of a very steep hill, past the quaint little school. Her car climbed the hill easily and she pulled into the driveway on the right. She got out of the car, keys in hand, and took in the sight of the brick house with its sturdy front door that the owners had put in with its fly-screen security door, although Carrie doubted anyone would ever bother to break in given there was nothing inside to pinch, including any fixtures or fittings. Behind the front door, she knew there was a shell that needed a hell of a lot of tender loving care to put it right again.

Carrie let herself in and stood in the hallway. She couldn't stop smiling. On auction day the place had been overrun with eager buyers and she'd been nervous. Lachlan had come with her and bid for the property, his poker-face giving nothing away until the auctioneer's hammer fell, when he'd turned to her and kissed her full on the mouth to say congratulations. But, now, it was nice to take the first steps inside on her own.

The floorboards weren't bad and thankfully there was only one old threadbare carpet to be taken up in the lounge, beneath which were more floorboards, which she hoped could be sanded and polished and brought back to life easily enough. The kitchen would need to be ripped out; same with the bathroom. Carrie touched a hand to the pine cupboards on the wall of the kitchen at the end of the hallway but immediately wished she hadn't when she felt the grease and grime signalling years of neglect. She guessed she'd done it because this was hers, and the thought had her buzzing for the first time in a long while.

She took some wipes out of her handbag as she walked back through the house and into the room on the opposite side of the corridor to the lounge. The floorboards creaked as she stood in the empty space with nothing but an ornate fireplace for company. She'd already decided to keep it because following the survey of the house she knew it was merely dust and dirt that made it look unusable, and beneath all of that it would come up as good as new with a superior cleaning solution plus a lot of elbow grease.

Carrie finished wiping her hands and, back in the hallway, followed the narrow staircase up to two bedrooms. The bathroom off the main bedroom was old – nothing like she was used to – but in a box in the car, along with a single airbed she'd use for a couple of weeks until the bedroom was ready, she had a tartan shower curtain she'd bought especially. She tried the taps and the shower attachment, and although not great, at least they were functional.

Excited to be here and eager to settle herself in, Carrie went back to her car and, beneath the autumn sunshine and pleasant outside temperature, opened the boot to pull out the few boxes she'd brought. She had cleaning cloths, liquids, rubbish bags and scrubbing brushes in one, along with a few pairs of marigolds. In another she had sheets for the airbed plus a pump. Another box contained tea towels and bath towels along with three bottles of liquid soap, one for the laundry sink, one for the bathroom and the other for the kitchen. She took the boxes inside, as well as a duvet and a suitcase full of clothes.

As she climbed the stairs with the cleaning equipment she noticed the banister would need repairing too and already she thought she might paint it white to brighten the place up. The existing wood was a nut-brown colour but she wanted the inside of the house to resemble a seaside cottage, a Cape Cod style house interior except on a smaller scale. She could see it in her mind's eye already – with soft furnishings and a rug in the lounge, plantation shutters at the windows – and she was glad that even though she had chosen a career in medicine, she'd inherited a little bit of her mum's passion for interior design.

Carrie got to work scrubbing the bath and the sink in the bathroom and although she couldn't rid it of years' worth of grime, it would do for now. She swept the floor in the bedroom and plugged a couple of holes in a floorboard with scrunched-up balls of newspaper, which she secured in place with duct tape across the top, laughing at her own ingenuity and way of keeping any spiders or creepy-crawlies at bay. She unfolded the airbed and pumped it up, covered it with a sheet, pulled the duvet cover on and the pillowcases, and for a moment she almost collapsed onto it. Cleaning the apartment, packing up, and now this, had taken most of her energy and all of a sudden the prospect of doing anything else seemed insurmountable.

Relieved to hear a knock at the door, she leaned her head out of the window in the bedroom. 'Owen, is that you?'

The figure down below stood away from the front door to show that her guess was right and he waved up at her. She galloped down the stairs and went to greet the man who'd become a good friend. He'd been kind enough to offer his services for renovations, having come to the end of a job only last week and without another lined up for at least a month.

'It's as great as I remembered,' he commented as soon as he stepped inside. He put his shades up on top of his head. 'I almost fought you at auction for it.'

'Is that so?'

He shrugged. 'I thought about it, but no. I could tell when you got in touch that you were in love with the place and I couldn't do that to you.'

'Well I'm glad you didn't. Did you watch the auction?'

'No, too busy putting in a new kitchen for someone up in Healesville.'

'You're a busy man.' She smiled. 'That's why I really appreciate you doing this for me.'

'Hey, it's my job – and working with someone I actually like has its benefits. The client I have at the moment is a hoverer. Tells me what to do, hangs around supervising.'

'That must be annoying.'

'I'm all for the client giving their input, it's kind of essential. But when they follow me too closely, it's as though they don't trust me to do the work properly.'

Carrie thought back to Lachlan's warning not to get ripped off with the renovations and already she was glad Owen was someone she knew and could trust.

'Nothing like a blank canvas.' Owen looked around again, touching walls, peering round corners, below windowsills and behind door frames.

'I can't even offer you a cup of tea I'm afraid, because I can't find the teabags.' She shook her head. 'Sorry, I'm no hostess. Back in the city, yes, but here – I'm already out of my depth.'

'No worries. It's a bit too warm for tea anyway.'

It was. Carrie had thought it was a mild summer's day but in here without air conditioning, and working away cleaning and trying to make it at least liveable, she was feeling the heat. 'I do have a few glasses with me. How about a water? The tap works.'

'Perfect.' He didn't follow her into the kitchen immediately. He was too busy looking at the wooden floors and the fireplace more closely. 'Mind if I go upstairs?' he called as he appeared in the hallway.

'Sure.' They'd discussed the preliminaries and Carrie couldn't wait to go into more detail once he'd had a really good look around.

'You're lucky,' he said as he returned from investigating upstairs. 'The windows in this place are all in pretty good condition, and secure, so they won't need replacing – except you may want frosted glass in the bathroom, but I know someone who can sort that for you.' He went into the laundry. 'The glass in this door is weak,' he said. When she poked her head around the doorway he was feeling a glass panel. 'I'd get that one done too, for security, although the panels in the door will stop anyone climbing through as they're so small. Nice touch with the balled-up paper by the way.'

She felt herself blush. He'd seen her handiwork upstairs. 'Sorry, I just can't bear the thought of spiders or anything else sneaking in when I'm asleep.' She shuddered. 'The additional wildlife around here may take some getting used to. I've already noticed the cobwebs in the trees out front, and another flapping away at the side of the house.'

'You're such a girl. Once the renovations are done you can get the place sprayed.'

She handed him the water when he came back into the kitchen. 'Believe me, I will. And I appreciate all the suggestions.'

'You're an easy client.' He smiled at her. 'Did you order the white goods?'

'I did. The washing machine is coming tomorrow, plus a fridge freezer, a microwave and a tumble dryer. I appreciate you saying you can work around them.'

'Easy. The washing machine and dryer can go in the laundry already as the cabinetry is almost non-existent in there. They won't have to move again. And the fridge freezer can go anywhere in the kitchen and I'll shift it about as I need to. Find a place for the microwave wherever you can and that'll be easy to move when we get going.' He paused. 'Can I ask you something? Why the rush? Why move in up here and put up with the mess? I know you, remember, and you don't live like this.'

Carrie shrugged. 'It won't be so bad. I can make decisions along the way without racing back and forth to the city; I'll be here to see the house evolve into something better.' She wouldn't tell him that the longer she stayed in the city, the more pressured she felt to go back to the hospital. Camping out in a grotty house and putting up with renovations going on around her would be easier than Lachlan's gentle, persuasive remarks or his suggestions aimed at helping her but actually doing the exact opposite. Last week they'd had lunch with an old friend of his and when it turned out the man was in Human Resources at the hospital, Carrie knew it was no coincidence. She was seething at being set up – but how could she really be that angry when all Lachlan was trying to do was help?

17

'Do you have a laptop here?' Owen's question interrupted her train of thought. 'You'll need to check out the websites I gave you and make some firm decisions on fixtures and fittings. I know you've chosen the main bits for the kitchen and bathroom but it's all the extras you need to decide on: taps, showerhead, tiles you'd like, et cetera.'

'I do have my laptop, but no WiFi in the house yet.'

'The joys of moving.' He downed the rest of his glass of water.

'It's OK, I can use the hotspot from my phone.'

'Great. Do it sooner rather than later.'

'I will,' she promised. 'I get a surprisingly good phone signal out here.' She looked at her phone again to see it had the full five dots at the top indicating coverage was the best it could be.

'Maybe it's a perk of living at the top of the hill.' He grinned. 'I'd forgotten what it's like to walk up here.' He sniffed his armpit. 'I'm gonna need another shower I think.'

'Yeah, you reek.' She pinched her nose for effect.

'Careful, or I'll leave you to cook meals in that stinking kitchen. Those cupboards are full of grease you know.'

'Don't you dare!' She pulled a face. 'When do you think you could make a start?'

'Next couple of days. I'll rip the kitchen out first, then the bathroom, then the floors, and I'll do the painting last. You can come over to the cottage when your shower is out of action; Rosie won't mind.'

'I hope this won't make things awkward between you and Rosie.'

'Because of our history?' He shook his head. 'Rosie is absolutely fine about having you around. In fact, she told me to invite you for dinner at the pub tonight, with both of us. You can't eat here so you have no excuse.' He looked around and pulled a face, stretched out a hand and trailed his fingers down the grease on the side of the oven. 'You won't need to buy any cooking oil – looks like this kitchen comes with its own.'

'Now I feel ill.' She passed him a wipe from her handbag.

'Will you come?'

She smiled. 'What time?' She wanted to make sure Rosie was as comfortable with having an ex-girlfriend hanging around as Owen said she was.

'How does seven thirty sound?'

'I'll be there.'

He sniffed his armpit again and made a face as though he couldn't believe he smelt so bad. 'I'd better get going and have another shower. Oh, and I've spoken to a local guy about the garden.'

She looked out of the kitchen window at the outside space. 'Jungle more like.'

'Well, yeah. It's a jungle now but this guy will give you a reasonable quote to sort it out. I won't have time to tackle it myself so I'll stick to the inside and leave him with the outside. You're entitled to shop around for quotes though. Don't feel obligated.'

Carrie already knew that unless Owen's recommended person charged a ridiculous price she wasn't going to bother shopping around. She didn't have the energy. 'If you're happy with this guy and say he's reasonably priced, let's go with that.'

'Anything for an easy life, eh?'

'Something like that.' The fact he hadn't asked about Lachlan or her reasons behind this move away from her normal life told Carrie that Owen probably suspected there was more to it than what lingered on the surface. But he was good enough not to pry, and that was the sign of a true friend.

He raised a hand to say goodbye at the door and turned before he was out of sight. 'Got something to tell you later by the way.' And he tapped the side of his nose.

'Tell me now!' she called after him.

'My lips are sealed!' And he disappeared behind the bushes to saunter off down the hill.

Shutting the door, she smiled inwardly. Owen had gone from boyfriend to friend and he was one of those people you could go for years without seeing and always know you'd pick up where you left off when you finally did. She didn't have many close friends – the result of a busy time concentrating on her studies – and already it felt good to know he was in her corner. She wasn't attracted to him anymore and she knew the feeling was mutual. They'd had their fun and that was that, and soon after things ended between them she'd met Lachlan and hadn't looked back.

She glanced around the kitchen again. Truth was, she couldn't wait to see this place ripped apart and put back together with her stamp on it. Lachlan owned his apartment in the city and was forever asking her to move in with him, but she'd always thought if she moved in with someone it would be to a place they chose together, somewhere special.

Her tummy grumbled loudly and she found an apple lurking at the bottom of her bag. It would have to do until dinner time. She leaned against the kitchen sink and enjoyed a brief rest while she ate, then she checked her watch and, with plenty of time until she was due to meet Owen and Rosie, went upstairs to tackle the jobs that still needed doing. She gave the toilet the once-over, put towels in the bathroom and arranged a few toiletries on the shelf behind the bath.

Enthused by the thrill of something that was just hers, she nipped outside and plucked a few stems of lavender from the bush taking over the front path. She put them in a glass, filled it with a little water and set it in the corner of the bedroom. It would be something to lift the aroma of grubbiness and neglect. She sat down on the airbed, amused by the unstable surface and the bounce you didn't get on a normal bed. And then she opened the diary on the floor and looked at the special photograph inside. This picture was her biggest reason to get away from everything she knew and try to find herself again.

She tucked the photograph away and went to hang the tartan shower curtain up so that she could start getting ready. The shower rod was reasonably new and she hoped it would last until the new bathroom was installed, and already the room looked better with her splashes of colour. She lined up shower gel, shampoo and conditioner, peeled off her checked shirt and put it in the cardboard box by the bedroom door, which would do as a laundry basket for now. She wiggled out of her jeans and put them in the box too, along with her bra and knickers. When a fleeting search for a hook produced nothing, she hung a towel over the bathroom door handle ready to grab.

Stepping into the bathtub, she turned on the taps and when the shower spat out a hopeful amount of nice warm water she stood beneath the flow, letting it fall through her hair and listening to the sound of the drops hitting the enamel surface beneath her. She washed her hair, lathered a grapefruit shower gel all over her body and by the time she'd finished the bathroom was filled with steam. There was no extractor fan so in an effort to clear the room and cool down before she completely overheated, she squeezed out her hair and, before she retrieved her towel, went to fling open the window to get some relief.

But relief wasn't exactly what she got when she came face to face with a man standing on top of a ladder the other side of the glass, hands cupped around his eyes, peering in.

Carrie screamed louder than she'd ever done before. And then she ducked. Her breathing heavy, she crawled to the door and seized the towel, careful not to let the man see any more of her than he already had. She was in the middle of nowhere and there was a pervert at the window! She'd left her phone downstairs so without even looking to see if the man was still lingering, she fled the bathroom and padded down the stairs as her hair dripped down her back and water from her legs left wet footprints on each step.

In the kitchen she reached for her phone and there was the man again, this time looking in the back door right at her. He had the audacity to knock but there was no way she was opening that door.

'I'm calling the police!' she yelled, waving her phone at him and then unlocking it ready to dial.

'Owen sent me,' he hollered back at her through the glass.

She stopped, her breathing rapid.

He pointed behind him to indicate the backyard space. 'To talk to you about the garden.'

She put her phone down and, clasping her towel tighter, opened the door.

'Thanks,' said the man. 'I was beginning to think you'd make me yell like that the whole time.'

She didn't miss his eyes stray towards where she was clutching her towel around her chest and then down to her bare legs. She bristled. 'Do you often go round the neighbourhood peering in through unsuspecting people's windows?' The start of a smile crept onto his face until Carrie's glare put a stop to it.

'I did knock first, but when there was no answer and nobody seemed to be around I thought I'd have a look at the place.'

'My car's out front – wasn't it obvious I was here?'

He shrugged. 'You could've gone for a walk; it's a beautiful evening.' When she didn't fall for his charm he said, 'You need to get the gate sorted, put a lock on it to stop people like me invading your privacy.'

'Well you've certainly done that!'

'I apologise.' His failure to stop the start of a smile suggested he wasn't sorry at all. 'I noticed leaves clogging the gutters and with this being a bushfire area I thought I'd clear them while I was here.'

'I know it's a bushfire area – I'm not stupid.' Actually, she had no idea of the precautions you needed to take in a town like Magnolia Creek, and she wouldn't really have given the gutters much thought had he not mentioned them.

'I didn't say you were stupid, but that's why I was up the ladder.'

For an awkward moment Carrie said nothing. 'Well, thank you for doing it.'

He leaned against the doorjamb, his muddy forearm against the paintwork. He held out a hand that was just as dirty. 'I'm Noah,' he said.

Gripping her towel with one hand, she reluctantly held out her other to meet his. 'Carrie.' His grip felt firm, strong.

23

'It's nice to meet you, Carrie.'

Blushing because this man had already seen her naked from the waist up and they were only just introducing themselves, she told him, 'I'm meeting friends for dinner so I'm not sure I have time to talk now. How about tomorrow morning? I'm free all day.' Owen had done her a favour by sending this man here so she didn't want to be rude. And shopping around for a gardener didn't thrill her in the slightest.

'Sounds good to me.' He stopped leaning and clasped his hands together, and Carrie couldn't help it but her eyes went to the paintwork by the door to see if he'd left it dirtier than it had been before. She couldn't tell. It was well and truly in need of a clean anyway, like the rest of the place. 'Mind if I clear the gutters while I'm here with a ladder?'

'That's very nice of you. Thank you.' Was he going to do it without payment? Surely not.

'You'll get used to it – out here in Magnolia Creek we like to look after each other.' Clearly he wasn't expecting any reward for his labour. He turned to go down the side of the house but turned back briefly. 'You might want to stay away from the windows if you're getting changed.'

Without replying she shut the door and scarpered upstairs. She grabbed her clothes and stood in the corner of the bedroom where she couldn't possibly be seen through any of the windows should he choose to pop up and surprise her again. And by the time she left the house to walk down the hill towards the pub for dinner, Noah was nowhere to be seen.

Chapter Three

Owen didn't even bother trying to conceal his amusement. 'That's priceless!'

'I'm glad you think it's so funny.' Carrie punched him in the arm as they sat with Rosie in the beer garden of the Magnolia Tavern. It was dark now and white twinkly lights woven between the branches of the trees sparkled in the moonlight.

'You must've been mortified,' said Rosie, not without amusement, as she lifted her glass of orange juice to her lips. 'I'm sorry, but you have to admit it's a tiny bit funny.'

Carrie let herself laugh and covered her face. 'He saw me completely starkers from the waist up! How am I supposed to have a conversation with him about my garden now?'

'You can talk about your lady garden.' Owen couldn't lift his pint he was laughing so hard.

'Stop it!' Carrie pleaded.

'I'm sorry, it was an obvious joke.'

She hadn't mentioned the encounter to Lachlan when he'd called as she walked down to the pub because she doubted he'd see the funny side. He'd be up here like a shot, whisking her back to the city, and she wasn't ready for that.

'Can we please change the subject?' Carrie requested. 'I'm embarrassed enough, so let's talk about something else.'

Rosie shot Owen a warning look that enough was enough. 'I'm glad you agreed to join us,' she said. 'It's really lovely to see you again.'

'It's been a while.' Carrie smiled. She'd wondered whether things would be awkward with Rosie given that

Owen and Carrie had been dating when Rosie appeared on the scene and stole his heart quite unexpectedly, but so far Carrie felt completely at ease.

'I hear the house is a bit of a wreck,' said Rosie. 'Owen will help you make it beautiful again.' Her straight copper hair hung down the middle of her back and trusting eyes rarely looked away from her man.

'I can't wait to get started.' Carrie paused. 'Actually, I'll rephrase that. I can't wait for it to be finished, but I guess I need to be patient. Tomorrow I'll talk to Noah about the garden —'

'Maybe do it with your clothes on this time,' Owen quipped.

'Ignore him,' said Rosie. 'You'll have to come and see Rosie Cottage. Owen did a brilliant job; he put in a gorgeous window seat, which comes highly recommended – especially if you like to curl up and read a book.'

Carrie was interested. 'I'd never thought of a window seat but I like the sound of it. There's plenty of room in the main bedroom for one.'

'You employ me now,' said Owen. 'Whatever you want, I'll do. Within reason.' He grinned.

'I almost forgot…' Carrie sipped her wine, a welcome treat after all the hard work over the last couple of days. '…what was it that you wanted to tell me?'

Owen put his arm around Rosie's shoulders and they both looked pretty pleased with themselves. 'We're having a baby.'

Carrie almost knocked the drinks over in an effort to reach them both and hug them. 'That's amazing! Congratulations! How far along are you?' She looked at Rosie wondering why she hadn't guessed. The girl was definitely glowing, even beneath the subtle lighting outside.

'Nearly twenty-nine weeks.'

'But you're hardly showing at all!'

At her comment Rosie took off her light-weave cardigan, turned to the side and pulled the fabric of her loose-fitting top against her.

Carrie laughed. 'You're showing now. I can't believe that slipped under my radar.'

'I told Rosie to wear a top that kept it a bit hidden,' Owen admitted. 'I wanted us both to tell you properly. I love seeing the look on people's faces.'

'So when are you going to make an honest woman of her?' Carrie asked.

'All in good time.' He looked admiringly at his girlfriend, stretched out a hand to her bump. 'We didn't plan this – it was something for the future – so we're being a little bit unconventional.'

When the landlord, Chris, called over to say their table was ready for dinner, they filed inside and Carrie asked Rosie all about her pregnancy. It was going smoothly, they weren't going to find out the sex, she'd had relatively little morning sickness and slowly they were collecting all the paraphernalia you'd need to bring a little one home. It was something Carrie knew she'd never need to think about herself.

They scanned the menus as soon as they sat down and ordered straight away.

'When do you start your new job, Carrie?' Rosie was already buttering a bread roll and Carrie did the same.

'I start Monday. I'm looking forward to it actually.' She'd explained the position to Owen and presumably he'd filled Rosie in on all the details.

'It'll be a big pay cut.' Owen whistled through his teeth. 'And the paediatric world will surely miss you. It was your dream career once upon a time.'

Sometimes she forgot that despite them both having a lot of fun in their relationship, this man had got to know things about her. 'It still is, don't worry. I just need some time out. And being here means I can focus on the house.' None of it was a lie but what was left unsaid was the complete truth.

'Good to know.' Owen, the typical man, didn't delve further but Rosie gave her a passing look that said she knew Carrie was holding something back.

Carrie told them all about the family she'd be working for in her nannying position, how it was less than a five-minute drive from her house, and she told them about the baby-cuddling program she'd be involved with at a newly opened hospital not far from Magnolia Creek.

'I don't think I've ever heard of baby cuddling.' Rosie shook her head at the offer of a second piece of bread, preferring to save herself for her main course.

'It's done quite a lot these days,' said Carrie, 'both in Australia and in several countries around the world. And it really is a good initiative. I've never been on the organisational side of paediatrics so I'm quite excited about nurturing the project to establish it as part of the hospital's plan.' It was also her way of returning to work in her own way. She'd fought to make a strong career and no matter how tough it was, she wasn't ready to give it up – she just didn't know how to find a way back in.

'You never know,' said Rosie. 'You may end up enjoying it so much living out here that you don't want to return to the city.

'It's different, for sure. Peaceful.'

They stayed in the pub for hours and both Owen and Rosie walked Carrie home. Rosie claimed she needed the exercise and Owen had insisted Carrie didn't walk on her own. When they left she searched the car and eventually found the box of teabags that must've toppled out. She made a cup of tea, lit a scented candle in the lounge room and plonked herself down on the leather beanbag she'd managed to cram into the back seat of the car for furniture until the house was ready. She had no television for company, only a big pile of books, so she'd taken relaxation to a whole new level and, sitting here in the dark, it felt like completely the right thing to do.

*

The next morning Carrie woke to sun streaming through the window, which had a lemon-yellow curtain hanging across it. The material was so thin it did nothing to block the light. Her mum would say it was no better than a summer dress hanging up there rather than a suitable piece of window dressing but Carrie, for once, didn't care. In the city she'd cherished her sleep, darkening the room until she could see nothing, using earplugs to block out the sounds of the city outside, even using an eye mask if she'd been on nights and needed to sleep during the day. But out here in Magnolia Creek she didn't want to do any of that. She felt alive in a way she couldn't describe – at least not to Lachlan, who'd think she'd finally lost it if she tried to explain.

She stretched her arms over her head and sat up. She'd slept surprisingly well in a strange house, on a bed that moved whenever you did. It was nothing like the plush-carpeted apartment in the city with its floor-to-ceiling mirrors in the bedroom, everything clean, neat and in its place.

In the bathroom she peered out of the window to check she didn't have any surprise visitors and, certain the place was clear, put her towel at the end of the bath, ready to grab before she went anywhere near the glass again. She'd learnt her lesson last time.

After showering and dressing she made her way downstairs. The dust inside was more shocking in the daytime. She'd forgotten all about it last night beneath candlelight, able to envisage what the place would be like once it was finished. There were no major structural changes to be made, a fact she'd ascertained when the house was surveyed pre-auction, so the work would be cosmetic, not overly expensive and, best of all, fast, so it would be a proper home soon enough.

Carrie plugged in the small toaster she'd brought with her and popped in a couple of slices of bread. She took out some butter from her small esky and although it wasn't completely cold it was good to use. When the toast was ready she scraped the golden spread across its surface.

Next, she switched on the laptop, got the personal hotspot functioning, and decided it was time to make a firm decision about the fixtures and fittings.

Shortly after nine o'clock, when Carrie was surfing the internet and deciding whether to go for a freestanding bath and separate shower cubicle or a shower over a contemporary bath to create more space, a knock at the door announced the arrival of the white goods she'd ordered. She smiled. She didn't mind living semi-rough, but there were some things you couldn't do without.

When the men left, the first thing Carrie did was make a list of things to buy. She'd have a cardboard box for dry goods, she'd fill the fridge freezer as best she could with food that required minimal preparation or cooking, and somehow manage around the mess. If you'd told her a year ago, as she'd cradled a glass of Baileys and curled her feet beneath her on her pale floral sofa in her apartment that she'd be living like this in the country one day, she would've laughed and said it was utter nonsense. Now, it seemed like a wonderful adventure, distracting her from the real issues in her life.

She jumped when a figure appeared at the back door. Her hand on her chest, she opened the door to Noah. 'Do you like scaring me or something?'

'Sorry, thought my whistling would be enough to alert you.' He smiled back at her. 'Ready to talk about the garden?'

'Sure.'

'You'd better do that up properly, looks expensive.' He nodded to her watch.

Carrie tutted. The clasp had come undone, again. It would be far easier to buy a cheap watch and then she wouldn't have to worry about losing it all the time.

'A gift was it?' he asked as she fiddled with the clasp to secure it.

'Er…yes, it was. Anyway, shall we?' When he looked down at her feet and the white, sparkly thongs she had on she asked, 'What's wrong?'

'It's overgrown out there; you'll probably cut your toes to shreds in those if there's anything prickly. Do you have anything else?'

With a sigh she went into the lounge and found her only other pair of shoes, slip-on ballet flats. 'It's all I've got,' she told him as she followed him out to the back.

Beneath the sun, bathing the overgrown backyard space and highlighting all its weaknesses, they talked about how they could transform the mess into something manageable. Decking would be laid across the back of the house, a new fence would enclose the garden, with trellises added on for more plants and flowers to give colour, and the old dilapidated shed in the corner would be torn down and replaced. Noah suggested a pergola with a base beneath it at the foot of the garden, with shade created from plants nurtured up its sides. They agreed on curved flowerbeds providing the perfect perimeter to add a splash of vibrancy, and by the time she and Noah had finished conferring, Carrie thought it all sounded wonderful.

'Just make sure it's fairly low-maintenance.' She drew a rough circle in the air with her hand. 'All of it.'

He nodded but the look on his face hinted he wasn't finding this job as easy as it should be and Carrie had no idea why. She was a dream client, wasn't she? She was giving him a virtually free rein after all.

'I'd suggest going for a deciduous climber such as bougainvillea for the pergola.' Noah was unable to resist pulling at existing shrubs and plants, casting bits aside, examining others more closely.

As they'd gone around the garden and he'd thrown various names of plants, trees and shrubs at her to tell her what had once been here, still was, or could be, Carrie's face had been blank most of the time. And although she had no idea what a deciduous climber was, she knew bougainvillea. 'I agree,' she said, if only to remind him that she was employing him so he should be polite and not give her any more strange looks. When he looked doubtful that she knew what he was talking about, she added, 'My boyfriend took me on a surprise holiday to the Greek Islands last year, and bougainvillea was everywhere. Set against the whitewashed houses it was gorgeous.' *Ha, that told him!*

'Fancy.' He seemed disinterested and Carrie couldn't work out whether the 'fancy' applied to the flower or Lachlan's gesture of taking her on holiday.
'Bougainvilleas come in shades of red, purple, apricot, orange, pink, cream – lots to choose from.'

'I think I'd like the pinky-purple I saw in the Greek Islands.'

He seemed to approve of her choice and indicated to each side of the garden, talking about how to fill the curved beds they'd talked about. He suggested clematis, which she'd heard of but had no idea what they looked like, and also something called a guinea flower, which she thought sounded revolting.

'It's a climber and produces big, bright yellow flowers, so if you want colour it's a great option. You could have it going up the fence.'

He ran through a few more species and they trampled around the space, Carrie doing her best to avoid any particularly muddy patches with her pale pink ballet flats and Noah lumbering through merrily in his clumpy steel-toe-capped boots.

Her shades firmly down she watched him as he made more notes on the pad he'd brought out here. He was grubby, not like the scrubbed, efficient and clean doctors she normally aligned herself with. He didn't give off a waft of aftershave but rather a smell of the sun, of the earth and a man scent that wasn't offensive in the slightest. She wondered then whether he had someone at home waiting for him. Someone who didn't mind dirt being traipsed through the house she decided, when he wiped the mud from his hand on his shorts.

'I think I've got all the details I need.' Noah slid his sunglasses on top of his head and turned in time to see her watching him, although from behind her own sunglasses she knew he wouldn't have been able to catch her looking at his bum in his khakis when he bent over. Gardening obviously kept him in good shape and even though he wasn't her type, she could still appreciate an attractive man when she saw one.

'I'll put everything together,' he said, 'draw up a design and price the quote, then get back to you. How does tomorrow sound?'

'Is there any way you could give me a rough idea now?'

'You're keen.'

'A ball park figure will be enough for me to know whether to give you the go ahead.'

'I'd hate to give you an amount and then find it changes, there's a lot to consider.'

'I'm happy with that. I know it won't be exact, but as long as it doesn't end up being thousands more, I can live with it.'

'I like a woman who's decisive.' His comment hovered between them until he pulled a scrap of paper and a pencil from his back pocket. 'Let me see what I can do.'

He wandered around the outside space, scribbling things down, his brow creased in thought. Carrie went inside for a drink of water and it wasn't long before he appeared at the back door and knocked gently.

He gave her an approximate cost. 'I can give you the exact figures tomorrow, but if you're happy with the quote, I'm happy to make a start in the morning. There'll be plenty of prep work to do. I had a client cancel on me yesterday and so all I've got on right now is finishing a garden over in Fernybrooke. I usually overlap jobs but that one is near completion so I'll be able to focus on you.' He looked uneasy. 'On this place,' he corrected.

Carrie did her best not to grin. 'I guess I'll see you tomorrow.'

'Look forward to it,' he called after her as she walked back towards the house.

Chapter Four

'He's a good guy, Carrie.' Owen pulled at the cupboard door in the kitchen until finally it came off its hinges. He discarded it on the pile in the corner.

'I'm sure he is.' After Noah left and Carrie chatted on the phone with Lachlan before he went into surgery, Owen had shown up to start the first stages of the renovations, which involved a lot of noise, a lot of physical strength and a great deal of mess. It hadn't taken him long to deduce from Carrie's conversation that she had her misgivings about Noah.

Owen ripped out a drawer and prised the runners away from the side of another cupboard using a chisel. 'You don't have to like the guy. But he'll do a good job in the garden for you.'

'I suppose you're right.'

'You know I am. And besides...' He wiped the sweat from his brow. Without air conditioning, physical work took its toll quickly. '...if he's seen you naked I'm sure he likes you.' He earned himself a clip round the ear from Carrie. Laughing, he said, 'I guess I deserved that.'

'Are you sure I can't help?' she asked when Owen reached to the top cabinet next and began to wrench its door off.

He looked down at her. 'I know you're just offering to be polite.'

'Of course I am. I think we both know it's best I stick to supervising you.'

'I don't need babysitting, but you've already helped anyway.'

'How's that?'

'By making firm decisions on what you want. Some clients take forever and change their minds over and over, but you've made your decisions and stuck with them.'

Before Owen had been allowed to get started, Carrie had taken out her laptop to show him the oven she liked, the cooktop, colours of the benchtops, the bath and the accessories she wanted. She'd spent hours choosing them but had enjoyed every second, visualising what the house would be like when it was complete.

The cabinet door finally came off and he lowered it to the ground, and with the kitchen stripped, Carrie insisted on helping move the wood outside to dump in front of the house ready to be taken away.

'It's like kindling,' she said as they surveyed the big pile at the front of the house when they'd finished.

Owen laughed. 'You obviously learned a bit from being with me.'

'Should I keep it all for when the fireplace is up and running?'

He shook his head and wiped his brow. 'It'll get wet out here and you've nowhere to store it. I've asked Noah to help get rid of all the debris as we gradually pull everything out.'

'That's nice of him.'

'I told you, he's a nice guy. Now, I suggest you get out of my hair or I might make you help me rip out those laundry cupboards, and I'm pretty sure I saw a huge huntsman at the back of one.'

'Dead or alive?'

'Dead.' When she breathed a sigh of relief he added, 'Not necessarily a good thing. You've got to wonder what killed it.'

'I'm out of here,' she grinned. 'I'll see you later.'

With the chance to escape, she picked up her bag and walked down the hill and into town. Magnolia Creek was a pretty place. She'd enjoyed the odd day here when she was with Owen and again for her sister's wedding at Magnolia House, set behind Main Street and beside a gorgeous lake. She knew that bushfires had done their worst in the next town and had tried to take this town too, but now the café had been rebuilt, and there were enough tall trees lining the sides of the roads to mask anything sinister that may have happened before.

The sun kissed her neck and shoulders as she walked down Main Street enjoying the gentle breeze that kept her cool in her long floaty multicoloured dress – a complete change from her usual everyday attire. At the hospital she'd always dressed smartly in a trouser suit or a skirt with a nice shirt, she'd wear heels and fix her hair in some kind of up-do to keep it out of the way. But now, with her thongs back on her feet, makeup-free, her hair hanging long down her back, there were no rules, no regulations, just the feeling of freedom.

When she spotted Rosie she waved. She crossed over outside the pub they'd had dinner at last night and immediately smiled. 'Pregnancy suits you. I can definitely see your baby bump now!' Rosie had on a summer dress too, and it clung to her shape to tell the world of the expected arrival.

'Thank you.' Rosie beamed. 'I was about to go and say hello to Gemma in the chocolaterie, if you're interested.' When Carrie said she'd love to, Rosie added, 'My chocolate consumption has gone up a notch – well, a few notches if I'm completely honest – and they've got some heavenly salted-caramel chocolate bars.'

'Now you're talking. I'm glad I have my purse.'

'Oh come on,' said Rosie, 'don't tell me you eat chocolate – not with your gorgeous figure.'

'I love the stuff!' She didn't add that she ate more when she was stressed, had the occasional breakout of spots on her face when things got really bad, and it was her anxiety that probably burned off all the calories before her body had a chance to even think about storing them away.

Inside the chocolaterie Carrie and Rosie browsed while they waited for Gemma to come through from out the back. They admired the individual chocolates beneath the glass-topped counter, the novelty chocolates made into different shapes including a handbag, a stiletto shoe and a tennis racket.

When a blonde woman appeared at Rosie's side, Rosie said, 'Carrie, this is Gemma.'

'It's lovely to meet you.' Carrie extended a hand.

'Likewise. I hear you're from the big smoke.'

'You make me sound like I'm a different breed,' Carrie smiled.

'Not at all,' Gemma dismissed. 'My husband and I were in the city for a long time too and this was a bit of a change for us when we first arrived.'

'You don't regret moving?'

'Not in the slightest. And I have a three-year-old now so living with all this open space – well it's beautiful, and a great place for her to grow up.'

Rosie elaborated on Gemma's story when Gemma served a customer wanting butterscotch ice-cream, which had run out at the front of the shop. It turned out Gemma had tried and tried to fall pregnant, had suffered miscarriages, but she and her husband, Andrew, had eventually adopted a little girl called Abby last year.

Gemma finished with her customer. 'Abby will be so disappointed not to see you, Rosie.'

'I have been roped into babysitting once or twice.' Rosie winked at Carrie, clearly not put out in the slightest. 'It's all good practice.'

Gemma and Rosie were completely at ease with one another and Carrie felt a pang of sadness. She had friends, she had family and she had Lachlan, but as she watched these women chatting away, she knew true friendship was something she hadn't prioritised before. Friends had come and gone from her life but her career had called the shots for a long while and she wondered what it would be like if that were to change.

Andrew came through from the back of the shop and introduced himself. He handed out chocolate samples to all three women, telling them about his latest creation, asking for opinions, and in the few minutes they were in the shop it was almost like the flick of a magic wand, because Carrie felt a part of something new and unfamiliar, something she wanted more and more.

After the chocolate shop, Rosie insisted on accompanying Carrie along Main Street so she could make introductions. Noah had told her earlier that in Magnolia Creek they looked after each other, and Carrie could already see how true it was.

Next up was the café, where they met Bella, the kind-faced woman with trademark red lipstick whom Carrie had definitely seen before, most likely at the pub on occasion when she'd been dating Owen. They met Mal from the gift shop; Stephanie, whose parents owned the pub and whom Carrie recognised as well; and they waved to Gus, who, according to Rosie, volunteered at the fire station with Owen.

They ended with a walk to Magnolia House and Carrie smiled as the big curved veranda came into view, remembering her sister's wedding. She'd helped with the organisation and had taken bonbonnière to Rosie, who worked here at the time.

Rosie was first to sit down on the low wall surrounding the lake. 'I swear my ankles get swollen if I try to do too much.'

'Are you still working?' Carrie sat alongside her, leaned back and trailed her fingers across the surface of the water.

'I'm still here at Magnolia House. I love it.' Her smile was a match for the sun. 'I do three days a week and I'll take six months off when the baby comes and then go back part time. We can manage it with Owen running his own business so I'm lucky.'

'He'll be a great dad. I bet he's really excited.'

'He is.' Rosie hesitated. 'Carrie, can I ask, is there another reason you're here in Magnolia Creek? I mean, apart from the job you lined up.'

When Rosie looked uneasy, Carrie realised what she was getting at. 'Oh, God, no! You don't think I'm trying to get Owen back do you?'

Rosie shook her head, frustrated with herself. 'Call it pregnancy hormones, but I've been feeling a tiny bit paranoid.'

'Rosie.' Carrie put a hand on her arm. 'I swear to you that I absolutely, categorically, do not want Owen back.'

'OK, so now I'm embarrassed.'

'Don't be. He's a catch, and when you met me before I was pretty much the kind of girl who always got what she wanted. But he chose you, remember? He loves you with all his heart.' She paused. 'But then you don't doubt his feelings. It's me, isn't it?'

'I shouldn't have brought it up.' She shook her head as though trying to erase the moment. 'It's just that, well,

41

I suppose it feels strange that you've turned your back on your career to come out here to a little town like this.'

Carrie wasn't about to divulge her real reasons but she liked Rosie, she wanted to keep her on side. 'Owen will always be special to me,' she admitted. 'He's a good friend, but that's all. The feeling's mutual. Even when you two got together I wasn't that upset about losing him as a boyfriend. We lost touch until recently, when I found the job and the house and made contact. But it's platonic, I absolutely promise you.'

The smile Rosie gave her was confident enough to tell Carrie she believed her. 'When I first met you, with your tanned skin, long legs, blonde hair and perfection, I wondered what you'd ever have to worry about. And finding out you were a paediatrician, I thought wow, this girl has looks and brains. She's got it all.'

Carrie harrumphed. 'I guess a lot of people make the same assumption.'

'So what really brings you out here to the country, away from the city and your life there?'

'The nannying job and the position at the hospital. Nothing more,' Carrie assured her. The clouds gathered overhead and she shivered. 'We should get going before it rains on us.'

'Come to my place – you can see the window seat.' Rosie stood up slowly, without another word about Carrie's personal life, and they headed back to Rosie Cottage talking about the plans for Carrie's own house all the way there.

'It's gorgeous! I love it.' Carrie admired the window seat in the bedroom the second she saw it. Covered in denim blue with cream cushions placed at intervals, it was inviting, and with a view over the bush it would be a great place to curl up with a good book and a glass of wine.

Rosie showed Carrie the fireplace, explained the work that had gone into restoring the floors, the choices that had been made in the kitchen and bathroom, and over a cup of tea they chatted more about the town and the community that held it all together.

'Are we OK?' Carrie asked as she stepped out of the cottage ready to return to her own house.

'Of course we are!' Rosie pulled a face. 'Ah, you mean after I asked you about your intentions with Owen? I'm really embarrassed I said anything.'

'No, don't be. It was a legitimate concern.' The bruised clouds hovered ominously and Carrie knew she wouldn't have much time to walk home before they spilled over. 'I'd better go.'

'Don't forget, Carrie, if you need to talk, you know where I am.'

Carrie raised a hand to wave goodbye as she walked away, along Daisy Lane and onto the road that would lead her back to town. Rosie was honest, down to earth and not afraid to air her concerns. It was a sincerity Carrie admired.

She made her way back to Main Street, treating herself to the couple of squares of salted-caramel chocolate she'd bought at the chocolaterie, but before she turned up the hill towards her own house she decided on a pit stop at the florist's next to the vet surgery. She returned the friendly greeting of a man walking his dog and then stopped to appreciate the pots and hanging baskets out front of the florist's. The scent was intoxicating and the riot of colour made her smile: purples, pinks, cream, green, orange, apricot – every colour you could imagine. She looked at labels not recognising a single one but she didn't care. If she could have any of these colouring up the pretty house she'd bought then she'd be happy.

'Carrie?' It was Noah, in the same shorts he'd had on earlier, looking a bit muddier but sporting a big smile as he carried out a tray of miniature plants. He seemed friendlier and she was surprised to find she felt a flush of relief.

'Hey.' She peered into the tray.

'They don't look much now,' he explained, perhaps sensing she was looking for something pretty in there but hadn't managed to find it, 'but they will be beautiful eventually. Every seed and plant has to be allowed a chance to grow.'

'I'll take your word for it.'

'What have you been up to?'

'Meeting the locals.' She smiled and recounted the route they'd taken around the town and the people she'd been introduced to, and when he extended a hand to touch her face she held her breath.

'You have chocolate on the corner of your mouth.'

She reached her own fingers up and wiped the same place he'd touched. 'Thanks.' She wondered whether she'd have mud there now but she'd caught the waft of soap and cleanliness when he'd lifted a hand to her skin.

She spun round in an effort to mask her awkwardness. 'What are these? The label's missing.' She pointed up at the hanging basket with glorious orange flowers spilling out of it.

'Those are nasturtiums.'

'Oh,' she managed, wondering if he realised how uneasy he made her feel. She turned back to find him watching her rather than the flowers but as she did, in the corner of her eye she saw a car she recognised and, rather than being elated her boyfriend had driven all this way to surprise her, she found herself forcing a smile as she waved at him, because the thinking space she'd found out here suddenly felt a whole lot smaller.

The powerful, agile and distinctive Jaguar convertible in glossy red stood out against the peaceful backdrop of Magnolia Creek and Carrie noticed the car had already drawn attention. Mal from the gift shop looked over in awe as he washed his front window, Andrew from the chocolaterie had appeared vaguely interested before retreating back inside to his customers, and a group of teenage boys who had sauntered along from the direction of the train station were taking a healthy interest, and Carrie suspected if she didn't get to Lachlan in the next few minutes they'd be asking him questions about the car's maximum speed, its acceleration from zero to a hundred kilometres an hour, or a thousand other questions she didn't understand or care for.

'What are you doing here?' She kissed Lachlan on the lips when he leaned in and she caught the familiar smell of his Gucci aftershave. It was the same scent he'd worn since the day they met. Even when he'd scrubbed for surgery the subtle aroma still lingered in some way.

'I thought I'd surprise my girl.' He slung an arm around her shoulder, pointed the remote at the car and bleeped to lock it and activate the alarm. He nodded to the boys walking past, who gave the vehicle another look of appreciation. 'I missed you.'

'You've been on nights, haven't you?'

'On again tonight,' he confirmed, taking both her hands in his.

Carrie knew Noah was hovering nearby so she had no choice but to introduce them. 'Lachlan, this is Noah.

Noah's going to be helping out with the garden up at the house.'

Lachlan stretched out a hand and shook Noah's. 'You've got a job there, it's in quite a mess.'

'It is,' Noah replied, 'but there's beauty beneath, I'm sure of it. We'll find it, won't we, Carrie?'

Was he deliberately trying to goad her boyfriend? 'Er…yes, you will. I'm afraid I won't be much help. Gardening and me don't see eye to eye – I'd kill a plant at a thousand paces.'

'She's not wrong,' said Lachlan, his conviction blotting out any remark Noah had intended to rock the boat for whatever reason. 'It's a cute town.' He looked down to the other end of Main Street and then peered at the shops opposite.

'I'll see you again soon, Carrie.' Noah clearly didn't want to hang around, and for that she was grateful.

'See you.' She didn't look at him, just cuddled in tightly to Lachlan. 'I can't believe you missed me so much you'd drive up when you should be sleeping.'

'You know me, I only need a good stretch of a few hours and I'm raring to go again.'

Both of them had been the same; working long hours at the hospital plus nights on call meant that sleep was often hard to come by, and you got used to it. But out here, Carrie had slept longer and better than ever before and already she was realising how good it made her feel.

'Let's have a coffee,' she suggested. Owen was back at the house and she hadn't briefed him on not telling Lachlan their history. Not that he would, anyway. It wasn't really the first thing he was likely to say: 'Nice to meet you and, by the way, I know what it's like to go to bed with your girlfriend.'

46

They walked on in the direction of the café and Bella was no less busy than before but she made enough time to come over and introduce herself to Lachlan. At almost six foot five with a very sure presence, as soon as anyone heard he was a heart surgeon it only made them more enamoured.

Bella couldn't chat for long, but she was able to nudge Carrie with an approving look and make Carrie realise how quickly she was making friends around here.

'Great coffee,' Lachlan confirmed after his first sip of macchiato.

She sipped her own cappuccino and made an approving face. 'Bella is famous for her scones too, apparently.'

'Go on then,' he grinned. 'I've got some healthy pasta back at the apartment to eat before work, but the scones will go down much better than that.'

With the legendary scones that came served with a generous pot of cream and another of jam, she talked to Lachlan about some of the local businesses she'd discovered that day, the people she'd met, the lake that was hidden from here and the holiday cottages at one end, surrounded by bushland and as peaceful as you could imagine. They moved on to talking a bit about the hospital and some more about Stella and Marco, their friends in the city who eloped last month and married in the Seychelles.

'They're both soaring in their careers. Stella's head of paediatrics now, Marco's aiming for Director of Cardiology.'

'Impressive.' Stella and Marco were two of the most dedicated doctors Carrie had ever met and two of the nicest people they knew. They didn't see much of them so Carrie had never got close enough to call Stella a true girlfriend, one of those women you could have a giggle with over something inconsequential. Mostly their conversations revolved around medicine, fine dining, property or exotic locations for holidays. Quite often Marco and Lachlan would drift off and discuss cardiology, while Carrie and Stella would turn to matters of paediatrics. Carrie guessed it was only natural.

'It could be you one day,' said Lachlan as she smoothed some jam onto the scone's surface. 'You're an amazing paediatrician and you have the drive to go as far as you want to go.'

Once upon a time she would've said the same. But now, she wasn't so sure.

'You do, Carrie. Just don't leave it too long to get back in the game.'

She turned down the offer of another coffee when Bella passed by their table. 'I'm not completely out of the game,' she told him, 'and remember I'll be looking after a project at the hospital near here, thanks to you and Serena.'

'Forgive the pun, but that project is child's play for you.' He dismissed a potential protest with his hand. 'I'm not saying it's not important, because I know it is and I've seen many successful similar projects at the hospital. But it won't use your talents in the way they should be used.'

He was only trying to be nice, but this was what she'd enjoyed about not staying in the city any longer and why she'd chosen to live in a total mess and camp out at the house. In the city she felt pressured. Lachlan was the most ambitious man she'd ever met – it was one of the things that had attracted her to him in the first place – but now she'd taken her own foot off the pedal, he seemed intent on making sure she pushed it down again and kept it there.

She distracted him by talking about the garden and what she was going to do with it. She even remembered some of the names of plants, shrubs and climbing things Noah had mentioned, which seemed to impress him.

'Come on.' Lachlan took out his wallet and left cash plus a healthy tip on the tray with a receipt that Bella had discretely brought over. 'I want to see this house again.'

It was exactly what she'd been dreading, and as she climbed into the Jaguar parked outside the florist's she wished she'd had a chance to forewarn Owen that Lachlan was on his way.

Chapter Five

Carrie asked Lachlan to drive her to the supermarket first so she could buy in the supplies she'd already made a list of, and they managed to squeeze everything into the boot alongside another couple of boxes of her clothes and a hanging rail he'd brought up from the city.

Back at the house, Carrie stocked the fridge and the cardboard box that was her only pantry for now and Lachlan assembled the clothes rail for her upstairs in the bedroom.

'You certainly have a lot of buff men helping you out.' Lachlan opened up the boxes when Carrie joined him and they began to hang the clothes on the extra hangers she'd bought at the supermarket.

She wiggled another coat-hanger into the arms of a cardigan and hung it on the rail. Carrie had briefly introduced Owen downstairs when they first arrived at the house, and meeting Noah plus Owen in such a short space of time was bound to be the cause of some contention so she tried not to let things escalate. 'They're working for me, Lachlan, nothing more, nothing less.'

It didn't take long before the makeshift wardrobe housed most of the clothes from the boxes. The rest would have to stay put until she got a more permanent solution, and when Owen hollered up the stairs that he'd need to get started on the bathroom, Carrie and Lachlan escaped downstairs.

'I'll rip out the cupboards,' Owen told her, 'but I'll leave the sink, bath and toilet intact for now.'

'Thanks, Owen. It's all yours.' With Noah elsewhere, Carrie took the opportunity to show Lachlan more of the garden and explain what was going to happen out there.

She pointed to where the pergola would be, the decking that would be laid beneath it and at the back of the house, the fences that would be repaired, and as they stood taking in the space, they could hear clattering about upstairs as Owen carried on with his destruction.

'How did you say you knew Owen?'

'Kristy.'

'Did she date him?'

Carrie shook her head. 'No, I can't remember how they met.' She hated lying, but she knew if he found out Owen was an ex-boyfriend it wouldn't go down well and these surprise visits would become too frequent to handle. She wanted to see him but she also needed some headspace to think, and not to feel constantly like she was letting her career fall apart, and therefore a failure.

Carrie pointed out where the curved flowerbeds would go. 'We can sit out here on a balmy summer's evening with a glass of wine.' Her eyes sparkled as he leaned down to kiss her.

'It's quiet around here.' He took her hand and led her behind the shed. 'We could do more than have a drink.'

She pushed him away playfully. 'Owen's right inside. And there's no gate on the garden. Anyone could turn up!' Giggling as he trailed kisses down her neck and deftly undid the first few buttons of her dress, she felt her desire beneath the heat of the day heighten. 'Lachlan, seriously…'

'I am being serious,' he murmured, pulling the material of her bra to one side and letting his tongue explore.

She felt guilty that she hadn't been more excited when she'd seen him pull up in his car on Main Street, because she did miss him, and the way she was feeling now was a big reminder of their relationship, their history, and how much he cared for her.

With the banging coming from the inside of the house and not another soul around, Carrie hoped, she didn't resist for too long and against the wall of the shed they both gave in to temptation.

Afterwards she breathed heavily, her lips against his neck. 'I swear I've got splinters in my butt cheeks.'

He laughed. 'I might need to go see Greg in orthopaedics. I don't think my knees are as up to taking my girlfriend against a wall as they used to be.'

She buttoned up her dress and ruffled her hair. 'Ouch.' She reached behind her. 'I think I've got something in my back too.'

He turned her round and pulled out a small thorny stem, then inspected her dress more closely as she held her hair out of the way. 'The material's fine, it's not ripped.' He kissed the back of her neck before she dropped her hair down and sighed with pleasure. 'I think you'll live.'

Lachlan was driven, ambitious, and he was also impulsive. She only hoped this latest escapade hadn't echoed all the way inside for Owen to hear.

When she went into the kitchen again it didn't look as though Owen realised what had been going on. He was in the lounge now, pulling out the shelving in the alcove, most of which was rotten. The frame was still intact so they'd leave that and repaint it. Carrie trotted up the stairs to use the bathroom and make sure she didn't have any stray twigs or other fragments in her hair and then she washed her face, put on some deodorant from her toiletry bag, and by the time she returned downstairs the men were chatting about floorboards, maximising a property's potential for resale value and the fireplace, which was already looking better now the cobwebs had been cleared away and the rotten mantelpiece removed.

'You won't recognise the place by the time I've finished,' Owen assured Lachlan, who seemed happier now, less threatened.

'I've said to Carrie it'll make a great weekender,' said Lachlan. 'We can come and escape the city when we need to, or we could rent it out.' He draped an arm around her shoulders and she put hers around his waist.

Owen jotted down details of any floorboards that were damaged and would need repairing before they were sanded to look completely unrecognisable. 'Holidaymakers do love it here. The town has a lot to offer with the functions at Magnolia House, the chocolaterie and pub, the café, the walking and cycling trails and the lake.'

As Lachlan nodded, Carrie knew in an instant that she was never going to rent it to anyone else. The thought had entered her mind once upon a time, but now she was here, it felt like hers and she didn't want anyone else intruding to enjoy the claw-foot roll-top bath or freestanding rainfall shower, or her solid oak kitchen with the farmhouse sink in front of the window looking out over the garden that would soon be filled with colour.

'I'll be out of your way tomorrow, Owen,' she assured him as he finished making notes on the flooring and moved to the narrow hallway.

'Ah, the new job.' He slipped his pencil above his ear.

'The new *temporary* job,' Lachlan reminded them both. 'This one deserves a break but she'll be back.' He planted a kiss on the top of Carrie's head. 'She's too good not to be. Patients and families adore Carrie.'

53

'I've no doubt they do.' Owen smiled at her. 'Now, if you'll excuse me I've got a pregnant girlfriend who's texted me to ensure I pick up ice-cream on my way home.' He rolled his eyes but Carrie could see he was loving every moment of it. 'Oh, before I go – my parents are throwing a bit of a town party on Friday night and we'd love it if you could join us. They do this every year; it's become their thing after the fires almost took the town from us.' He shrugged. 'It's a lot of effort for Mum but she thrives on it.'

'That sounds lovely,' Carrie beamed. 'I'll definitely be able to make it. What time?'

'Any time from seven thirty until late.'

'Lachlan?' Owen asked. 'You're welcome to come along too.'

'Oh, yes, please do.' Carrie knew the best way to not have her boyfriend worry about this change of direction was to involve him in her life, at least part of the time.

He checked his iPhone calendar. 'I finish at four o'clock that day. I'll have work on and off for a few hours after that but I should be able to make it up here by eight, nine at the latest.'

'Great.' Owen nodded to each of them. 'See you at the weekend. I'd better get that ice-cream over to Rosie.' He shook his head, amused.

After he'd left Lachlan pulled her towards him. 'I'm looking forward to the party. I can see what other men Magnolia Creek has secretly hidden away. There are too many around here for my liking.'

'Nonsense.' She hit him on the arm playfully. 'Now you'd better go or you'll be late.'

He kissed her goodbye. 'Good luck with the new job tomorrow.' And he left it at that, although Carrie suspected he wanted to say more.

Outside, she waved him off as he reversed the Jaguar and it trundled over the uneven ground to meet the hill he'd drive down towards town before turning right for the city. And with the evening drawing to a close she felt the exhaustion of another busy day take over and followed the stairs up to her airbed.

*

Maria, the ten-month-old baby Carrie was employed to look after for three days a week between the hours of eight and three o'clock, turned out to be a delight, at least for the first morning. Carrie entertained the baby in the high chair by pulling faces, singing and passing various toys that Maria either shoved in her mouth or threw across the kitchen. Carrie was allowed to help herself to ingredients to make a sandwich for lunch – handy when your kitchen was non-existent at home – and after she'd made one for Maria and one for herself, giving Maria mashed-up banana to follow, Carrie was happy with how the day was going.

By early afternoon it was a different story. Maria, content on the play mat for well over half an hour as she'd gazed up at a mirror dangling from her play gym, was beginning to get fractious and most likely had the same cabin fever that Carrie was experiencing.

'What do you say?' Carrie scooped Maria up in her arms. 'Is it time for a walk? Time to get outside?' As a paediatrician she had a way with children and babies, but that was at work. She wasn't sure how any adult could stand doing this all day every day with no other adults for company. She'd go stir crazy if she didn't know she was leaving at three o'clock – there was only so much smiling you could do, pulling faces, cajoling the baby to please not turn over when you were trying to wipe her bum and put on a fresh nappy. Carrie felt as though she needed eight eyes like a spider, eight limbs to multitask and a brain that was happy to operate down a gear. Even getting out the door was a rigmarole. Maria put up a protest at going in the pram and as for putting the harness on, she wasn't having any of it. Carrie had to use brute strength to hold her in place and see her safely in so she could turn her back and get the change bag and bottle she'd need.

But out in the sunshine, walking the short distance to the main area of Magnolia Creek, past the train station and round the bend, she knew why so many mums paraded around Albert Park Lake with their little ones, or walked the Tan Track near the city. It was for their sanity; one hundred per cent necessary.

When she passed the fire station Owen called over to her. 'How's the first day going?'

She smiled. Adult company. But the smile wavered when she saw Noah close behind him, because she had no idea what this man thought of her. 'It's going well, but let me give you a warning. And I should've known this, given my chosen profession. These things…' She pointed at Maria. 'They are not easy.'

Noah crouched down and let Maria take hold of his finger. She curled her fingers around it and gurgled. It seemed she'd already discovered men, and Noah had no qualms with this girl.

'Aren't you two supposed to be at my place?' she looked at Owen and Noah, the man with a natural affinity to babies.

'Yes, boss,' Owen joked. 'We've both been there this morning but I dragged Noah up here to the station to introduce him to a few of the other guys. He's decided to step up and volunteer. About time he had the balls.'

56

Noah stood up. 'I should've done it sooner, I know. But better late than never.'

'Do you live around here?' she asked Noah, if only for something to say.

'Up the hill, about five minutes on from your place.'

For some reason his proximity made her heart skip a beat. Maybe it was the idea of him peering in her windows unannounced again and seeing her naked. At the thought she blushed and stroked Maria's head now as a distraction. Maria had quietened down on their walk so Carrie guessed the walking brigades of mummies she often saw around the city were necessary for the child as much as the parent.

They talked more about the training session Noah was in for on Sunday and chatted about progress on the house. Noah had demolished the shed apparently, so no more shenanigans behind that if Lachlan got any ideas, and next up he'd be yanking out more plants and digging the soil to get rid of any debris lurking beneath. Owen had got hold of some wood to replace the lounge room shelves so he'd be building those, and in the next couple of days the kitchen would arrive so he could get going putting in the units and sorting out a plumber to do the bits he couldn't manage.

Carrie left them to it. Owen had assured her they'd be hot-footing it back to her place but Noah had had more to say to Maria than he had to Carrie.

The rest of Carrie's week with baby Maria went much the same as the first day, with smooth mornings, a walk after lunch to settle them both, and a happy escape at three o'clock.

By the time Friday came around Carrie felt ready to tackle something new, and as she pulled into the car park of the modern hospital facility to meet Serena, a pang of nostalgia hit her unexpectedly: she saw herself in her smarter clothes, clipboard in hand, making rounds on the wards, talking with families and children about their ongoing medical needs. It was like being on the brink of her old life – one she wasn't sure how to step back into again.

Owen's text with a photo of the first stage of kitchen installation brought her out of her trance and she replied to say how good it was looking. Each day she returned to the house, he and Noah had made such progress. Noah had pulled most of the old shrubs from their stubborn positions and cleared to the ground beneath, while Owen had pretty much created a blank canvas to work with inside the house.

She took a deep breath, locked her car and walked towards the front entrance of the hospital. Inside she followed the signs to reception and eventually located Serena.

'Carrie, hi!' Serena shook her hand vigorously and Carrie hoped she didn't manhandle all her patients the same way. Her mannerisms were as over the top as those fake eyebrows of hers but she seemed genuine and Carrie felt she was in good hands.

Serena gave Carrie a brief tour, showed her where the NICU was. 'We're lucky to have the Neonatal Intensive Care Unit,' Serena explained. 'Not all hospitals have one and it makes it easier for families if they don't have to travel all the way to another facility.'

Carrie scanned the NICU, which looked as busy as any other, and Serena introduced her to the neonatal nurse in charge as well as the nurse educator, who would be providing the training for the baby-cuddling program.

'I understand you're after a change of scene,' said Serena.

Carrie wasn't sure what Lachlan had told Serena – she assumed not much – and she was grateful for the relative anonymity. 'I've done some travelling, just bought a house that I'm renovating and, with a nannying job close by, the baby cuddling will keep me busy.'

Judging by the way Serena's eyebrows lifted, Lachlan hadn't told her about Carrie's newfound employment that was at odds with her paediatric skill set.

'I thought I'd get on the property ladder while I can.' Carrie tried to keep the conversation light, make this move more about the house than anything else.

Serena's eyebrows seemed to come down in gratitude that this paediatrician hadn't walked away from a stellar career only to do something anyone could do. 'It's way too expensive to buy in the city, so you're doing the right thing. And you're young,' she smiled. 'Do it now and then you've got plenty of time to work your way up the ranks in paediatrics.'

'That's the plan.' Carrie smiled as they continued their tour of the hospital and chatted about what Carrie's role would be.

'I've had approval for the program from the powers that be,' Serena explained. 'It's been a long time in the planning stage, but finally we have negotiated the terms. The baby-cuddling program will need to be publicised in newsletters, media releases, that sort of thing. We'll need to put in place a system to hold details of volunteers, who will each need to be screened to make sure they're suitable for our precious babies, and once we have the volunteers we'll need to arrange the nurse educator to deliver the training. There'll also be parental consent forms to be completed.'

Carrie's own eyebrows responded by pulling into a frown. 'From what Lachlan said, I hadn't realised the baby-cuddling program was so close to getting off the ground. I thought that's what I was here to do.'

Serena didn't seem phased at the confusion and as she went into a bit more detail about what Carrie would need to do, Carrie realised how overqualified she was for this position. She was tempted to delve further and ask whether Lachlan had begged for some kind of job to get her back in the hospital environment, but the fact she was in a hospital and still relatively calm showed that however this had happened, it was good for her. She hadn't fled from the building in a panic. She hadn't fallen to her knees and sobbed, declaring she couldn't be here. Instead, she'd calmly taken in the environment and talked about the program and the different patient cases she might encounter.

Perhaps Lachlan's way of throwing her in at the deep end and pushing her was exactly what she needed.

*

Following her session at the hospital, Carrie drove back to Magnolia Creek and stopped at the café for sustenance. She'd brought away a heap of reading material from Serena, the bumf she'd thought she would be a part of producing as they negotiated with seniority at the hospital and got the program off the ground.

As she waited for her scone with cream and jam, Carrie wasn't sure how to feel now. She'd left Lachlan an upbeat message to say her meeting had gone well and to say thank you for setting it up, but did she really think that way?

She drummed her fingers on the pile of papers until Bella brought over the scone, fresh from the oven, and the condiments to go with it.

'That smells heavenly.' Carrie closed her eyes to inhale the comforting smell. 'I mustn't keep having these – they'll wreak havoc with my waistline.'

'Nonsense,' Bella assured her with a smile. She glanced at the paperwork in front of Carrie and whistled through her teeth. 'Now that's a lot to get through.'

'It sure is.' There was information about the history of baby cuddling, the way it would work at the hospital itself, details on how volunteers would be screened, guidance they'd be providing for parents.

Bella nodded in greeting to another customer. 'I'll leave you to it, Carrie.'

'Thanks, Bella. Are you going to the party tonight?' If she was honest, she'd be happy to stay at home and wade through this file of information, but she wanted to make the effort with this town, not lose herself in work the same way as she once had.

'I sure am. I'll see you there.' Tea towel in hand, she went behind the counter to take another order.

Carrie flipped through as much of the information as she could while she devoured the scone and when her phone rang and the caller display told her it was Lachlan, she took the call and reiterated what she'd told him in her message.

'I'm glad,' he said. 'You sound happy.'

'I am, but I thought I'd be taking the program from a much earlier stage.' She wondered if he'd admit to anything. 'It all seems to be set up and ready for the final push before it goes live.'

'That's a good thing, surely?'

'I appreciate you putting in a word for me.' Was there really any point in grilling him over the specifics? 'I'm going to be crazy busy for a while.'

'You thrive on being busy.'

'You know me so well.'

'I'm going to be a little late tonight, I'm afraid.'

It came with the territory. Surgeons didn't earn their stripes or their generous pay packets without putting in the hard yards. 'How late is "late"?'

'An hour, tops. But you go ahead – go to the party and I'll be there as soon as I can. Oh, and I booked us into a little cottage by the lake, so pack an overnight bag and take it with you. I'm not sure I'm up to squeezing onto a single airbed with you, much as I love you.'

Carrie grinned. The cottages by the lake were exquisite. This way she'd get to see inside one, and secretly she liked managing her renovations all on her own. 'I'm looking forward to it already. I love you.'

He returned the sentiment and when he hung up Carrie gathered up her papers, climbed into her car and headed back to her house to see what progress had been made.

*

Rosie and Owen were hosting the gathering that night alongside Jane and Michael Harrison as though they were all in the party-planning business. Drinks were continuously topped up, guests were chatted to and introduced seamlessly, and canapés cruised around the room with a practised ease. It was vastly different to the highbrow gatherings Carrie usually found herself a part of, with some of the guests here nipping out for a swim in the backyard pool at the host's insistence, and with George the cat loving company so much he moved from one lap to another and probably intended to do the same for the rest of the night.

'You'll love staying in them,' said Gemma when Carrie told her Lachlan had booked them a cottage for tonight. 'Which number did you get?' Gemma kissed

Andrew on the cheek as he went through to find the men at the party and take the enormous basket of chocolates he'd brought with him to the hosts.

'I don't know. Lachlan booked us in so I guess it'll be a surprise.'

'Well, enjoy the chocolates.'

'On the pillows?' Carrie guessed.

'Not quite. But there'll be a small bowl filled with them, I can guarantee it. It's a nice welcoming gesture and plenty of guests see the wrapping and come into the chocolaterie for more, especially to take home as souvenirs.'

'Sneaky.' When Gemma laughed Carrie relaxed in the woman's company and they talked some more about Gemma's previous life in the city before they'd made the move out here.

'Don't get me wrong, I absolutely love Melbourne,' said Gemma, 'and I make sure I meet my girlfriends there for a big lunch and get-together every few months, but when you drive away and arrive back out here in the fresh air with so much space around, it just feels so welcoming.'

'I'm beginning to know exactly what you mean.' Carrie talked more about the city itself, favourite restaurants, walking along the Yarra or around Albert Park Lake.

As they were chatting she looked around to see if Owen was here yet. He'd already left the house by the time she'd arrived home but she thought she'd better mention to him not to discuss their history with Lachlan. Not that he would. He hadn't said anything so far and she'd never met his parents until tonight anyway, so they were unlikely to spill the beans, but she wanted to be doubly sure he wouldn't let anything slip. She didn't want to upset Lachlan – not when he was doing so much for her and going out of his way to help her after she'd fallen apart so spectacularly.

When Rosie joined them she said that Owen had been at the fire station late after getting a call but he'd shower and change at the cottage and be there as soon as he could. 'Where's your handsome boyfriend tonight?' she asked Carrie.

'He'll be here soon.'

'I always imagine the hospital life to be exactly like *Grey's Anatomy*. Owen bought me the box set to watch when my ankles get so fat with this pregnancy that I can no longer do much apart from sit around and wait for my baby to make an appearance.'

Gemma grinned. 'Make the most of it, girl. I didn't have Abby at the baby stage but toddlerdom isn't much easier, let me tell you.'

'I think having kids is hard work full stop,' added Carrie. 'Take Maria, the baby I'm looking after. She's happy one minute and sitting in her high chair gurgling away, the next she's thrown her toy either at me or to the ground, then I think she's hungry so food will work for a couple of minutes until she decides it's much better for smearing across the tray or in her hair. Then I take her for a walk and she'll be loving the sunshine and fresh air, then suddenly she's grizzling again and yawning, and I'm thinking why don't you just go to sleep if you're that damn tired?'

She hadn't realised she was ranting but Carrie and Rosie were falling about laughing. 'What?'

'Love your job then?' Gemma asked.

Carrie saw the funny side. 'Maria is one feisty boss.' She accepted the top-up of champagne from Jane, whom she'd been introduced to along with Michael when she first arrived.

Carrie clinked her glass against Gemma's and then Rosie's, containing water.

'Do you think you and Lachlan will start a family?' Rosie helped herself to a canapé with cheese and a caramelised onion relish.

Carrie was used to being asked. Even her own family made enough remarks, and as she did with them, she shrugged the question away with a 'who knows?'

'Is he the one, more importantly?' Bella joined in with the conversation and sat on the arm of the sofa.

Carrie found it odd having this much female attention around her. She was used to it from men but not from other women.

'No need to say anything,' said Bella, 'if that's him there.' She pointed and stood up. 'I'll quiz him myself.'

Lachlan had walked into the room and Carrie watched on in amusement as Bella commandeered his attention and probably barraged him with endless questions. Carrie stayed where she was and helped herself to a couple of canapés as they talked about Rosie's pregnancy, and when Rosie had a FaceTime call on her iPad, which was sitting on the table, she jumped at Rosie's apparent excitement.

'It's Molly!' Carrie noticed a few others in the room seemed to be just as elated.

'Who's Molly?' She asked the question of Gemma.

Gemma smiled. 'It's a long story, but she's Andrew's biological daughter and Owen's brother Ben's girlfriend. They're working in London and flit between here and there, but who knows where they'll settle eventually.' Gemma quietened as Rosie chatted on the iPad and Andrew made sure he didn't miss out on saying hello.

65

Magnolia Creek seemed to have so much more going on than Carrie had realised and with so many people vying to say hello on the iPad it showed how friendly people were. It had scared Carrie at first, the thought of everyone knowing your business, but from the second she'd met up with Owen, and Rosie had introduced her to so many people, she'd felt surprisingly at ease.

Carrie looked around for Lachlan and hoped he was as relaxed as she was, but when she saw him she realised he definitely wasn't. He was still talking to Bella, but even from her position on the sofa Carrie could see his jaw stiffen – the twitch he got when he was annoyed that something wasn't going his way.

And a feeling of dread pooled in her stomach.

Chapter Six

'You lied to me.' Lachlan stared ahead. They were outside in the darkness, surrounded by the scent from the beautiful roses.

The sounds of others frolicking in the pool echoed into the evening air and Carrie nervously put her hand on her boyfriend's arm. 'I didn't tell you because I knew how you'd react.' Bella had let it slip that Carrie had been a part of Owen's life before Rosie came along.

'You should've mentioned it. Being blind-sided isn't what I had in mind when I came here tonight.'

'Tell me something…' She trod carefully. 'Would you have been comfortable with Owen doing the renovations at my place if you knew we'd dated?'

The tension in his jaw was still there. 'I don't suppose I would, no.'

Carrie leaned her body against his and put her arms around his waist. 'Owen only has eyes for one woman now, and that's Rosie.'

'I met her, she seems nice.'

'She's lovely. They met when I was dating Owen.'

He pulled back, intrigued. 'Really?' And over by the rockery she told him the entire story before they made their way inside to mingle some more. But as they reached the door Lachlan leaned in and said, 'I just don't like knowing he's seen you naked.'

'Yeah, sorry about that mate. I didn't realise she was there.' Noah had appeared in the doorway just as Carrie was about to reassure Lachlan that he had nothing to worry about. He smiled, oblivious. 'And then the next minute there she is on the other side of the window, dripping wet from the shower. I think we were both as shocked as each other.'

Carrie's insides plummeted and Lachlan wouldn't even look at her this time. She asked him if he wanted a beer or a wine and he grunted a response but Carrie couldn't wait to get away. Noah sensed he'd put his foot in it somehow and escaped the second Carrie went to get the drinks, leaving Lachlan talking to Owen's dad, Michael – a safe bet for a good chat given he'd been a doctor too, once upon a time. Lachlan could talk about medicine until the end of time. It was his life. His reason for being.

Rosie filled two glasses with sauvignon blanc and Carrie turned to take them outside, almost bumping into Noah as he reached for a beer from the selection on the kitchen benchtop.

'Did I cause a problem back there?' he asked.

Carrie smiled although she was a little embarrassed at having had her naked body brought up in conversation again, especially after she'd only just settled things between her and Lachlan over her history with Owen. 'Not at all.'

'Only your boyfriend seemed shocked I'd seen you naked. From what I'd overheard, I thought you'd just told him the whole story and were laughing about it.'

'We weren't talking about you.' She went to leave but he obviously hadn't finished and as he moved in to talk to her again she caught a waft of aftershave she wouldn't usually associate with him. She was used to seeing him with mud over his legs, his hands and face showing signs of his work as an outdoor labourer, but here he was in a freshly laundered shirt, ironed impeccably, with jeans that didn't give any hint as to his occupation.

'Then who?' he asked, but it didn't take long for the penny to drop. 'Ah, he's jealous of Owen.'

She shushed him. 'Keep your voice down.'

'The jealous type is he?' He swigged his beer.

'That's none of your business.'

'Fine, I'll go shall I?'

'I think that would be best.' She scurried through the throng of people, most of whom she didn't know, and found Lachlan looking less tense as he spoke to Michael Harrison. She stood patiently by his side like a sports widow, except instead of talking wickets, goals and tries they were discussing the latest techniques in cardiothoracic surgery.

'He's a good man,' said Lachlan when Michael excused himself to talk to Bella's husband, Rodney, who'd spotted the resident blue-tongue lizard scarpering across the back of the rockery. The rockery was all lit up and looked equally impressive as the rest of the garden.

'He's nice,' Carrie agreed.

'I guess you'd know that already. You've obviously briefed him though because he didn't say a word about you. And who knows, maybe he's seen you naked as well.'

'You're being ridiculous.' She snapped at him but then her voice softened. 'I haven't briefed him, Lachlan. I've never met the man before.' She took his hand and led him to the other, less populated, side of the deck. 'Owen and I were never serious, it was a bit of fun.'

Lachlan raked a hand through his hair although it was so short it daren't move. 'Sometimes I wonder if by you coming up here, it's the beginning of the end between us.'

Carrie gulped.

'If you stay here, in that house, you'll rarely get back to the city, and with my shifts at the hospital I don't see how we'll survive.'

She didn't know what to say. How could she reassure him when she had no idea what was going to happen long term? There was the house now, her career, her feelings. So much to consider, and she was beginning to feel stifled again with no clear path through the fog.

Lachlan leaned closer and planted a kiss on her lips, a kiss that said he hoped everyone around could see that she was his. And although not entirely comfortable with the display of affection at someone else's house, she couldn't be too annoyed at him. He was a strong, together surgeon and often described as unflappable, but that was at work. When it came to his home life, Lachlan could be entirely different.

'No more men seeing you naked.' Lachlan took her wine glass and put it on the table. He pulled her against him again. 'Unless it's me, agreed?'

She sighed against his chest. 'Agreed.' She moved to go inside the house but he pulled her back.

'How about we get out of here? The cottage is waiting for us and from what I've been told it's got a corner tub for two.'

She smiled. 'All in good time, but I want to see a bit more of the girls first.'

He made a sound as though he was pained but it was short-lived as Michael reappeared and the two men, with Rodney, launched into conversation about football.

'Your boyfriend seems to be hitting it off with everyone,' said Gemma when Carrie went inside. 'And he's gorgeous too. I wouldn't mind him being my doctor.'

'Get in line.' Bella joined them at the kitchen bench as they helped themselves to the mini cheese and bacon quiches. She leaned closer to Carrie as Rosie came over and poured three glasses of champagne. 'I'm sorry if I put my foot in it earlier, with Lachlan,' said Bella. 'I assumed he knew who Owen was, what with him working at the house.'

Carrie shook her head. 'Absolutely no need to apologise. I should've told him in the first place, but we're all good now so please don't give it another moment's thought.'

Rosie handed the champagne to Carrie, Gemma and Bella and they moved outside with their drinks. Lachlan looked comfortable with the men and so the girls made their way down to the gazebo at the back of the pool and sat on the bench overlooking the water.

'You going to swim tonight, Carrie?' Rosie looked at many of the town's residents making the most of the fine March weather, the warm endless evenings that would soon disappear when autumn was upon them.

'No, not tonight.' She'd bought her swimmers as instructed on the invite Owen had dropped round, but getting near-naked in front of all these people would surely be too much for Lachlan to cope with.

'She's in trouble,' Bella whispered, and Carrie had to laugh. Her delivery was clearly fuelled by too much of the fizzy stuff.

'Why?' Rosie and Gemma wanted to know.

'She didn't tell Lachlan she'd dated Owen,' Bella explained.

Carrie took it from there. 'He's a little uncomfortable. I mean, he's just found out the host's son was with his girlfriend once upon a time...' She hesitated but Rosie dismissed her concern. '...sorry, Rosie.' She laughed then, the bubbles going to her own head. 'The man renovating my house used to be my lover, and the man doing my garden has seen me naked. It's too much fuel for the fire, shall we say.'

Gemma's mouth fell open. 'What?' Rosie had already heard the story but Gemma and Bella were intrigued. 'Noah? What was he doing seeing you naked?'

Carrie enlightened them. 'I was so embarrassed. No, mortified. I mean, I thought I was in the middle of nowhere and then there's a man the other side of my window.'

'How much did he see?' Bella wanted to know.

'From my waist up, so enough.'

Bella sniggered. 'I bet he got excited…bet he needed a cold shower of his own after that.'

'I'm not surprised Lachlan is feeling a bit threatened,' Gemma surmised.

'He must think we're all a bunch of interbreeding weirdos.' Bella's giggle echoed into the night.

'OK, no more of those for you,' said Rosie, pointing to Bella's empty glass. 'You should eat something.'

'I will, I will. I'm letting my hair down for once. Managing your own business is tough and although I'm glad the café's up and running again, I'd forgotten how your time is never your own. You're either in there serving, or you're cleaning up, or you're cooking and planning menus, and then doing the books in every spare moment you have.'

Gemma nodded. 'You sound like Andrew. But I bet, just like him, you wouldn't have it any other way.'

'You're right, and I'm doing it with Rodney so that makes it easier.'

'How's the nannying going?' Rosie asked Carrie. 'Still hard work?'

'It is, but I think Maria and I are starting to come to an understanding. No longer does she say jump and I ask how high.' She laughed. 'Actually, that's bullshit. Whatever Maria wants she pretty much gets. She's not even a year old so I don't think the art of manipulation will enter her mind for a long time yet.'

'And what about the baby-cuddling program you mentioned?'

'I was at the hospital today, and the organisation of it is much further along than I thought.' Carrie went into detail about the program, what the aim was, how it would roughly work.

'So you'll be advertising for volunteers?' Bella asked. 'Will you do a shift yourself?'

'I hadn't thought I would,' Carrie confessed. 'But reading more about the program and being in charge of bringing it to fruition, I think I might.'

'Are there any qualifications volunteers need to have?' Gemma wanted to know.

Carrie shook her head. 'Not at all. Volunteers will be screened to check backgrounds and their suitability, but all training is given and really it's a case of whoever wants to volunteer can.'

'It'd be good practice for you.' Bella nudged Rosie. 'Then again, it might scare you off. I mean, how sick are these babies, Carrie?'

'I won't lie to you,' – she wanted to be as honest as possible – 'there are some really sick babies and that is the hardest part. Some babies are born to drug-addicted mothers and might be going through withdrawal.' Bella gasped. 'I know, it can be confronting. All these babies have one hell of a journey ahead and they can be agitated, have difficulty sleeping, they're jittery. It breaks your heart to think about it, but what they really crave is being tightly swaddled, held, and that's what the program is about.'

'Are all the babies in the same position?' Gemma asked.

'Not all. Often the cuddling program helps parents of multiple births because obviously they can't hold all three or four babies at once, or it offers parents who live a distance away and who have other children to care for the chance to be at home with their family and know their baby is being held and looked after at the hospital when they can't be there.'

Rosie's face fell. 'I can't imagine what it must be like for those mothers.' She looked at Carrie as she touched her baby bump. 'I would hate for this little one to be at the hospital without me.'

'If you had another child at home then it might be what you had to do. Some of these parents don't have a choice. The hospital opening means families aren't having to travel into the city all the time but, still, it's often a distance from where they live.'

'You know,' Rosie began, 'you hear parents talking about wanting their kids to join certain clubs, be at a particular school, succeed in their exams, but, at the end of the day, none of it matters, does it? You just want children who are happy and healthy.'

'I'll raise a glass to that.' Bella lifted up her glass with the others to toast but collapsed in a fit of the giggles when she realised the vessel was empty.

'Here.' Gemma poured some of her own champagne into the glass for Bella.

'Thank you.' Bella sounded as though she was verging on the emotional. 'You know what we should do?'

'What?' Gemma grinned and rolled her eyes at Rosie, as they wondered what would come out of Bella's mouth.

Bella raised her glass and looked at Carrie. 'I think we should do it. All of us.'

'Do what?' Carrie jerked back slightly when someone bombed into the pool and sent water over the jacuzzi and onto her legs.

'We should go cuddle those babies. Poor little mites.'

'You know, she's actually talking sense,' said Gemma.

'I think for once she might be.' Rosie earned herself a playful slap from Bella.

'You're serious?' Carrie asked. 'You all want to sign up as volunteers?'

'Not just us, you too. You're one of us now.' Bella was on her feet and gestured for the others to do the same. She raised her glass and waited for the other girls to follow suit. 'To us. The volunteers of the baby-cuddling program.' After they'd clinked glasses she jumped up and down on the spot in excitement. 'What should we call ourselves? We need a name!'

'I don't know – we'll have to think, won't we?' Rosie leaned back from her seated position and plucked a bottle of water from the fridge in the gazebo.

This time it was Carrie on her feet, in amongst a group of friends and taking the lead. 'To the Magnolia Girls!' she declared.

'That's it!' Gemma smiled.

'It's perfect,' Rosie agreed.

Carrie looked at each of them as they all smiled excitedly at their new collective title. And when she held up her glass they followed suit, their vessels meeting mid-air.

'To the Magnolia Girls!' they chorused.

Chapter Seven

'Come in.' Carrie still felt a bit groggy when she opened the door to Noah the next morning, and already she was glad she wasn't on Maria duty today.

After the party last night Carrie and Lachlan had walked over to the cottages by the lake and let themselves into the most exquisite holiday accommodation. The walls were painted a pale lilac and a white jug filled with lavender perched on the windowsill in the tiny lounge, spreading its scent throughout the cottage. As Gemma had promised, there was a small bowl filled with treats from the chocolaterie and Carrie had laughed as Lachlan fed her one after the other, before they made love and fell asleep until the sunlight woke them this morning and it was time to get back to the house. They'd gone via the pub for a cooked breakfast, desperately needed after last night's revelry, and Lachlan had returned to the city much calmer than he'd been during the party. Putting herself in his shoes, she knew it had to be hard seeing your girlfriend with all these new, super-friendly people who welcomed her as though they'd known her for years.

Noah came through the front door now and sidestepped the sink from the bathroom that Owen had ripped out yesterday. 'How's the head?'

'It's fine.' When he looked at her she said, 'OK, so I may have had a few glasses too many, but it was a great party. It was lovely to meet more people.'

'They're a friendly bunch in Magnolia Creek.' He looked sheepish. 'I wanted to say again that I'm sorry if I caused waves with the boyfriend.'

'It's all good.' Carrie dismissed his concern and nodded to the drawings in his arms. 'Are they for me?'

'I've put together proper plans and the formal quote. These will help you visualise what the garden will look like when I've finished.'

Carrie looked around. 'We could do with a table.'

'No worries, the floor will have to do.' He got down on his knees and unrolled the plans while Carrie reviewed the written quote. It wasn't too dissimilar from his verbal estimate and so she was happy to proceed.

Carrie had no choice but to join him and on her knees she listened to him patiently explain all the plants, shrubs and flowers he was planning to include and she asked as many questions as she needed to without looking completely daft. Her fingers were about as green as the soil beneath the grass so as long as what he had in mind added a bit of colour, she'd leave him to it.

'I think you'll be very happy with it.' He patiently rolled up the plans as they both stood up. 'I'll get out there and get on with it.'

'On a Saturday?' she quizzed.

He smiled. 'It's supposed to rain Monday and Tuesday so if you don't mind, I'll put in a day today and maybe again tomorrow after my training session down at the fire station.'

He seemed about to say something else but, instead, disappeared outside and when he noticed her watching from the window she busied herself washing the cups by the sink, dried them and stowed them in the cardboard box she had for such items. She swept the floor in the kitchen even though Owen would be here soon and it'd probably get ten times worse, because despite what she'd claimed about being happy to live in a mess for a while, it turned out it was quite stressful, especially after the night in the cottage, with its brand-new bath, a basic but fitted kitchen, floors that shone and that you could walk on without needing shoes.

By the time Owen came to get stuck into ripping out some more of the bathroom suite, yanking old tiles off the walls and dismantling the grotty cupboard that had once been beneath the sink, the kitchen was looking as clean as she could manage. He had a mate coming to help him sort out the spare bedroom's new en suite, which would go in the far corner and required new stud walls with timber frames and plasterboard, and another contractor to come and do the wiring and the plumbing. Owen said his talents were expanding but he always did anything complicated under the guidance of a professional, and Carrie was happy he took such pride in his work. He also assured her he'd be concentrating on the upstairs today so the kitchen would look exactly the same when she returned.

Feeling happy, she decided to get outside and make the most of the sunshine before the rain came next week. She walked down the hill towards Main Street and past the chocolaterie.

'Carrie.' Gemma poked her head around the doorway. 'It's my break time.' She beckoned Carrie inside and when she followed said, 'I've already texted Bella and Rosie and they're on their way over. I didn't have your number or I'd have sent you a message too. Do you want to come upstairs to join us?'

'That sounds lovely.'

The others arrived as they were chatting and Gemma soon had everyone organised in the café that sat on the floor above the chocolaterie. The first thing she did was to get Carrie to give them all her number, and Carrie felt delighted to be included in the friendship group.

'I'm tired after the party,' Rosie claimed the second she sat down. 'And I didn't even drink!'

'You're carrying a human being inside of you,' said Carrie. 'You're allowed to be a little tired. How's the head, Bella?'

Bella had stumbled in shortly after Rosie. 'Fine, fine. Plenty of water before I went to bed and it worked a treat.'

'I had a great time last night,' said Gemma. 'I took over a basket of chocolate for Jane and Michael this morning to say thanks.'

Outside on the balcony, with a perfect view of the bush that stretched for miles, they chatted over coffees, hot chocolates and fresh fruit juice.

'Isn't this your competition?' Carrie asked Bella.

Bella shook her head and told her about how Andrew had approached her when he and Gemma first moved to Magnolia Creek. 'He didn't want to tread on any toes when the café reopened.'

'Andrew wanted us to fit in with the community,' Gemma added. 'He's always been one to do the right thing. And Bella here gave us the go-ahead and they agreed what items he'd sell.'

'You'll never lose customers if you keep baking those scones,' said Rosie. 'They're so yummy. I intend to introduce my little one to them as soon as he or she is on solids.'

Laughing, Carrie said, 'I don't blame you. I've had the pleasure of tasting them on a couple of occasions and I'll definitely be going back for more.' She loved the way this community worked. People were welcoming but not overly nosy and she suspected that if you wanted to keep yourself to yourself you could but, equally, if you needed support or a friend to lean on, help would be there in spades. She thought back to her time with Owen when he'd talked about volunteering for the CFA as a firefighter and it all made sense now. His unwavering commitment to the community was something you absorbed the moment you drove past the sign with curly writing welcoming you to the town.

'So, Carrie, what's the plan for the Magnolia Girls?' Gemma said the title of their group with enormous pride. 'I can't wait to get started. I work part time up at the school and with Abby in playgroup a couple of mornings a week I have time. How flexible will the schedule be?'

Carrie put down her apple juice and enjoyed the warmth of the sun on her arms and face. 'It's really flexible. Basically, baby cuddlers are there to make it easier for the nursing staff who can't cuddle the babies all the time. So we'll fit around you, perhaps draw up a roster depending on your availability.'

Bella produced a sparkly notepad and pen and they went through times and days. Gemma would be needed in the chocolaterie a couple of times during the week, more in the school holidays, Rosie had to factor in the work she did at Magnolia House but she tended to finish early, and then there was the imminent arrival of the baby of course, and Bella pinpointed the café's quieter times, not that there were many, but there were some slots where Rodney could manage on his own.

'Thanks for that, girls.' Carrie tore off the couple of sheets of paper, folded them and put them in her handbag. 'When I'm at the hospital next week I'll get everything organised and we'll know what we're doing. Then it'll be screening for you all and paperwork before we can really start.'

'We're not going to be strip-searched are we?' Bella guffawed. 'Only if we are, make sure it's a handsome doctor like your man, Lachlan.'

'I'll do my best,' Carrie laughed, and added, 'but strip-searching will not be required.'

'Tell us more about this man of yours,' Gemma insisted.

'You met him last night.'

'I know we did, but we need to know more. Is it serious? Are there wedding bells on the horizon? Babies?' Bella certainly liked to keep on top of things.

'Leave the poor girl alone,' Rosie admonished. 'Or you'll have her packing up her things and moving on.'

They launched into a more comfortable conversation about the renovations at the house, and the garden that was nothing but dirt and mess right now but would eventually be a little haven. Carrie could already imagine what it would be like to sit out there at her own place, sipping a glass of wine in the evening and watching the sun go down.

She shook herself out of her reverie when Rosie said, 'You're working heaps of hours, Carrie. Aren't you exhausted doing it all and trying to renovate a house?'

'I like to be busy.' She'd never been one to sit around; weekends back in the city had mostly been filled with shifts at the hospital, going out on the town with Lachlan or attending work functions to meet new people. 'Maria is full on during the day, but she's sweet too. And I'm looking forward to being at the hospital in my new role. And as for the renovations, Owen and Noah seem to have those organised between them so I try to stay out of the way.'

'Noah seems lovely,' Bella said with a twinkle in her eye.

'You're such a stirrer,' giggled Gemma. 'But she's right, he's a hottie.'

'Yep.' Rosie grinned. 'I bet Lachlan would rather you had an old man as a gardener. Freddie, he'd do.'

It was Bella's turn to laugh, before she explained the comment to Carrie. 'Freddie is Mal's father.'

'Mal who owns the gift shop?' Carrie asked.

'That's him. Anyway, Freddie is a gardener by trade but older than some of those trees out there.' She pointed to the bush. 'Mal is forever telling him to retire properly but the man doesn't know how to sit still. I saw him only yesterday buying plants to spruce up the garden at Mal's home. Anyway, at almost eighty years old, if it were him rather than Noah hanging out at your place, Lachlan would be a lot less threatened.'

Carrie changed the topic of conversation back to baby cuddling and before too long they declared their first Magnolia Girls meeting over, but not without Andrew coming upstairs with samples of his latest creation – dark chocolate with crushed, dried raspberries and some other ingredient Carrie didn't quite catch the name of. All she knew was that it tasted delicious and if she wasn't careful she'd be stacking on the weight before the renovations were even finished.

Carrie walked up the hill towards the house, marvelling at the king parrot foraging in the trees outside. It looked her way but then turned its distinctive red head away to carry on looking for food. She shut the door behind her and was pleased to see Owen must have swept the hallway. It tickled her inside because she doubted he'd have bothered if he didn't know her so well. But when she reached the kitchen her heart sank. It was a total mess. Nothing like the organised room she'd left – which, fair enough, looked dreadful and was only a shell, but at least the floor had been clear with no visible dirt.

She looked on in horror, barely able to keep moving into the room itself, because now her clean floor had mud and clumps of dirt traipsed through, and it was only as she braved taking a step closer that she realised Noah was in the kitchen.

'What the hell do you think you're doing?' She couldn't keep the agitation out of her voice. 'I left this place neat at least so I could walk in without getting covered in mud.'

He grimaced but didn't stop washing his hands in the sink. 'I'm sorry about that. I'll clear it up.'

'Too damn right you will!'

'Keep your hair on! There's no need to lose your temper.'

'I've got every right to lose my temper! You're hired to do the garden, out there' – she jabbed a finger towards the window – 'not employed to bring the outside in!'

'Haven't you heard of indoor/outdoor living? It's all the rage.' His attempt at a joke fell flat.

The water was still running. How long did it take to wash your hands? 'I have to pay water bills you know – try not to use all of it.' She turned on her heel but stopped at his voice.

'OK, princess.'

'Hey, you don't get to talk to me like that.'

'Of course not,' he quipped. 'Because I *work* for you.'

'What?' What was his problem?

'Your house is being renovated. It's ridiculous trying to keep it neat and tidy. I mean, talk about anal,' he muttered, but her hearing was good enough to pick it up.

'I am not anal!'

His look said otherwise.

'Just clear everything up, will you? And turn that bloody tap off!' She moved closer and it was only then she realised there wasn't just mud on the floor but something red too and when she saw the blood washing down the sink as the water flowed, she realised Noah had cut himself badly. 'What did you do?' She was close enough to pick up his manly smell, strangely familiar and mixed with the scent of the earth from outside, the sunshine from the sky.

'What do you care, Princess Carrie?' Rather than saying it in a mean way, he actually smiled and his voice wasn't as hard as it had been.

Ignoring his jibe, she turned the tap off. 'I'm not worried about the water supply,' she told him before he could jump to conclusions, 'but I want to take a look at your wrist.'

'I'm not a child. Don't your patients' credentials usually include being under the age of eighteen?'

'I studied medicine for long enough to know what's what, whether this wrist belongs to a man or a boy.' Her eyes flickered away from his when he looked at her, seemingly forgetting to be in pain any more. She inspected the cut and gently examined the area around it. 'We need to use disinfectant to clean this up properly and then I'll assess whether we're good to cover it with a plaster or bandage.'

'I don't exactly carry disinfectant in my toolbox.'

'Well good job I have some in my first-aid kit then.'

'OK, but first you might want to look at this too, Doctor Carrie.' He turned slightly and looked down but kept his wrist over the sink.

Carrie looked in the same direction and saw blood trickling down his shin. 'What on earth did you do?'

'I was lifting those paving slabs from the foot of the garden. I caught my wrist on one and it scraped the skin away. Then I stupidly tried to keep lifting it before I came inside to sort myself out. It slipped from my grip and scraped all down my shin.'

'Idiot.' She said it with a smile before she turned to go find her first-aid kit, which was still in the car. 'By the way,' she called behind her, 'I much prefer the name Doctor Carrie to Princess Carrie, it's what all my friends call me.'

Back with the first-aid kit, she tended to his leg first, cleaning it up to assess the damage. She covered it with a special dressing and then saw to his wrist. He spent the time talking about the garden and how much he'd progressed and prattled on so much it was only when he eventually turned and stopped looking out of the window and beyond that she realised he was squeamish at the sight of blood.

'You think I'm a big sissy, don't you?' he asked, all cleaned up. There was no need for stitches and the blood had made the wounds look far worse than they actually were. 'It's just that I'm not keen on the sight of blood.'

She packed away the first-aid kit. 'A lot of people aren't.'

'I bet some of your younger patients are tougher than I am.'

'They are,' she confirmed, but at least it made them both smile. 'My mum's the same. If she sees blood, on her or anyone else, she almost faints. She's always been that way. When I was little she'd try to put on a brave face if I grazed my knee, cleaning out the dirt, putting a plaster on, but I'd do it myself a lot of the time.'

'Aren't you scared of anything?' His question hung between them.

Carrie looked away but then grinned back at him. 'I'm terrible with vomit.'

'Really?' He seemed to appreciate the admission. 'But you're a paediatrician – don't you have kids puking all the time?'

'Not always, and when it happens we catch it most of the time, thankfully, but if they vomit down themselves I have to step up and put my own reservations aside. Seriously, I gag clearing it up but I can't let the children know that. They're scared enough; they don't need me making it worse.'

'I'll bet you're a great doctor.'

She pulled on her marigolds ready to clean the floor. 'I do my best.'

'I'll clean up. It's my mess.' He reached for the cloth before she did.

She snatched the cloth back. 'No you won't. I've only just patched you up and I don't want you aggravating the cuts, especially the one on your wrist – it's quite nasty.'

'But you said it looked worse than it really was.'

'And that was true.' She filled a washing-up bowl with water and threw the cloth in. Then she found some kitchen roll from her box of cleaning supplies and proceeded to pick up the clumps of mud and put them in the bin, which was a black rubbish bag in the corner of the room, before she did anything else. 'Using your wrist a lot might make it bleed more and I'd hate it to get worse. Make sure you check it tonight and tomorrow and change the dressing using what I've given you, and you should be back to normal soon.'

'I've got work to do.' He nodded out to the garden.

Carrie got down on her hands and knees and began cleaning up the floor, conscious it was his blood she was wiping up. Somehow it felt intimate, a part of him. 'No

86

gardening for you, not for a couple of days. Let yourself heal. And if you're interested, I'll make us both some tea.'

'Wow, I'm really getting the gold-star treatment.'

'Hey, don't push it.' Her look sent him scarpering to the lounge room and when the floor was acceptably clean she took two mugs of tea through, seeing Noah immediately move to get up from the beanbag.

'Don't you get up. Rest your leg. I'm fine sitting on the floor.' She put her cup of tea down. 'I'll just get an old towel; I have a few upstairs.'

When she returned they drank their tea and talked more about Magnolia Creek and the training he was doing with the CFA.

'Owen has been trying to get me into it for a long time,' he admitted. 'I wasn't sure I'd be up to it but they're a good group of guys and I'm glad I gave it a go.'

'Must be frightening though, fighting fire.'

'Owen has told me some stories, but he's still in one piece. If he can do it, so can I.' He looked down at his leg. 'Although maybe I'll have to start being more careful.'

They talked about the house Noah had bought a few years ago, another renovation project that had been brought back to life and was now a home.

'Owen did the inside for me and I focused on the garden.'

'You're a good team.'

'Working with mates always helps. What were your work colleagues like?'

'I'm not sure I'd class any of them as mates but they were all friendly enough. To be honest, I didn't have much time to do anything apart from work or talk about work.'

'I'll bet that's changed out here.'

'It certainly has.' She smiled.

'How does your boyfriend feel about you buying a place in Magnolia Creek?'

'He knows it's something I wanted to do, so he's on board.' Was she trying to convince Noah, or herself?

'You know, it's funny…' He slurped his tea. '…I never took you as someone who'd remotely enjoy the countryside when I first saw you. Well, not when I *first* saw you of course, because —'

'No need to elaborate,' she said quickly. 'I think we both know what you mean.'

His eyes danced. 'Anyway, you've begun to surprise me by how settled you seem already. Despite the mess and flying off the handle when you find a bleeding man in your kitchen, you kind of fit in.'

She looked at him over the top of her mug. 'It's not a bad town.'

Magnolia Creek was growing on her by the day, but worse than that, so was Noah's company. And that could only spell trouble.

Chapter Eight

Carrie's relaxing weekend got busier when Kristy decided to make an impromptu visit.

'I've brought supplies!' Her sister grinned as she climbed out of her car and pushed her sunglasses onto the top of her head. She leaned into the back to grab her belongings and pulled out a Tupperware box that she took straight over to Carrie.

Carrie peeled off the lid when Kristy returned to the car for the rest of her things. 'Oh you're so bad! You know I'm a sucker for your lamingtons.'

'Voted best lamington two years in a row at the local school,' Kristy confirmed, now armed with a folded-down airbed, a sleeping bag and a pillow.

'You'll make a good school mum.'

'Let me enjoy being married for a bit but, one day, let's hope so. That Lamington title is mine!' she claimed, eyes wide enough to make Carrie giggle. 'Get the wine, would you? There's two bottles in the back, in a special bag to keep them cold. Oh, and I brought a beanbag with me too.'

'Good thinking.' Carrie grabbed the beanbag first and then returned to fetch the wine. 'I had too much last night,' she told her sister when she had the wine in her arms.

'Well it's your obligation to drink with me tonight – it's a rare occasion I get my sister all to myself so I'm making the most of it. What else does a girl need apart from wine and lamingtons?'

'It's a tip, I'm warning you,' Carrie called after Kristy as they filed into the house, but her sister wasn't nearly as fastidious as she was so she wouldn't be sensitive to the state of the inside. The girl loved to go camping with her husband, and when kids came along in the future they'd no doubt be like the Brady Bunch and far more adventurous than Carrie would ever be.

'It's a bit messy for you,' Kristy remarked. 'I'll put up with it though.'

'You're used to roughing it, that's why. How was Halls Gap?'

'Best camping trip ever.' Kristy stood in the kitchen looking around at the bare walls and floors, not a cupboard in sight. 'Please tell me you have wine glasses somewhere.'

Carrie's lips twisted. 'It'll have to be cups I'm afraid.'

'No chance. I even take wine glasses camping – I'm not behaving like a student.'

'So you got a bit of the princess gene too,' Carrie observed.

'The princess gene?'

'I'm a princess because I hate getting dirty,' she explained when her sister looked at her vaguely, 'but you can't drink out of a different vessel. I'm shocked.'

'They're decent bottles of sauvignon blanc,' Kristy declared, taking them out of the insulated bag and slotting them into the fridge. 'They deserve glasses. Come on, this is a matter of extreme urgency.'

Carrie laughed. 'I've missed you.'

'I've missed you too. You know, you're looking the most relaxed you've been in a long while.'

'I'm knee-deep in renovations – how can I be relaxed?'

'I'm wondering the same thing myself,' said Kristy. 'What are you doing?'

Carrie had taken out her phone and fired off a text. 'I've texted Gemma, Rosie and Bella, so one of them should be able to sort us out.'

'Who are they?' Kristy helped herself to a lamington.

'Friends who live here in Magnolia Creek.'

Kristy stopped chewing. 'Hold on a minute, you've made friends, already?' Her look of mock horror wasn't lost on Carrie.

'I'm not that terrible.'

'No, you're not, you're lovely. But usually outside of your and Lachlan's circle of friends/colleagues, or whatever you'd describe them as, you don't want to know.'

'I'm usually too busy, that's why.'

'Everyone needs friends, Carrie.'

'Thanks. They're lovely girls actually.' She giggled.

'What? What aren't you telling me?'

'We've called ourselves the Magnolia Girls.'

Kristy sniggered but then stopped smiling. 'Oh, God, you're serious, aren't you?'

'I am.' Carrie explained all about the enthusiasm at the baby-cuddling project.

'Well good for you. It sounds as though you've chosen the best place to be. I love this town. My wedding was more dreamlike than I ever could've imagined. Hang on, isn't Rosie the name of a girl who works at Magnolia House? In fact, isn't that the girl Owen ended up with?' She finished the last morsel of lamington, eyes wide and eager to find out all the gossip.

'The very same. She still works there. She's loved up with Owen and they're expecting a baby.'

Kristy took a deep breath. 'Well, for a small town, it's all happening.' When Carrie's phone pinged she said, 'Oh please let that be news of our wine glasses.'

Carrie nodded. 'Bella says she has some for us, we just need to pop into the café. Come on, you can come and meet her, and hopefully some of the others if they're

91

still hanging around. And we can work off some of the lamingtons.' She grabbed one to devour on the way.

*

Carrie and Kristy had always been close as sisters, with similar temperaments yet enough differences to stop them competing against one another. Now she was here in Magnolia Creek, Carrie realised she could've probably confided in Kristy much earlier, but not today. Not when the sun was hanging in there before the forecast rain tomorrow, and when she had friends to introduce.

Kristy met Bella, then Gemma and Andrew, followed by Rosie, whom they bumped into at the gift shop. The pair returned to the house armed with wine glasses and as they pumped up the extra airbed they sipped on sauvignon blanc, which they then took downstairs to the lounge where Kristy had installed her own beanbag.

'It'll be amazing when it's finished.' Kristy looked around the room, another shell in a house that would come back to life in a few short weeks. She patted her beanbag. 'And you can keep this here as long as you need.'

'Thank you, that's kind.'

'You're lucky you've saved up and have the funds to really make this place something.' Kristy couldn't stop looking around in awe, most likely imagining the transformation. Neither of them had gone into interior design but they were both their mother's daughters. 'And how's the nannying? Sorry' – she shook off the laugh clearly about to escape – 'I just can't imagine you spending every day with someone incapable of meaningful conversation. It's like imagining Dad flipping through fabric samples instead of Mum, chatting about what sofa would look good and which curtains hung the best.'

Carrie joined the laughter. 'You're right, that is weird. But I was…*am* a paediatrician. It shouldn't be that much of a shock.'

'It's completely different and you know it.'

She had a point.

'I like the mix of nannying plus the baby-cuddling program.' Carrie was eager to keep the air of positivity rather than share the truth just now. 'It'll keep me busy for a while, and it's good to be at the house here to see it evolving. Owen will be taking the rest of the bathroom out this week so I'll be over at the holiday cottages by the lake, just for two nights, to give him a chance to get the new toilet and bath in at least. The finish won't matter, as long as it's usable.'

Kristy remembered the cottages and they chatted about the gorgeous view of the lake from each of them with their miniature verandas out front.

'So what's the plan long-term?' Kristy asked.

'When the house is finished?' She might have known her sister would delve further. 'I haven't thought that far ahead yet.' As far as anyone was concerned, they could look at her CV and see she'd taken a break from work, which she could explain away by talking about her travels. Then they'd see the nannying and the part-time baby-cuddling program coordinator as jobs she took to keep her hand in while she renovated a country property: again something she could easily explain.

They talked some more about Rosie and Owen and Kristy was impressed at how they all seemed to be friendly enough. Carrie explained colour schemes she'd selected, what she'd do where, and how she'd position furniture when all her belongings finally arrived.

'Do you miss the city?' Kristy wanted to know.

'Sometimes. I miss how much there was going on, but out here it's the opposite end of the spectrum and I'm enjoying the tranquillity. It's really something else.'

'It sure is. But I'm craving Chinese takeaway right now, and I'll bet there's not one in a ten-mile radius.'

'I'm actually not sure.' Carrie took out her phone and after a good search declared, 'hallelujah!'

'You found one?'

'Sure have. It's quite a way but they deliver for a small fee. I'm craving one now too. Spring rolls, crispy duck…'

'Sticky pork…oh my goodness, I'm salivating!'

Ten minutes later they'd placed their order and were well into the second bottle of wine by the time the food arrived. And for tonight, Carrie couldn't be happier. Here she was in the middle of nowhere with no massive responsibilities weighing on her mind, no paediatric case giving her sleepless nights, and just for a while longer she wanted to enjoy it and pretend everything was fine.

*

'Oh why did you let me drink so much?' Kristy groaned from the airbed against the far wall on Sunday morning.

'Totally your fault,' Carrie moaned.

The sun streamed in through the window and Carrie could hear a faint clattering sound. 'Who's that? It's Sunday!' She stumbled into the bathroom following the sound coming from the back of the house. She peered out the window and saw Noah down below, clattering a collection of tools. She groaned. He was a bit early wasn't he? And she'd told him to take it easy. Still, he wouldn't be training at the fire station since he'd hurt himself so she supposed he was putting in the hours while he could.

She pulled on her jeans and an old T-shirt and offered to make some tea for Kristy and herself. She gave her hair a quick ruffle with her fingers on the way down the stairs so it looked half presentable. In the kitchen she filled the kettle on the floor and flicked the switch and, after waving a quick hello at Noah, she took two cups of tea upstairs and headed straight for the shower.

With fresh hair and now properly dressed, she took the empty cups downstairs and left Kristy to get ready, warning her not to stand too close to the window when she was naked. She rapped her knuckles against the kitchen window when she saw Noah lifting part of a paving slab again and when he looked she wagged a finger at him.

He came to the back door. 'You caught me.'

'How's the wrist?' She gestured to it and then looked at his leg, both of which had been properly dressed again. He'd obviously showered because he was completely clean and the hairs on his legs shone in the sun, matching the lighter shades in his brown hair that came from working outside so much. His hair was fresh too, so the wrist was clearly operating well enough to keep him presentable.

'It's not feeling bad at all, and the wound looks clean. I used disinfectant again today and then redressed it as instructed.'

'And the leg?' She felt self-conscious zoning in on the limb as he stood there in his shorts and work boots.

'Same. I'll be back to normal soon. I'm not going to do much today, just wanted to move this last slab out of the way, collect up my tools and then when the rain stops mid-week I'll be ready to go again.'

She was about to ask what the next stage was now the shrubs and shed had gone when a dog came sauntering around the corner of the house.

'Norma!' Noah made a grab for the dog as it wagged its tail and pushed past him into the kitchen, seeing someone new. 'Norma, no!' He looked at Carrie as she crouched down to make a fuss of the dog. 'I'm sorry, she sleeps in the back of the truck but obviously had other ideas today.'

Norma looked old and though her tail wagged, it lacked the ferocity of a younger canine's. 'Hello there.' She fussed Norma's head and ears, which seemed to go down well. 'Noah and Norma – the names sound good together.'

'Very funny. You like dogs?' He seemed surprised.

'I don't mind them. What sort is she?'

'A golden retriever.'

'I've never owned a dog. In fact, I've never had many friends or family who did either. But she's gorgeous.' Carrie stayed where she was and stroked Norma, who had taken to lying down in the sunny spot inside the kitchen by the back door.

'Come on, Norma, let's put you back in the car.' Noah began to walk away but the dog was having none of it.

'She's no bother, really.' Carrie was quite enamoured with her. 'She can lie there as long as she wants.'

'Really?'

'I'm not that horrible, am I?'

'You're not horrible at all. I suppose even princesses have dogs.' His grin warmed her more than the sun from above and off he went back to the garden. Norma, evidently not entirely confident in new company, trotted obediently after him.

Kristy appeared and made straight for the fridge.

'I can make toast if you like,' Carrie suggested. 'Or we could go to the pub for a cooked breakfast.'

Kristy's face broke out in a smile. 'Now we're talking. It's a bit much after the takeaway last night but, hey, I'm on holiday. I don't have to leave until mid-morning so it'll be a perfect start to the day.'

'Just let me grab my purse and keys.' Carrie moved to go upstairs, where she kept her bag, when Norma's nose nudged the back door open again. 'Hey, what are you doing, you gorgeous thing?'

'It's a dog!' Kristy was horrified.

Carrie collapsed into fits of laughter. 'The look on your face!'

'Who does it belong to? And, more to the point, what are you doing embracing it?' She stepped forward and fussed Norma. Ever since Kristy had met her in-laws and been introduced to their two German shepherds, Kristy had become a self-confessed dog lover. 'Oh, you're beautiful. And so gentle.' She stroked Norma around her ears, which the dog seemed to adore. 'What is our Carrie doing being so kind to you?' She lowered her voice. 'Between you and me, you're a bit smelly and covered in hair for someone like my sister.'

Carrie sighed. 'I like a tidy house, but I'm not completely intolerant. And Norma here is very polite – she's not leaping up at me, catching my clothes, there's no slobber in sight and she smells pretty OK to me.'

'Well, I never thought I'd see this side of you.' Kristy smiled genuinely. 'Coming to Magnolia Creek really has done you the world of good.'

Just then Noah poked his head around the door. 'God, I'm so sorry, Carrie. Norma, come here.' The dog reluctantly went to her master, who made just as much

97

fuss of her despite his reprimand. 'Oh, and sorry again, I didn't realise you had a visitor.'

'No need to apologise. This is my sister, Kristy. Kristy, this is Noah – he's working for me…transforming the garden,' she added. She didn't want him thinking she was looking down on him again.

The pair shook hands and Carrie didn't miss Kristy's look of approval and another look Noah's way when they both bid him goodbye to head for the pub.

In the Magnolia Tavern after they'd ordered the breakfast – poached eggs on toast for Carrie, and the same for Kristy with a side order of mushrooms and bacon added for good measure – Kristy looked at her sister. 'Well?'

'Well what?' She thanked Chris, the landlord, for the freshly squeezed orange juice and took a welcome sip.

'Noah!' Kristy leaned towards her in case another customer heard. 'I kept quiet all the way down here, waiting for you to make the first comment, but I can't keep it in any longer. He's pretty hot, don't you think?'

'He's my gardener.' But she didn't disagree. 'And anyway, I'm attached. Fully attached, to Lachlan. Remember him?'

Kristy gulped down her juice and swiftly ordered another. The pub was pretty empty now but Carrie suspected it would fill up later for Sunday lunch and the beer garden outside would be awash with customers.

'He has a gorgeous body,' Kristy added. 'Well, come on, don't tell me you didn't notice! Even in a T-shirt I could see muscle definition beneath.'

'I'm gonna tell on you, have a word with your husband and tell him you've got your eye on another man.'

'Don't be ridiculous,' said Kristy. 'You can look at the menu, always. So have you been, looking at the menu?' She raised her eyebrows. 'Would you ever sample what's on offer?'

Carrie laughed out loud. 'Oh my goodness, stop it. No I wouldn't. The only menu I'm interested in is the one here,' she told her sister.

And when their eggs arrived she did her best to change the subject, because as she'd stood talking to Noah and making a fuss over Norma that morning, she knew his injuries hadn't been the only parts of him she'd inspected.

*

Back at the house, Carrie waved her sister off. Her company had been amazing this weekend, truly what she'd needed, but she went straight inside and called Lachlan when she realised that since yesterday morning she hadn't replied to either of his texts. He seemed fine, but when she mentioned she'd stay at the holiday cottages while Owen pulled out the bathroom she could tell he wasn't happy with the arrangement and found herself agreeing to ask Owen to hold off until the weekend, when she could go to stay with Lachlan in the city and see him around his work commitments.

Noah knocked on the back door as Carrie hung up the call.

She smiled. 'Is everything OK?'

'It's all good. I've been in touch with a fencing company so I wanted to run it by you first. They'll be here later this afternoon to give me a quote.'

'No problem, although I'm surprised they've agreed to come over on a Sunday.'

'Us tradies all know each other, and we're slaves to the weather. We'll work hard now and look forward to some down time when it pours with rain for three days straight.'

When Norma appeared and walked in through the kitchen door as though she lived here, Carrie laughed.

'She likes you,' Noah observed.

'I like her too.'

'Do you mind if I use your bathroom?'

'Sure, go ahead.' She watched Noah wiggle off his boots and leave them on the back step. She was about to tell him not to bother as long as they weren't caked in mud, but she appreciated the consideration so kept quiet.

She fussed over Norma for a while and the dog rolled onto her back so Carrie could tickle her tummy.

'You know,' she said as Norma's back leg twitched when the scratching tickled her a bit too much, 'you are the most beautiful dog I've ever seen. I know I haven't seen many – I've never had a dog of my own – but you I could get to like. Maybe I'll get a dog, what do you think? Do you think a dog would enjoy my little house up here on the hill, do you think the garden would be nice for a dog?'

Carrie spun round when she sensed Noah behind her. Without his boots he was amazingly quiet. 'I wasn't talking to myself,' she explained.

'I know, you were talking to Norma.' He couldn't keep the grin off his face and crouched down beside her to fuss his dog too. 'You were talking in the same way people talk to babies.'

'I bet you talk to her like that all the time.'

'Of course. Norma and I go back fourteen years – I got her as a pup. She's my best friend and we have great conversations on our travels around here. Out of all the women I know, she talks the most sense.' He seemed glad to have made Carrie smile so much and when he stood up he asked, 'Who's the little boy?'

Confused, Carrie looked out of the window. 'I don't see anyone.'

'Not out there. The little boy with you in the photograph.'

She hardly dare ask. 'What are you talking about?'

'I wasn't nosing around. I was about to tread on it on my way to the bathroom so I picked it up and put it on top of your airbed.'

'Thanks, it must've fallen out of…anyway, if you'll excuse me I need to go to the supermarket. I've got nothing for dinner and despite the enormous breakfast I know I'll be ravenous later.'

He reached a hand out to her arm to stop her scurrying away. 'Who is he? A nephew, yours, a friend's kid?'

'Why do you need to know?' She hadn't meant to snap but she definitely didn't want to talk about it. Why couldn't her brain process things faster and make something up? She could say it was a friend's son, or a relative. But, her mouth dry, she couldn't get any words out.'

'Judging by your reaction, he's someone who means something to you, so I'm curious.'

'It's none of your business.' She tugged her arm away when she realised his hand was still touching it. The photograph must have fallen out the back of her diary beside her airbed upstairs. She looked at it most days but was usually sure to tuck it away safely each time.

She needed to leave the house. She didn't want Noah to read any hurt or distress on her face, anything to give away how she felt about that little boy.

'Fine. Be like that.' His voice took her by surprise. She wasn't used to men biting her head off. Kristy had always joked that Carrie's blonde hair, tanned skin and attractiveness cast a spell on any man who crossed her path and rendered him incapable of doing anything but bow down to her.

Clearly Noah was different.

He tugged on his boots, did up the laces and beckoned Norma outside. 'Come on, let's leave this lady alone. Clearly that's the way she wants to be.'

And when he left she went straight upstairs and cradled the photo to her. Lachlan had once snapped at her in a similar way as she'd clutched the photo in the same way she was doing now. 'It's not natural,' he'd told her with such disdain it had stopped her tears. 'You're not his mother, his sister, or any part of his family. I know it hurts, Carrie, but get a fucking grip.' His words had stung almost as much as if he'd slapped her and since then she'd kept the photo hidden away.

Chapter Nine

After the run-in with Noah yesterday Carrie kept her distance from him, and, it seemed, he was thinking the same way. The fencer came and quoted but there was no knock on the door to discuss anything, and Noah and Norma had packed up and gone on their way before Carrie even returned from the supermarket. She'd heated up a rice dish in the microwave, tried to read her book upstairs on the airbed but when the words on the page morphed into one, she shut it and had an exceptionally early night.

Maria was in fine form the next morning. 'Teething', her mum had described it as, but with the rain lashing at the windows and without the promise of escape into the fresh air today, Carrie was tearing her hair out by lunchtime and so she bundled Maria up and drove into Magnolia Creek, where she started with a visit to the café and a coffee to keep her sane. Bella fussed over Maria, and all the cuddles made the baby so much calmer by the time they left. With the rain cover over the pram and a waterproof for Carrie, next stop was the gift shop, where Maria watched a mobile moving above their heads. Mal gave her some leftover bubble wrap to play with while they were browsing, although Carrie wouldn't let her have it when she wasn't watching in case Maria thought it a good idea to shove it in her mouth. After the gift shop came the chocolaterie and a quick hello to Gemma, and they ended their outing with a dash over to the florist's so they didn't get soaked as Carrie picked up a bunch of orange gerberas for Bella to say thank you for saving her sanity that morning.

'Maria was a challenge today, so thank you.' Carrie handed Bella the flowers when they reached the café.

'You didn't have to do this.' Bella was touched and immediately took the blooms out back to put in a vase and returned to put the display next to the till.

'I did, because I was going crazy earlier.'

'It was my pleasure,' Bella smiled. She leaned in and let Maria grab hold of her hand, fascinated by her watch.

Carrie and Maria had a good afternoon after that and although the both of them got wet on the transfers from pram to car and car to house, it had been worth it.

After Maria it was busy, busy, busy, and on to the hospital. Today Carrie was collating information on volunteers. Serena was impressed she'd already coerced friends to take part, although Carrie had claimed no such thing, and there were fifteen women and one man who had signed up to be baby cuddlers in all. It was a lot of admin entering all their information, arranging for checks, sorting people into groups so they could come into the hospital for training, but by the time Carrie left that evening the rain had stopped and shooting up from behind the roofs of the stores on Main Street was a rainbow of indigo, red, yellow and blue strips, all the different colours in the sun that you didn't usually see.

At the house, she parked next to Owen's motorbike and went inside to see what the progress was.

'I've nailed down the loose floorboards in here,' he said from his position on the floor in the second lounge room, 'I've knocked in any protruding nails and I've had to take up a few of the floorboards that weren't salvageable.'

'Thanks again for changing your schedule,' she told him, referring to the change of plan for when he'd tear out the bathroom suite. 'It's just easier for me to go and stay with Lachlan at the weekend.'

'No worries at all.' He pulled up one more floorboard, which was rotten at the end and had another hole in the middle, and leaned it against another board beside the wall. 'I'll replace the missing boards and fill any small holes, then we can get on to sanding. This room hasn't taken much work at all, but the architrave is rotten.' He took her over to the window. 'The window is fine, but see here?' He crouched down and she did the same as he pointed beneath the architrave where half the wood was missing. 'It's not expensive, just another thing to do before we're ready to finish the floors and start painting.'

Standing up, she looked around. 'This is a nice room. Smaller than the other but cosy.' A sudden thought entered her mind. 'I can see this room as a snug, perhaps with a wood burner.'

'That's what I call vision. You must get that from your mum.'

Carrie smiled. 'That's about the extent of it though. I'll have to get her out here to sort furnishings and colour schemes.'

He picked up a bottle of water from next to the pile of boards and took a swig. 'You sound as though you'll be making this homely enough.'

'You know, I never thought I would.'

'You've always liked things just so,' he said, 'so why has it surprised you so much that you want to do the same here?'

She shook her head. 'I don't mean wanting the place to look good. I mean doing it all so far away from the city. I always thought I'd buy my first place in inner Melbourne – Toorak, Albert Park, or somewhere like that. I never thought I'd come this far out.'

'It's something else, isn't it? You always said it was beautiful when you came up to visit me.'

'But that's not the same. I was visiting briefly each time – totally different from immersing yourself in a place like this, getting to know people.'

'People seem to like you.' He started wrenching off the architrave at fault, using sufficient force but gentle enough not to damage anything else around the window. 'And Rosie can't wait to do this baby-cuddling thing.' He grinned, and without turning away from the architrave said, 'I hear you're all calling yourselves the Magnolia Girls.'

'Hey, don't mock.'

'I'm not!' He put the offending piece of wood next to all the others. 'I think it's a great thing. You know me and the community – I like to be involved, and it's great to see you doing it too. Not just because it's a good thing to do for others but because I think it's good for *you* as well.' He was clearly about to ask more but she changed the subject.

'What happens here then?' She nodded to the bare parts of the floor that now had nothing stopping the outside from coming in. The house wasn't built on a concrete slab but on stumps and as Carrie stood next to where one of the floorboards had been ripped out, she could see the ground half a metre below.

Owen came and stood next to her. 'I told you, I'll get some replacement boards, tomorrow most probably.'

She looked up at him as though her query should be obvious. 'No, I mean what can it be covered with in the meantime? I don't want anything crawling inside and taking me by surprise.'

'Ah yes, the balled-up paper upstairs should've told me that.'

'Seriously though,' she said, 'I don't feel comfortable leaving it like that.'

Owen scratched his head in thought and then went into the other lounge and returned with his tools. Screwdriver in hand, he began unscrewing the hinges of the door to the room. 'This has to come off anyway, to be sanded and then painted, so may as well take it off now.' When the door was off he manoeuvred it until it was near the gap in the floor and then laid it down flat.

'Perfect,' Carrie grinned.

Owen went to the kitchen and removed that door too, bringing it into the room and doing the same on the other side of the floor, and with the addition of a flattened old cardboard box, they'd covered all the area they needed to.

Noah chose that moment to knock at the front door with the fencing quotes. 'Just wanted to check you're OK to go ahead with this one.' He handed her a piece of paper with figures written on it and she gave it straight back to him.

'Whatever,' she told Noah. 'You've got the budget so whatever fits in is fine by me.'

He rolled his eyes much like she'd rolled hers at Maria that morning when she threw half a muffin on the floor for the third time. 'I meant the style of the fence. If you turn it over there's a sketch of how it'll go around the property.'

She took the paper back but it made no sense to her. 'You'll have to show me.' Turning the paper around at different angles she said, 'I don't even know which is the start of the garden and which is the end.' She walked through to the kitchen and waited for him to follow. Impatiently, she stood, hands on hips, looking out the window and over the back garden, which was becoming one sodden mess with the rain that had drenched Magnolia Creek today. With more due tomorrow, and the day after that, she wondered what sort of a quagmire she'd be left with by the end of the week.

Noah stood next to her and she tried to ignore the warmth coming from his skin, the accidental brush of his arm against hers as he leaned over to point to the far corner and explain how that was where the fence would be a slightly different shape because of the land boundaries.

'The land isn't completely rectangular,' he said, unaware of how he made her feel. 'So the fence over there will be cut off at the corner. I'll put in a shed and a lilly pilly on either side of it, which should grow well, and you'll forget all about the peculiar shape.'

Carrie nodded, but really she wasn't thinking about the garden or lilly-whatever-they-were-calleds. Instead she was wondering whether Noah was thinking about the photograph he'd found, or her reaction and refusal to tell him who the little boy was. For some reason she found herself hoping that he was, but when he announced he'd give the fencer the go-ahead and turned to leave, she realised he probably hadn't given it much more thought and just assumed she was a rude princess who liked things her own way.

*

Come Friday afternoon, following a busy week with Maria, the rain that had made everyone miserable and some busy afternoons at the hospital, Carrie was glad to escape the renovations and head away from Magnolia Creek, back to the city.

It felt weird letting herself into Lachlan's apartment. She'd done it plenty of times before, but she'd quickly got used to an entirely different routine.

With Lachlan not due home for another couple of hours, when they'd head out to a restaurant, she made the most of the luxury. She ran a heavenly bubble bath and soaked for as long as she could before the water turned lukewarm. She made herself a fruit salad – Lachlan was surprisingly domesticated and healthy, keeping his fridge stocked with fresh ingredients at all times, which had always surprised her. Most doctors she knew ate on the run so often they mostly had convenience on tap, but here was her boyfriend with a plentiful supply of grapes, berries of multiple kinds, and even Greek yogurt to go with it.

After she'd had a snack, Carrie unpacked her outfit for that evening. Lachlan had always approved of her dress sense. With high heels and tailored dresses, she always felt empowered, sexy and like the Carrie she'd always strived to be. A lot of her smarter clothes were in storage but she'd kept a few smarter outfits for times like these.

She pulled on the designer inky-blue and purple dress. With its high waist and overlapping V neckline, it was flattering and comfortable. It seemed like forever since she'd worn heels and she grinned as she slipped her feet into the nude patent pair. There wasn't much call for them in Magnolia Creek and she realised how out of place she'd appear if she walked down Main Street looking like this, or attempted to walk up the hill to her house.

Checking her watch, she sighed. Lachlan was late as usual and she was unsurprised when her phone pinged as though it could tell what she was thinking. He'd been held up at the hospital but their friends Stella and Marco, Flora and Dean were at an Italian restaurant in Southgate not far from the apartment and he asked her to meet them there and he'd get there when he could.

'Great.' She looked down at her heels. Her feet were already feeling a little uncomfortable. Once upon a time she'd strolled so serenely from her apartment to the hubbub of Melbourne's city dressed for occasions such as these, but now she realised her feet had quickly got used to being at home in more appropriate shoes.

She giggled at the thought of slinging on her jeans and multicoloured checked shirt with a pair of Skechers, knowing it wasn't going to be the kind of restaurant that would look favourably on such a dressed-down look. She was back in the city now, back to the life she'd once been a big part of, so it was time to shake off the doubts. She compromised. She'd wear her Skechers to walk from the apartment all the way past the casino and towards Southbank and then discretely visit the Ladies bathroom in the Crown Casino complex, where she'd change into her heels for the remainder of the walk to the restaurant.

Nobody would be any the wiser.

Her plan went without a hitch and as soon as she arrived at the Italian restaurant, Flora was first up out of her seat to greet her. 'Great to see you!' She air kissed Carrie once on either side of her face. A paediatrician in the hospital where Carrie had once worked, Flora was one of those women who seemed to keep a lot bottled up inside and emotions were kept in check.

Stella kissed Carrie on both cheeks. 'The men are waiting at the bar,' she said. 'They wanted to give us ladies a chance to catch up. So come on, Carrie, I can't wait to hear all about this little house of yours.'

Carrie described how it looked now, what it would become after all the hard work was finished. 'Magnolia Creek is a beautiful town.'

Stella voiced her approval. 'It does sound quaint. But it's so far away.'

'Not really. It takes less than a couple of hours and it's so beautiful up there. Apparently it's stunning in the spring so I can't wait to see it then.'

Stella and Flora agreed it sounded lovely, but these two women were the least likely people Carrie could ever imagine living in a mess, sleeping on an airbed as men worked around them. Carrie had been like that not so long ago, but she was gradually changing and already she felt one step removed from the gathering tonight.

'Is Clare coming along this evening?' Carrie asked. Clare was single, gorgeous and the most relaxed of the crowd – or at least she had been until she'd lost her job when her position was phased out following a restructure at the end of last year.

Flora shook her head, crossed one tanned leg over the other and adjusted her black dress that revealed a bit too much with the movement. 'We asked, but…' She shrugged as though even that had been too much effort.

Carrie changed the subject and told them all about her garden and the pergola she planned to have installed.

'You'll be fighting us off,' claimed Flora, 'because that does sound good. A long evening relaxing beneath a pergola with a glass of wine sounds perfect.'

'She's right,' said Stella. 'My new role is full on, so a glass of wine sitting in a quiet house in the country sounds the business.'

'How's the new job going?' Carrie asked.

She sighed. 'Tonight is the first evening I've been able to relax for a while.'

'Tell me about it,' Flora sighed, not daring to miss out on the conversation.

And, just like that, it was on to hospital talk.

Carrie did her best to chat with the other women about life at the hospital but when they asked her about the baby-cuddling program – they weren't interested in the nannying job – she almost didn't want to tell them anything. But that would be churlish, so she explained about how it would be run and coordinated, the recruitment of volunteers and the red tape that had to be tackled. She didn't mention that most of the red tape had already been overcome – because for now she wanted them to talk to her as though nothing had changed, as though she hadn't taken a huge step back in her career.

'I think it's a wonderful thing,' said Stella. 'As you know, we run a similar program at the hospital, but we've had to close the waitlist because it's so long already. Have you got many volunteers?'

'The number is slowly building. I got a small group together from Magnolia Creek, and as soon as I wrote a media release that appeared in the local newspaper, word spread.'

Stella touched a hand to her husband Marco's knee as the men rejoined them but the focus was still on Carrie. 'Well I'm impressed. I thought it would take far longer to get through the bureaucracy.'

Carrie said hello to Marco and to Flora's partner, Dean. 'The plans have been under way for quite some time,' she was forced to admit.

'Forgive me,' Flora began, reaching out for her wine, 'but I thought that was your new job – to set up the program in the first place.' Her shiny red talons splayed around the glass.

'I'm happy to jump in where I have. It's crazy busy already, and with my other job and renovating the house, it's more than enough to manage.' She wished Lachlan would show up for a distraction or that they'd simply change the subject, but luckily for Carrie, Marco came to the rescue.

'You sound like you're juggling a lot.' Marco smiled across at her. He'd always been her favourite of the bunch. He aimed high in his career, but he was much easier to talk to than the rest of them. 'Is it full on, looking after the baby?'

Thank goodness he'd saved her from the discomfort of having to admit it was no managerial role she'd taken at the country hospital but more that of a lackey. Not that she minded, but these women might. She moved away from the subject and chatted about Maria, pondering how a ten-month-old could keep a grown woman on her toes. 'She really is the boss of me.'

Marco turned to Stella. 'Someday we'll have to get ourselves a little boss baby.'

'One day.' Stella touched the side of his face affectionately before excusing herself to go to the Ladies.

'Is everything OK with you guys?' Carrie hadn't missed the underlying tension.

'Kind of.' He lowered his voice. The others were now embroiled in conversation about an upcoming conference. 'I want to start trying; she wants to be in her new role for at least a couple of years first. We're not fighting, but we also don't have time on our side. I'm forty-one this year, Stella will be thirty-eight. I'm worried that if we leave it too long, it won't happen.'

Carrie patted his hand as she saw Lachlan finally heading their way. 'I really hope it all works out for you.'

Lachlan only had eyes for Carrie when he arrived. He complimented her dress, her hair, and whispered in her ear to tell her how good she looked tonight, making her feel special and happy to be here. When they were all seated he continued in fine form. He was attentive to her but part of the overall conversation and Carrie found herself relaxing into it, with the help of a few glasses of wine. She talked to Dean about the bathroom renovations as he and Flora were redoing their own, she talked more about the baby-cuddling program when Lachlan insisted on boasting about his girlfriend who could achieve anything she put her mind to, and she told the group more about Magnolia Creek, a place none of them had ever been.

'You should definitely visit,' she said to Stella when dessert arrived. Hers was chocolate mousse, the lightest option but she didn't think she could even manage that. The food here was delicious but three courses was too much. 'There are cottages by the lake, there's a wonderful pub that serves yummy food, and there's a café, a gift shop.' She blushed, realising she was blabbering on like an information guide touting for tourists.

Stella smiled at her. 'Even paediatricians take holidays now and again, so I'm sure we'll visit. It sounds like quite the place.' The way Stella looked at Marco told Carrie there was a lot more to this pair than she'd realised before. There was a deeper level, a current that ran beneath the talk of fast cars and expensive holidays.

Flora and Dean on the other hand were different, or at least Flora was. Dean was down to earth, if a little old-fashioned, and when they'd talked about renovating he wanted to know what Carrie had chosen for the bathroom, whether chrome fittings were all the rage, whether a roll-top bath would be impossible to clean around the base, if Victorian taps were a total no-no nowadays. But Flora was preoccupied. She'd been interested in talk of skiing in Vail, been the instigator of a discussion about test driving a new car, the make and model of which Carrie had let go completely over her head because she was so disinterested, but when it came to the normalities of everyday life Flora withdrew as though all it did was remind her that they were all regular people and life didn't always operate at full speed.

Carrie made the group laugh with her tale of stuffing newspaper in holes at the house to stop spiders coming in, and Owen covering gaps in the floor downstairs when she worried about the same. And when there was a lull in conversation Flora asked, 'When are you coming back?'

'To the city?' Carrie put down her fork, defeated by the second half of the chocolate mousse.

'To the city, and to be a paediatrician. I mean, come on, organising the baby cuddling and looking after someone else's kid is admirable, but it's not what you want for the rest of your life, is it?' Her eyes danced as though putting someone else in an uncomfortable position was a joy. But looking at the others, expecting them to hold the same opinion as Flora, Carrie noticed they all looked a bit embarrassed for the woman even though they knew Carrie well enough to know she'd stick up for herself. After all, Carrie hadn't completely lost her identity.

'Life is full on right now with two jobs and a renovation,' Carrie explained diplomatically, 'but one day, yes, I'll be back to paediatrics.' The firmness in her voice was enough to put a stop to the line of questioning and Dean steered the conversation onto safer ground by discussing paint colours and the merits of wooden floors as opposed to tiles.

Over coffees at the end of the meal, talk turned to their friend Clare, who Carrie wished was here tonight, being almost an ally in her absence from the medical profession.

'It's terrible,' Stella began. 'She hasn't worked in four months. All that training – it's such a waste, and she doesn't seem to be able to find another position.'

'Has she applied for much?' Flora wanted to know.

'Would she consider looking outside of the city?' Dean was curious.

Lachlan frowned. 'She lives in the Eastern suburbs, doesn't she?' When Marco confirmed it he said, 'They're screaming out for doctors like her at two, even three, facilities that I know of.'

'Maybe she's taking a break,' Carrie put in. She may as well have said Clare had torn up her medical degree and put one finger up to her career judging by the looks she was getting now. 'She's only been out a few months, give her a chance.'

'She needs to get back in the game,' Flora insisted as though Carrie's point was ridiculous. 'If she's out too long, nobody will want her. And I saw her a couple of weeks ago.' She looked at Stella as though what she was about to tell them was the worst thing in the world. 'She was wearing baggy tracksuit pants, an old T-shirt and trainers – nothing like the Clare we used to see around the place. She's really let herself go.'

Carrie almost fell about laughing, because she'd done pretty much the same. These women had no idea how liberating it had been. *Don't knock it till you try it*, she wanted to yell, but instead gulped the rest of her wine so she wouldn't say anything more.

At the end of the meal, when coffees had been drunk and the bill delivered to the table, Flora turned to Carrie. 'We all feel like we need a break sometimes, but she's not doing *anything*.'

'How do you know?' Carrie kept her voice level because Flora was winding her up this evening. As she suspected, Flora didn't have an answer. 'What did she say when you called her about tonight?'

'I emailed her.' Flora took her napkin from her lap and bunched it up before setting it on the table. 'I'm not chasing her. If she doesn't want to come to these things, I'm not going to be the bitch that hounds her until she does.'

'Maybe money is tight – have you thought of that?' Carrie began. 'Or maybe she's stressed.'

'Carrie…' Lachlan's look told her she was going too far.

'I'm sorry,' Carrie continued, 'but you're her friends. Why not call her and ask her if she's OK? Pick up the phone and actually have a conversation.' She held up a hand before Flora could respond. 'And don't tell me you're too busy. She was your friend long before I ever knew her – you guys go way back. She deserves more than us sitting around a table claiming self-righteousness.'

'Carrie, stop.' Lachlan's voice held steady.

Flora stood up. 'I'll be outside, Dean. I'm not going to sit here while I'm attacked for voicing my opinion.'

'I'm sorry,' said Carrie to everyone else around the table. They'd never had such an outburst within the group and it seemed nobody knew how to handle it.

They settled the bill between them and Dean went outside to join Flora. When the other men filed out of the restaurant in front of Carrie and Stella, Carrie said, 'I shouldn't have laid into her.'

'Between you and me,' Stella confided, 'she deserved it.' She winked. 'Flora speaks before she thinks; she has no filter. I don't know why she gets so high and mighty all the time – maybe she feels like she has to compete. Sometimes I feel like I should be doing the same, but I have enough of that in my career. I'm getting too old to be thinking about doing it anywhere else.'

Carrie appreciated the frank conversation. It was the most open Stella had ever been, but by the time they all went their separate ways she knew she owed Lachlan an apology too. He hated confrontation at social occasions and this was supposed to be a nice weekend, some quality time together. Truth be told, she'd wanted to stay in tonight, have a takeaway and cosy up on the sofa watching a movie, but she'd gone along with dinner plans after he told her everyone wanted to see her.

'It's a beautiful night.' Lachlan draped his suit jacket across her shoulders and they walked along Southbank.

Carrie looked across the river to Flinders Street Station and its dome that shone at night. She loved this city, from the tinging of a tram's bell to the whooshing sounds the trams made as they whisked people from street to street. She loved the way the city stayed alive even in the dark hours, the gentle tinkling of cutlery from restaurants and the murmurs of laughter from crowds that didn't seem to ever want to go to sleep.

She'd not had much time to appreciate it up until now, forever in a work frenzy, rarely stepping back.

'I'm sorry about what happened at the restaurant.' The breeze lifted her hair as they walked on, the night sky lit up by the flames coming from tall columns outside the Crown Casino complex. 'I shouldn't have had a go at Flora.'

He put an arm across her shoulders. 'I think she often feels threatened when she's out with everyone else.'

'In what way?'

'You know she went for the Head of Paediatrics position too?'

She turned and looked up at him. 'I didn't know that. And Stella got the job.'

He nodded. 'Flora and Stella went to medical school together and according to Marco they've been close friends ever since, but there's always been competitiveness between them. They both claim it fired them up at university but I think that's more from Stella than it is from Flora. Flora has always been one step behind.'

'But she's got a brilliant job, earns a good salary, Dean is gorgeous and loves her to bits, he's an anaesthetist and top of his game. She couldn't want for much else.'

'Don't get me wrong, I know Flora and Dean have a good relationship – but she was never going to go for anyone outside of the medical profession unless they were in law or banking.' Lachlan offered more insight from before Carrie had come on the scene: he'd known these people quite a bit longer. 'Stella once set her up on a blind date with a carpenter.'

'Oh no, was it terrible?' They turned the corner away from the crowds and headed towards the apartment.

Carrie's feet already hurt and she couldn't wait to take off her shoes.

'No, it wasn't terrible. She was smitten. It all seemed to be going fantastically well – we even gossiped in the staff lounge that an engagement could be imminent – but then Stella and Marco got together.'

Carrie stopped, if only to rest her feet. 'Why would that affect Flora's relationship?'

'Marco was new to the hospital and, let's face it, he's not bad to look at.'

'Did Flora like Marco?' She didn't need to add that, yes, the man was incredibly good looking.

'No, nothing like that. But it was what Marco represented. He was a doctor, drove a flashy car, earned great money, and I really believe it became another level of competition. Things eventually fizzled out with the carpenter and, shortly afterwards, Flora found Dean.'

Carrie stopped outside the apartment building and stood on the first step so she was level with Lachlan. 'You seem to know a lot about this.'

'Believe me, I don't make a habit of being so in touch with the inner workings of the female mind, but Stella confided in me recently.'

'Oh?'

'Marco's pressuring her to start a family and she wants to focus on her career a while longer. But it's more than that…for a while she's been worried about Flora, and this was why I stopped you laying into her tonight. Stella's concerned that if she tries to start a family, Flora will do the same. Both of them had always been adamant they didn't want kids, but Stella says that in the last few years her feelings have changed.' He looked at Carrie and she wondered if he was thinking it may happen to them, too, one day.

'I don't understand why it's a problem if they both have babies. It might bring them closer together.'

Lachlan shook his head. 'Stella knows Dean doesn't want children so she's worried Flora will trap him and it'll kill their relationship.'

Carrie shook her head as they made their way through the foyer and into the lift. Inside the apartment she kicked off her heels and lay down on the sofa. 'I enjoyed Stella's company tonight,' she said as Lachlan sat down and lifted her feet onto his lap to massage them.

'Don't you usually?'

'I do, but sometimes I find I'm a bit out of the conversation. I certainly am with Flora.'

'Like I said, she has issues.'

Carrie was amazed Stella had changed her mind about babies in her future. In their previous conversations between all three of them, it had been the one thing they'd all had in common. But, it seemed, you never really knew people deep down unless you pulled apart the layers and took a closer look.

Lachlan ran a hand up her leg, past her knee and on further. 'Come on, let's go to bed. You look hot tonight and all I kept thinking about was what I could do to you when we got home.'

Carrie pulled him closer as he moved above her, but she was distracted. 'I hated the way Flora talked about Clare tonight.'

'That was uncalled for.' He kissed the skin below her ear lobe and she shuddered with pleasure.

'I sometimes wonder if you all talk about me in that way.'

He pulled back. 'What?'

'Do you all gossip about me, the reasons I left, talk about how I'm throwing it all away?'

121

He stopped what he was doing and climbed off. The moment was over. 'Now you're being ridiculous.' He got up and went to the kitchen area to get a drink of water.

Carrie sat up. 'What if I never went back to paediatrics?' When his glass paused mid-air she said, 'That's not my intention, but what if I left and only did nannying, or became a carpenter like Flora's boyfriend who she walked away from because he wasn't good enough?'

'You're being ridiculous, Carrie.'

'Am I? I wouldn't fit in though – you can see that, can't you?' She wondered if Noah saw her in the same way she was beginning to see Lachlan and their friends, as people out of reach, with jobs and lives they deemed superior. She hoped not. She hoped he could tell she was a good person.

But why did she even care?

'Just stop, Carrie,' Lachlan growled. 'You're making this into an argument between us. Jesus, this is supposed to be a nice weekend together. God knows we don't get much time, with you buggering off to the middle of nowhere so you can play house with beefy men in shorts and clumpy boots.'

She stood up, furious at his remark, but soon realised she had a small blister on her toe from the shoes she was no longer used to. She winced. 'I'm not *playing house*. What a ridiculous thing to say. I'm working two jobs and organising a renovation.'

'I'm going to bed.' He slammed the glass down. 'I can't talk to you when you're in this mood.'

'Can't or won't?' she yelled after him, but he'd already shut the bedroom door.

Carrie left her makeup on and took off her dress. She covered herself with a blanket on the sofa and shut her eyes, tried to make it all go away. If she hadn't had so much to drink she'd drive up to Magnolia Creek right now, to her airbed and the smell of freshly dug soil outside, the smell of wood from the wrenched-off floorboards, the sounds of the birds in the morning instead of the city coming alive at some ridiculous hour. She wouldn't even care that Owen had ripped out the bath, toilet and sink so she had no basic facilities.

Soon enough, Lachlan came out and kneeled by the sofa. 'Carrie, come to bed. This is silly.'

She sat up. 'Is it? I think you're on Flora's side.' She shouldn't push it much more or he'd walk away, go to sleep, go out on shift tomorrow and then where would it leave them?

'I'm not, but Flora kind of had a point. There are jobs around so I'm surprised Clare hasn't secured one yet. And, yes, I do agree that she doesn't want to stay out of the game too long or her skills will get rusty and it'll be even harder for her.'

'Is that why you set me up with the job with Serena?'

'She needed someone.' He didn't flinch until her stare forced him into submission. 'OK, fair enough, I pulled some strings. She could've easily recruited some help from within, but she took you on as a favour to me. You should be flattered. Serena isn't stupid – if she thought you weren't right, she'd have told me no. Her balls are as strong as her eyebrows.'

Giggling, she wrapped her arms around him. 'Well, thank you for doing it.' The thank you was genuine but as he took her by the hand and led her to the bedroom, she knew she was more thankful that she'd formed a group of friends in Magnolia Creek than anything else, that she'd seen a different side to life for the first time. And although she didn't have a solid plan about anything, she felt as though slowly she was getting on the right track.

Chapter Ten

Owen was surprised when Carrie turned up at the house in the early hours of Monday morning given she wasn't supposed to be home until much later. She and Lachlan had spent the day together yesterday but if Carrie had had a choice, she'd have come home the morning after the restaurant. Being in the city with the people and the familiarities she'd known before, she felt under enormous pressure to get her life back to where it had once been. And the more she was pushed, the more she panicked and realised it may never be the same. In the end she'd used the excuse with Lachlan that she wanted to get back to the house before going to her nannying job because Owen needed her to confirm he'd purchased the right toilet unit before he installed it.

'Is there no end to the man's talent?' Lachlan had asked, turning over in bed. He had a rare late start and always made the most of the lie-in.

Carrie kissed him on the lips and assured him, again, that their friendship was platonic. 'Anyway,' she said, 'who wants to get it on with the man looking after their drainage systems?'

He laughed and pulled her in for more of a kiss before she made her excuses again and left.

Owen looked at the mess in the hallway now and then back at Carrie. 'You're early.'

Carrie kept hold of her overnight bag and tiptoed over the dust and debris. 'Don't worry, I'll dump my bag and then I'm off to Little Miss Maria.'

'I hope you don't need to use the toilet,' he called up the stairs. 'It's not exactly fully functioning yet.'

She reappeared without even peeking into the bathroom. 'No need to explain, but it will be ready tonight won't it?'

He nodded. 'The bath is in, not the shower – that'll need someone more expert than me to do the frame, so the fitter is coming to do that in the morning. And the toilet should be done in the next hour or so. Same goes for the new en suite in the spare room.'

'That's great. And thanks again for working on a weekend.'

'No worries. I couldn't rip out the bathroom while you were here so it worked out well.'

'I hope Rosie doesn't mind how much I commandeer your time.'

He picked up some peculiar-looking black piping to take upstairs. 'Rosie knows the deal. I've always been like this. Crazy busy for a few weeks, even busier during bushfire season, and then there's a lull. She's waiting for the lull.'

'Let's hope you have a big lull when the baby comes,' Carrie smiled. 'Are you excited?' Ridiculous question, she could tell he was.

'I can't wait. You know, I never thought I'd be a dad. I don't know why. I mean, when we were together, you and me, if someone had suggested it we would've laughed at them.'

'Damn right. You with your motorbike, zipping here, there and everywhere, not letting a woman stay with you for the night.' She tutted, teasing him. 'Who would've thought?'

Funny how life could change when you least expected.

*

Carrie's week with Maria went well despite the baby's snuffles and low-grade temperature. Now that they were into April, the sun did its best to warm them but a chill had crept in and Carrie had taken to walking with the pram laden with blankets ready to bundle around Maria if she felt the cold.

Carrie hadn't seen much of Noah all week. He arrived early and left early, meaning their paths didn't tend to cross. If she did see him he'd smile and wave, remain well-mannered, but since she'd more or less told him to keep his nose out of her business, she couldn't help feeling he was giving her a wide berth. And who could blame him really?

The annual Easter egg hunt at Magnolia House took place and Carrie went along with the girls, Abby in tow. Carrie had nabbed a basket from Andrew and been just as enthused hunting for eggs as three-, four- and five-year-olds were, never mind the grown adults. She still had a collection of mini eggs now and had set them on the kitchen windowsill, telling Owen to help himself, please, so she didn't finish them all up herself.

The baby cuddling was well under way and on Friday the first training session came around. Carrie had scheduled all four of the Magnolia Girls for this one because it meant she could be thorough with her feedback and they would likely give fully honest opinions so she could tailor anything in the training that wasn't clear enough. Bella, Rosie and Gemma congregated in the reception area of the hospital and were soon shown through to the room where the nurse educator would start the training. They were taught ways to hold and settle babies, found out about the medical side of things that Carrie mostly knew but got to see from the layman's point of view, and by the end of the session the girls were in good spirits.

'What did you think?' Carrie asked them all as they gathered in the canteen afterwards. They'd scheduled a post-training Magnolia Girls' night at the chocolaterie tonight and Carrie wanted to get the formalities out of the way now so she could relax with these women who were becoming better friends with every passing day.

'I was impressed,' said Bella. 'She was friendly, told us all we needed to know but not so much that we'd be scared off and run in the opposite direction.'

Carrie smiled. 'It can be confronting to see and hear about babies who are so sick.'

'I thought the use of videos was helpful,' added Rosie. 'And it was better than having us all stand and gawp at a real patient. I think it's good we got to understand more about the sort of babies who need our help.'

'That's exactly right,' Carrie agreed. 'That's the whole point of the cuddling program. You are *helping* and it's fundamental to understand how you can make a difference. How did you feel, Gemma?' She was concerned about the fourth member of the group, who'd been quiet for a while.

Gemma's eyes filled with tears. 'They're so innocent, so tiny. I can't even fathom how any mother can take drugs while pregnant.'

'It's only in a few cases,' Rosie comforted her friend.

'I know.' Gemma shook her head. 'But it's still unimaginable.' She looked at the floor.

Carrie knew it would get to someone but her money would've been on Rosie, attuned to impending motherhood in a way the other two weren't. 'Those mothers you're referring to are addicted. It's hard to understand, I know.' She put a hand on Gemma's arm. She knew of Gemma's struggle to have her own baby, which probably heightened her sensitivity to the issue. 'The important thing is that the baby-cuddling program is about the babies themselves, regardless of why they need holding. Sometimes you may be cuddling a baby and not know much about them; other times you may see parents and they'll tell you as much as they want to.'

Gemma wiped her eyes. 'I'm not being very helpful with feedback, am I?'

Carrie put a hand on her arm. 'Nonsense. Every bit of feedback is important.'

'I was impressed with the training on how to settle a baby,' Gemma added more positively. 'A big tick for that, because I think a lot of people signing up think all they have to do is pick the baby up and, as if by magic, it'll quieten and sleep.'

'Yes, not quite as easy in some cases. Many babies are difficult to pacify but once they're settled, believe me, it's such a reward.' She squeezed Gemma's arm.

'You know, from the moment I got Abby I put my arms around her and couldn't believe how lucky I was. But we had some terrible nights with her in the beginning.'

Bella smiled kindly at her friend. 'You've done a good job there, you're a great mother.'

Rosie agreed. 'I'm expecting lots of tips from you when my little one arrives. And you, Bella, you're a natural.'

'I'm not a mother, but I think loving babies helps a lot.' She beamed. 'So, when can we get started?'

Carrie gathered up the feedback forms they'd completed and to which she'd added extra comments. 'Very soon. We've got the security checks to run

through and in the next couple of weeks, look out for the
Magnolia Girls!'

A collective cheer went up before they realised they
were probably too lively for the hospital environment
and went on their way.

*

Carrie bumped into Noah, literally, as she went round
the back of the house. Owen had blocked the front door
with tools and another tradesman had been there all day
helping with the bathroom and the extras that Owen
couldn't manage on his own.

'Oh, man, sorry,' Noah gasped. Carrying a shrub,
he'd bumped into Carrie and now she had mud all up the
front of her white shirt. 'I didn't see you coming. You
usually go in the front.'

She began to brush the front of her shirt but realised it
was futile. If anything, it seemed to be spreading the dirt
further. 'No worries, it'll wash.' Her tiredness made her
sound more peeved than she really was and he retreated
quickly enough. She opened her mouth to ask how his
leg and wrist were but she'd noticed there was no
dressing anymore so she suspected he was fine. She
looked around for any sign of Norma but when there
wasn't any she went inside.

Owen came through to the kitchen and noticed her
shirt but she shrugged, said it would wash, and asked if
she could get upstairs to grab a change of clothes at
least.

'I'm sorry. I thought we'd be finished by now but
we've a little way to go.' He wiped sweat from his brow.
'Everything seems to take longer than you think. The
new kitchen sink is in' – he nodded in its direction – 'so
that's something.'

Carrie looked back over her shoulder, feeling guilty at all his hard work that she hadn't even commented on. 'It looks great. And so does the cabinetry.' She grinned when she noticed the empty bowl on the windowsill. 'And thank you for finally finishing up the Easter eggs.'

'Happy to oblige.' He patted his taut stomach beneath his T-shirt. 'The tiler is booked for Thursday and Friday, is that OK?'

'All sounds good to me.'

'How did the session at the hospital go? Rosie wasn't too freaked out thinking about helpless babies, was she?'

'Rosie was actually fine. Gemma was a bit shocked at some of the cases we talked about, but the training went down well and we'll be able to start soon.'

She decided it was best to leave him to it. 'Do you think Rosie would let me have a shower at your place?' she asked.

'Be my guest. She won't mind at all.'

'Great, I'll grab a change of clothes.' She went up the stairs as Owen returned to work on the bathroom. She found a clean pair of jeans and a long-sleeved top plus her denim jacket and stuffed them in the overnight bag. She grabbed her towel and washbag, which had been put in the bedroom out of the way.

'Come and take a look.' Owen beckoned from the other side of the door.

She went in and smiled. 'Wow, I am going to like relaxing in that!' She knew now without a doubt that she'd selected the best bathtub. 'And you've put a shelf in behind!'

'I hope you don't mind but I thought an inset shelf would be useful.'

'You have great taste. It'll be the perfect place to put all my fancy bubble baths.'

'I'm glad you're happy with it. But don't tell Rosie. I didn't do an inset shelf at Rosie Cottage and something tells me she'll see this and want one.'

'Well, female solidarity and all that…I'm afraid I may have to. She did, after all, tell me about the window seat for the bedroom.'

He grinned. 'Go on, leave us to get on and you'll be able to admire this a bit more tonight when you're home.' He took out his phone. 'I'll text Rosie, tell her you're on your way. And have a great time with the girls.'

The Girls. His words sounded so normal but Carrie couldn't stop smiling, both inside and out. She walked down the hill and onto Main Street, turned right, nodded a hello to Gus, who was on his way to the fire station, and then took a right again into Lakeside Lane. She waved at Michael and Jane Harrison, who drove past her on their way off somewhere, and went on to Rosie Cottage, where Rosie welcomed her in and not only plonked freshly laundered towels in her arms, insisting she use those instead of her own, but also made her a quick omelette for dinner as she figured Carrie was relying on too many instant meals with her house in a shambles.

'Don't ask,' said Carrie when Rosie clocked the dirty white shirt. 'Run in with a gardener.'

'Oh, do tell me more,' Rosie called after her.

'Nothing to tell,' she shouted back, closing the bathroom door behind her.

Once they were ready and Carrie had dried her hair, grateful for the warmth of this house compared to her own that was starting to feel the autumn chill if you weren't working hard, they made their way down the hill and into Magnolia Creek. They called out a hello to

Chris, who was collecting glasses from the picnic tables outside the pub, and greeted Mal, who was closing up the gift shop for the day, and when Andrew let them into the chocolaterie and told them to go upstairs to find Gemma, Carrie told Rosie to go on ahead as she wanted to check out the chocolates.

Once Rosie went on her way, Carrie spoke with Andrew after he brought the chalkboard in from the pavement and left it tucked inside the doorway ready to have its message altered; at present it detailed ice-cream flavours and the latest creations but soon hot-chocolate season would be upon them and she bet Andrew already had plans for some delicious changes.

'Is Gemma OK?' she asked.

'I assume you mean after being a bit delicate this afternoon?' He turned the sign on the door to Closed.

'The details of patients can be distressing.'

He checked out the back to make sure Gemma was definitely upstairs.

'I'm sorry.' Carrie looked at her watch. 'I know I'm a little early.'

Andrew dismissed her concern. 'It's not that, it's just that I wouldn't want Gemma to think I'm gossiping, even though she'd probably tell you what I'm about to tell you herself if she were here. Gemma told you we adopted Abby,' he began, 'but I don't think she told you why Abby isn't with her biological parents.'

'No, she hasn't said a word.'

'Abby's mother was a drug addict. Abby was neglected for a long time, left in her cot for hours on end and was taken away from her mother when a neighbour reported her to the police for leaving Abby alone most of the night while she went out to get her next fix.'

Carrie gasped although she'd heard far worse in her job. She guessed it was all the more poignant when it was part of the life of someone you knew personally. 'No wonder Gemma found it difficult today.'

'Keep an eye on her for me, won't you?' he asked when they heard footsteps coming down the stairs.

'Of course I will.' She smiled at him and went to answer the door to Bella, the final Magnolia Girl to arrive for their night of fizz and chocolate.

After hot chocolates upstairs on the veranda, beneath outdoor heaters, the girls gathered in the workshop downstairs and Andrew left them to it. Gemma had already set everything up earlier, so it was all systems go.

'Whoever knew getting messy could be so much fun,' Carrie giggled. She had an apron on, but already it was streaked with dark chocolate that she'd dangled from a spoon and waved back and forth to make a pattern. 'Why don't mine look any good?' she complained.

'Let me see.' Gemma came over, equipped with her glass of champagne. 'It's not so bad, you've just used too much chocolate there and probably went too fast. Try another.'

Carrie was decorating smaller pastille-size chocolates rather than anything big. She positioned another white chocolate disc, about twice the size of a dollar coin, and then with a spoonful of melted milk chocolate and under Gemma's guidance she slowly tipped the spoon and moved methodically back and forth. 'Ha! I think it's working!'

'See, a bit of patience and you've done a good job. Who are they for?'

'They're for Lachlan. White chocolate is his absolute favourite.' She wanted to give them as a bit of a peace

134

offering after the last time they were together and she'd left beneath a veil of tension. She believed him when he said she wasn't judged for taking a break from her job, but what he said and what really went on in their world of high-flying friends and a life that rarely took a breath were different things entirely.

Gemma moved on to see what Bella was up to. 'That looks heavenly. The raspberry pieces will taste good against the dark chocolate heart.' She moved on to Rosie. 'Wow, I'm impressed.'

'I'm not exactly artistic,' Rosie claimed.

Gemma shook her head as Bella and Carrie came over. 'I think you are exactly that!'

'Rosie, that's gorgeous.' Carrie admired the round of chocolate decorated with smaller pieces of freeze-dried raspberries arranged into petals, along with caramel sprinkles, which looked like flowers on its surface.

'Can I take a photo?' Gemma was already taking out her phone.

Rosie blushed a shade not too far off her straight copper hair. 'I'm embarrassed now.'

'Don't be,' said Bella. 'You should be proud – it's a masterpiece compared to my effort.'

Carrie grinned. 'And mine.' She nudged Bella conspiratorially. 'But I figure it'll all taste the same on the way down.'

Happy with the photos she'd taken of the workshop and now Rosie's finished flower, Gemma said, 'We'll need to leave the chocolates to set so we may as well go relax upstairs again.'

'What did you make?' Carrie wanted to know and moved around to the bench Gemma had been working at. 'It's beautiful,' she said when she saw the chocolate heart Gemma had decorated with gold lustre dust. She'd piped the word 'love' in white chocolate and sprinkled finely crushed freeze-dried raspberries across the surface. It was beautiful in its simplicity. 'Now that should definitely go on the website. And Andrew will want to see it.'

Gemma set each chocolate aside in turn. 'He'll see it. It's for him.'

'You two are so romantic,' said Bella as they took off their aprons and grabbed their champagne glasses. 'Are you going to leave it on his pillow?'

Gemma's eyes sparkled. 'You know, I might just do that.'

Following the girls upstairs, Carrie wondered what it was like to be so in love. She thought she loved Lachlan. She cared for him, she was attracted to him. For a while they'd worked so well together, but she'd always worried there was something missing, something she couldn't quite put her finger on. And being here in Magnolia Creek she was beginning to question her relationship all the more.

Carrie shook away the feeling and upstairs she helped turn on the outdoor heaters while they swapped champagne for a second hot chocolate each and sat slurping them beneath the stars.

'I think my stomach might pay for this in the morning,' said Bella. 'All this chocolate, champagne…'

'Rubbish,' Rosie declared, gently stroking her tummy. 'The baby has been doing somersaults in here, so I'd say he or she is pretty happy. And chocolate is so good for you, isn't it Gemma? All those antioxidants!'

Carrie grinned. 'I'm not sure of the health benefits in the amount us lot have picked at tonight are particularly vast, but I like the way you think.'

136

'Is it true what else they say about chocolate?' Rosie directed her question at Carrie. 'You're in the medical profession so I thought you'd know. Is it an aphrodisiac?'

The others burst out laughing.

'I work with babies,' Carrie answered, 'not chocolate. Ask Gemma.' She was buzzing right now, from the champagne, the chocolate and the company.

'Andrew would say yes,' Gemma smiled. 'All I know is that it makes people happy, it brings people together. Chocolate has been in Andrew's family for years and we're already hoping Abby takes to it and wants to carry on the tradition – but if she doesn't want to, we'll accept that too.'

'You look happy, Gemma.' Bella put a hand on her friend's arm.

'I really am. Abby makes me smile every day. Even when she's being a little madam – which, believe me, she can be – I still love her to bits and wouldn't change anything for the world.'

'Have you spoken to Molly since the party at the Harrisons'?' Bella wanted to know.

Gemma smiled. 'I have. She's deeply envious of the Magnolia Girls so I should warn you that when they're over here next she wants a piece of the action.'

'Isn't she a midwife?' Carrie asked.

Rosie nodded. 'You'd really like her. She and Ben flit between the UK, where her family are, and here, where Andrew is.'

'They've got good careers to do so,' said Carrie. 'At least the medical profession will always be needed. A bit like property renovating,' she directed to Rosie, 'or drinking coffee,' she told Bella. 'Some careers are being replaced and it's quite scary. My sister's other half is in computing and he's moved jobs a few times but from what she says, he's only just managing to hold down a job. Lots of the work is outsourced to other countries now.'

'It's sad, isn't it?' said Bella. 'I wouldn't want to be in that position. It's tough having your own business – I think Gemma will attest to that – but at the same time we are in control, and at least out here in Magnolia Creek it's a small community, bringing in enough custom yet not the crazy competition you get elsewhere. But you'll surely have a job for life, won't you, Carrie? Paediatricians will always be in demand.'

'I'm sure they will. I think there are plenty of positions in the city and surrounds. I was always glad I had a job I could do anywhere, if I wanted to.' She looked at Rosie. 'What about you? Are you still enjoying Magnolia House?

'I am, and I'm lucky. I work part time, and in quiet times the owners get me to do any odd jobs required rather than not having any work. It works well for each of us: it means I'm not without pay and they don't have to find another employee. I've helped with everything from organising weddings to washing up in the kitchen when they were short-staffed.'

'Well, I think the Magnolia Girls are incredibly lucky.' Bella sipped her hot chocolate. 'We all seem to have our lives sorted in one way or another, and, more importantly, we have each other.'

'You know, I've never really had that.' Carrie found the words flowing out of her mouth before she could think about whether she really wanted to say them.

All eyes were on her.

'Had what?' Rosie asked.

'I've never had a group of girls, like this.' Her hand swept a circle from left to right, encompassing the other three women. 'I've got friends, but since university and medical school I was always so focused on my career that I'll be the first to admit I let friendships slip. Not just that, but the women I hung out with were all just like me – we were all pretty intent on striving to new heights in our careers.'

'It's understandable though, pet.' The term of endearment from Bella highlighted the differences in all these women, from their ages to their professions and personal circumstances. Somehow, they complemented one another.

'Is it?' Carrie couldn't stop now she'd begun to talk. She'd never once admitted to feeling lonely, not to anyone. When she was with Owen she'd been high on career, on life, on being young and free. But that had all changed in the blink of an eye. 'I always blamed myself.'

'I'm not in the medical profession,' Gemma began, 'but it's the same with any job that becomes a passion. It was, or is, a passion, am I right?'

Carrie nodded. 'I wanted to be a doctor right from when I was little. You know, I had one of those plastic boxes, the pretend medical kit, and I'd forever be taking people's temperature, checking blood pressure. I used to keep charts too,' she admitted sheepishly. 'I had a pink sparkly notepad for mum that I'd record my findings on, a blue one for dad, a purple one for Kristy. They were great, always willing to play along. Paediatrics became something I was interested in somewhere along the way. I was so enthralled by the idea that these tiny humans couldn't tell you what was wrong; they didn't have the

139

words as babies and then with older children I wanted to form that bond and solve the puzzle together.'

'It must be a rewarding career,' said Bella.

'Even at the start, it really was. The first patient I bonded with was a little boy called Jasper. He was the one who made me realise the career was definitely for me. He came in with a rare heart condition and turned up to his first appointment in a Spiderman outfit, to the second dressed as Superman, and on the third he was wearing a Batman costume. For the fourth appointment, when he was incredibly sick, he turned up in regular jeans and a T-shirt because the superhero outfits were all in the wash. He looked a shadow of the boy I'd seen. I knew it was because he was so unwell, but I missed his smile. Between seeing patients that morning I phoned around, got a costume delivered, and when I went to see him late afternoon and subject him to yet more tests, I was dressed as Supergirl.

'I'll never forget his grin that day.' Tears sprung into her eyes, but they were happy tears. 'He went on to have his operation, eventually got better, and months later at a follow-up appointment he turned up as Superman. His mum had hired me a Supergirl costume again and he made me pose for a photograph with him. He said he would remember me forever and that we both had superpowers.'

'Kids can be so gorgeous, can't they?' Gemma smiled.

They certainly could, and Carrie knew it was the case she should remember, the one that should've kept her going. Except it wasn't.

'Do you ever hear what happens to your patients once they leave your care?' Gemma asked. 'Or is the end of their treatment the time when you part ways?'

140

'It depends. Some of them love to keep in touch and come in all tall and proud to say hello to doctors and nurses they saw every day for a while, others, particularly those who live some distance away, get on with their lives and don't look back.'

'And what about the not-so-good cases?' Gemma swirled the hot chocolate in the bottom of her cup before drinking it. 'Do their parents ever contact you again? Do you remember them? I mean, how do you cope with the cases that aren't so nice, when you can't save them?'

Carrie took a deep breath and this time she couldn't find the words.

Gemma put a hand to her head. 'I'm sorry, that was really insensitive. It's just that, well, after being at the hospital the other day, I realised how hard it must be.'

'It's really hard,' Carrie managed.

Rosie began shifting herself about and offered to take the cups down to the kitchen. 'I need to move. I'm getting heavier and more uncomfortable by the day.'

Carrie wondered whether she was affected by the difficult topic of conversation or whether her discomfort was a mere coincidence but, whatever the reason for Rosie's actions, she was glad not to be the focus any longer as they moved on to happier topics.

'Are you still up for the movies tomorrow night?' Gemma asked as she lent a hand with the clearing up.

Rosie called over her shoulder. 'I sure am.'

'Carrie?' Gemma dropped a discarded teaspoon into the nearest mug.

'Sounds good to me.'

'I'm driving,' said Bella, making them all laugh when she added, 'but no arguing over who gets to sit in the front.'

Chapter Eleven

Noah missed a few days' work during the week, some because of rain, some because of reasons he hadn't shared with Carrie. But the morning after the movie night with the girls, Carrie showered in her new bathroom that only needed a fresh lick of paint and a mirror cut to fit above the sink, before peeking out of the window to find Noah making an early start.

She dressed quickly because Owen always made an early start too, and when she got downstairs gave Owen the go-ahead to begin construction of the window seat now she was out of the way.

Standing in the partially completed kitchen, she washed cups at the sink but found herself looking up every now and then out the window to where Noah stood, the sun kissing the skin on his neck and making the dust on his arms sparkle. The garden was taking shape and he was busy putting up the pergola. There were posts lined up on the ground and a few days ago she'd seen him repeatedly thrusting a spade into the ground, pushing it down with his foot and scooping out the soil to make holes that Carrie deduced were the foundations for the structure. Now, four poles stood tall in their corners.

It was April already but the sun made it feel hotter than it really was, and when Noah stood up from where he was fitting the last part of the pergola's base and lifted his T-shirt to wipe his face of sweat, Carrie didn't miss the toned stomach of a man who didn't sit down much during the day.

She jumped at a knock on the front door, but at least it meant Noah wouldn't catch her staring. She turned, walked down the corridor inhaling the waft of paint that told her this house was well on its way, and opened the front door to Rosie.

'Hey, what brings you here?'

'Owen forgot his lunch.' She smiled. 'I don't usually make it, he does it himself, but we had leftovers and I didn't want him to forget them. Which, of course, he did.'

Carrie took a Tupperware container from Rosie's outstretched hand. 'I'll give it to him, or you could do it yourself – he's only upstairs.'

'I won't disturb him. I'm on my way to work and the walk is always nice at this time of year when it's not too hot.'

'It's much more pleasant, I agree. Do you want to come in and see the progress so far?'

'I'd love to.'

'The floorboards are all repaired,' said Carrie in the smaller of the two rooms at the front. 'This will be a snug, or library if you like, and Owen's found me a wood burner, which will be installed next week.'

'That'll be cosy come the winter months.'

Carrie took her through to the other lounge, where Rosie admired the fireplace that hadn't needed anything apart from cleaning. She explained the paint colours in here, subtle and neutral beige tones. 'I add colour with accessories.'

'Good idea,' said Rosie. 'It means you can change your mind as often as you like.'

'Ha, spoken like a true woman!' Carrie led Rosie through to the kitchen next.

'Now I like this.' Rosie ran a hand across the surface of one of the cupboards. Most still had their plastic coverings on but this one had come off during the fitting. 'It's classic and really gives the house a country feel.'

She admired the farmhouse sink and looked up when she spied Noah through the window. 'And you've got to admit,' she said conspiratorially as she returned his wave, 'Noah kind of lifts the garden.'

'He's not bad, but believe it or not, I don't stand here leering at the man.'

'I would if I were you.' Rosie was still watching him. 'Bella said she saw the boys training on Sunday and she was speechless when Noah changed his T-shirt. "Rock-hard abs" I think was her exact description of his torso, and a few things I simply can't repeat in case my unborn baby hears me talking that way.'

Carrie laughed. Already she knew Bella well enough to know Rosie wasn't exaggerating. 'How are you feeling anyway?' she asked after they took a quick look at the laundry with units matching those in the kitchen.

'Pretty good.' She smiled.

'Do you have everything you need?' Carrie led them back through the kitchen and turned to go upstairs.

'We've already bought everything we need for the hospital dash – white Babygros because we don't know the sex, a couple of nighties for me, a music tape, some lavender oil. Molly laughed. She says expectant mothers turn up fully equipped and then the baby has other ideas – all birthing plans go out the window and it becomes a case of doing whatever you can to get through it.'

'You'll be fine,' said Carrie as they got to the top of the stairs and found Owen constructing the rectangular box that would become the window seat.

'What brings you here?' He came over to give Rosie a quick peck and a hug.

'I brought you leftover frittata.'

He smiled. 'I forgot to bring anything.'

With a roll of her eyes Rosie told Carrie, 'he usually dashes home but this way he'll be able to work harder for you.'

'I like the sound of that.' Carrie grinned. 'I think she's the boss of you, Owen.'

'Yeah,' he sighed. 'If the baby turns out to be a girl I think they'll both be the boss of me.'

When they heard footfall on the stairs they turned to see Noah. 'I need to borrow Owen,' he said.

'Owen's working hard up here, but I can help with whatever you need.' Carrie was determined to put their run-in behind them both.

'I really need Owen,' he reiterated.

Hands on hips, Carrie wanted to prove yet again that she was no princess. 'Anything you want him to do, I'm sure I'm perfectly capable of.'

Noah opened his mouth to say something but then clearly changed his mind and cocked his head. 'Come on then…we'll see how long you last.'

Carrie didn't miss the look pass between Rosie and Owen and she wondered what she was in for.

Outside, sunglasses pulled down, she waited for her next instruction. 'What do you want me to do?'

'I need you to hold the support beam in place while I put a spirit level on top. Then, when we're sure it's completely straight, I'll drill it in on either side. It'll take a few minutes.'

'Right, where's the support beam?' She looked around the garden, around the dirt and the huge lengths of wood, for whatever he was talking about.

'You're standing next to it.' He checked the sides of the construction and found a spirit level and his drill that he'd moved into position. 'Ready?'

'Are you sure your leg and wrist are all better now?' She asked, but when he shook his head at her she sensed it was time to be quiet.

'Don't you worry about me. You ready?'

'Sure.' If he was going to laugh at her, she'd show him. How heavy could a piece of wood be anyway? She'd lifted pretty hefty kids in her time, she was no wuss.

She heaved the wood up and felt the tendons in her arms strain but, delighted, she got it standing tall. 'Now what?'

'Now we'll take one end each, lift it to the top, and then you stand and hold it in position for me.'

'OK, let's do this.'

With a shake of his head he took the other end. 'Are you OK?' he asked.

Through gritted teeth and ignoring the audience of Rosie and Owen in the upstairs window, she urged him to carry on and they walked the wood over to the pergola posts.

'Now lift up,' he instructed.

She got it to shoulder height, changed her grip and then lifted it up over her head. Ha! Who said girls couldn't do anything men could do? Of course they could. Sometimes they could do it better!

But her jubilation was short-lived when she realised he needed her to stand in the middle of the piece of wood and take not half of its weight but all of it – and, more than that, she had to hold it for quite a time while he drilled it into position.

'Now move along,' said Noah, 'so you're in the centre of the wood. Then I'll let go.'

She moved along but as she felt his grip lessen for her to take the weight, the words gushed out of her mouth before she could stop them. 'No! God, please! Help me!'

Between them they lowered the wood to the floor.

'It's so heavy!' She couldn't help it. Admittance of feelings wasn't exactly what she'd intended to do but the weight of the wood had forced it out of her.

'Now shall I get Owen?' He could barely contain his amusement.

'Fine.' She turned, looked up to the bathroom window where Rosie and Owen were completely tuned in to the entire show, and waved Owen down.

'Thanks anyway,' Noah called after her as she stalked back into the house. She passed Owen and he patted her on the shoulder in commiseration.

'Bloody men,' she said to Rosie as she glanced at her watch. 'I'd better get going too, or Maria will think I've forgotten about her. I'm walking to their house today. I need the exercise after my chocolate consumption has gone up tenfold since moving to Magnolia Creek. What? Why are you looking at me like that?'

Rosie shook her head. 'Nothing.'

Carrie collected her bag. 'Come on, it's not nothing, spit it out. We're Magnolia Girls – we don't shy away from honesty.'

Rosie picked up her own bag as they left the house. 'Take it from someone who went out with the wrong guy for a really long time and didn't want to hurt him until it became inevitable.'

'What *are* you talking about?' Carrie shut the front door behind them and they set off down the hill towards Main Street.

'Noah. I'm talking about Noah. I've seen the way you look at each other, the way you bicker, the way your face lights up when you talk about him even though you're not saying anything particularly complimentary.'

'He's an attractive man,' Carrie said honestly. 'I'll be the first to admit that. But he's not my type. Lachlan is my type, and we have our ups and downs but doesn't everyone? I'll bet you and Owen do.'

'Of course we do.' They both waved at Gemma, who was herding children into a line in the school playground when they walked past. 'But I'd tell him anything and he'd do the same, and unlike when I was with Adam, I'm never daydreaming about what it could be like with someone else.'

'What, you think I go to bed every night dreaming of Noah?' Carrie laughed. 'I think the pregnancy hormones are affecting your judgement.'

By the time they reached the white signs pointing down the path that led from Main Street to the lake, Rosie was full of apologies rather than ribbing Carrie about Noah. 'I didn't mean to offend you with what I said about Lachlan and Noah.'

'You didn't offend me at all.'

'Well, I apologise anyway. Part of me was teasing, but the rest of me was poking my nose into something that really isn't any of my business. Lachlan seems lovely, genuine and kind, and it was wrong of me to make a judgement based on what little I know of either of you.'

'Quit worrying, we're friends, and absolutely no offence taken.' She hugged Rosie because it felt right and when they waved each other on their way and Carrie continued her walk to Maria's beneath the sunlight of the day, she realised that, yes, Rosie had made a judgement based on very little information but that's exactly what Carrie had done back when Rosie was with the man who came before Owen. And Carrie had been spot on when it came to both Rosie's and Owen's feelings.

What if Rosie was spot on about hers?

*

When Lachlan came into town a few nights later, Carrie booked a table at the pub for dinner. Chris had put them in the farthest corner as requested and, with the darkness outside creating a romantic ambience, the candle in the centre of the table flickered away between them as they talked.

'This is one of the nicest country pubs I've been to,' Lachlan admitted. 'And the food's good.'

'You seem surprised.' She smiled.

'Do you remember the hotel we stayed in when we went to Adelaide one year?' Lachlan picked up his glass of red wine as they finished their main course. They'd both gone for the red snapper and, served with a basil cream sauce and thick-cut chips, the meal was cooked to perfection.

'The food was terrible.' She pulled a face.

'It was a hotel with a pub beneath and not too dissimilar to this place at first glance.'

Carrie looked around. 'Actually, you're right.'

'When you suggested the local pub for dinner I wanted to drive you back to the city and a fancy restaurant, but I'm glad we're here.' His voice lacked its usual confidence and Carrie moved a hand across to his, gripped his fingers. Whatever her uncertainties at the moment, this man had been there for her for a long time and she'd never doubted her relationship before now. Her feelings were all down to her own insecurities and her need to escape the norm, which wasn't fair on Lachlan. And thinking so much about Noah wasn't fair

149

either. Besides, a physical attraction was totally different from a full-on relationship. Everyone knew that.

'I'm glad you like it here,' she said. 'Should I order some more wine?'

Her hand was still on his and he squeezed it. 'I've got a bottle in the car. How about we take it back to your place?'

She grinned. 'I still can't believe you've agreed to stay there.'

'I almost booked a cottage again but decided to step outside my comfort zone. I bought an airbed and I've brought a duvet and pillow so I'm all set. This is probably the closest I've been to camping since my days at university when a group of us went to Canberra.'

Carrie smiled. 'It's kind of romantic when you think about it.' She was glad they seemed back on track although she was nervous about having him in her space tonight. 'Dessert?' The menus had been discretely slipped in front of them but they hadn't given them a glance yet.

'Maybe back at the house,' Lachlan suggested.

'I don't have anything.'

He raised his eyebrows. 'I was thinking of a different sort of dessert.' He couldn't pay the bill quickly enough and they laughed their way up the hill, fuelled by wine and the heady promise of sex.

The next morning Carrie woke up feeling quite refreshed. She and Lachlan had pushed their airbeds together but because they were separate, the lack of bouncing created by the other person's body movements during night had meant a reasonably good night's sleep.

But now there was a snuffling sound that reminded her of baby Maria, yet more forceful. She opened her eyes and sat up to see Norma in the corner of the room, sniffing Lachlan's clothes they'd piled on top of an empty cardboard box.

Carrie clutched the sheet against her bare chest. Because if Norma was here, that could only mean one thing…

Footsteps confirmed her suspicions. 'Carrie…' Noah stumbled over his words. '…jeez, sorry…' He coaxed Norma towards him but she was wagging her tail, thinking the whole commotion was heaps of fun.

Lachlan stirred and opened his eyes. 'What's going on?' He saw Carrie first, then the dog, then focused on Noah. 'What the fuck? What are you doing in here? Give us some privacy!'

Noah turned. 'I'm sorry, didn't realise anyone was home. Just saw Norma wander up here.' He began to go downstairs. 'Come on, Norma.'

Norma ambled past Carrie closer to Lachlan, who was unimpressed at the dog sniffing his clothes, and when the dog followed her master Lachlan swore again before getting out of bed to go to the toilet. Carrie lay back on the airbed and shook her head.

'Do you want to tell me what that was about?' Back in the room Lachlan was tugging on his jeans and doing up his belt, inspecting his shirt for stray dog hairs. 'What makes him think it's OK to come up here, to your bedroom?' He put an emphasis on the word bedroom.

'Judging by his face, Lachlan, he had no idea we would be here. The last I told him and Owen, we'd be in one of the cottages again tonight.'

'Don't you think that makes it all the more weird?'

'In what way?'

'Well, he thinks you're not here so he assumes he can come upstairs, like some kind of stalker.'

Carrie laughed. 'He's not a stalker.' She pulled him down onto her own airbed and, not caring that Noah would be outside the house and Owen most likely not far away either, wrapped her legs around his torso. 'Now, I know you don't have to leave until much later than this, so be quiet and show me a good time. Just like you did last night.'

And although it took a bit of persuasion, he did as he was told.

While Lachlan showered, Carrie made them both poached eggs on toast. The cooker was installed, she had benchtops along one side of the kitchen as well as a cutlery drawer, and things were really taking shape.

'Get off, you're all wet,' she squealed when Lachlan joined her and snaked his arms around her waist.

'After the rude awakening this morning, that was the perfect way to start the day.'

She used a slotted spoon to remove the eggs from the pan and gently placed two on his plate and two on hers, atop the already buttered toast.

In the absence of any pantry shelves, Lachlan rummaged in the cardboard box on the floor for black pepper. 'This place will make a perfect holiday rental – you could get a good income from it.'

She chose to ignore his remark by announcing she'd take their breakfasts out to the front of the house, where they could sit side-by-side on the doorstep. Lachlan followed and, with Owen upstairs painting the window seat and Noah out back, it afforded them a little privacy as they ate.

As they tucked into their eggs she successfully avoided any talk of the plans for this place by asking instead about another conference Lachlan was booked to go on. But she couldn't put off the inevitable forever.

'That was good.' She finished eating and wrapped her cardigan around her torso as the autumn breeze kept her cool. 'I'm not sure I want anyone else in this place apart from me, or us,' she said.

Lachlan stacked the empty plates on top of one another. 'That's understandable, it'll be amazing when it's finished. But like I said, you could generate a really healthy income from it and, really, once you're back in the city, how much time will you have to run away for a few days?'

She didn't rise to the hint about her returning to work. 'We could make time. It'd be the perfect escape at a weekend.'

'Away from the city, eh?' He smiled at her and kissed the top of her head, reminding her of when they first got together and her mum had joked she could ask him to do anything and he'd melt on the spot and do it for her. But over time she'd realised he had quite the knack for coercing her round to his way of thinking. Since she'd left the city, however, she wasn't quite so easily persuaded, and she wondered how he'd take it in the long run.

'Away from the city,' she repeated.

Between them they took everything inside and Carrie put it all beside the sink. She knew what Lachlan was looking for when he scanned the kitchen. 'There's no dishwasher.'

'When's it coming?'

'I'm not having one.' She smiled at the surprise on his face. 'There's not much room and I chose to have a bigger pantry instead.'

'Don't tell me you've turned domesticated out here in the country. Are you going to turn into some kind of Nigella Lawson? Actually, she's pretty hot.'

Carrie grinned. She opened the back door to let the air circulate and clear the smell of eggs from the atmosphere.

He pulled her to him before she had a chance to start the washing up. 'When *are* you coming back to the city?'

'There's the job at the hospital remember.' She hoped her simple answer would buy her time but it didn't work.

'I know full well that once the program is running along nicely you won't need to be there the whole time.' He grabbed her hand before she had a chance to move away. 'What happened to the Carrie I first met, the one with fire in her belly, ambition to rival my own?'

She knew this little speech must have been brewing for a while. 'That Carrie is still here.'

'Is she?' He wouldn't let her pull away this time. 'Come on, you're better than this. Maybe I'm not saying it in the right way, but what I mean is you're a clever, talented paediatrician who had a scare and is burying her head in the sand.'

'I am not!' As usual he was taking this a step too far, as though he'd used up all his patience. 'I needed some time, Lachlan, and you coming over here hassling me isn't helping one bit.'

'I wanted to spend time with my girlfriend! I didn't realise I was hassling you, but I care about you and the career you've worked so hard for.'

'Well what if what's best for me is staying here in the country, working in a low-stress job, working fewer hours for not as much money but being happier than I ever was in the city?'

He harrumphed. 'You can't mean that, surely.'

'Why not? Why is that so terrible?' She couldn't help it. When they fought, she liked to give as good as she got.

'Because it's wasting the talent you've got!'

'Stop yelling at me!' Although her own voice wasn't exactly quiet. 'I feel like you're pressuring me, all the time.'

'I hardly ever mention it, Carrie.'

'Sometimes you don't say anything – it's just this vibe, this air of disapproval.'

'Oh, so now I'm supposed to tiptoe around you am I? For fuck's sake, Carrie.' He never swore at her, never. 'Get real. This isn't you!' When he raised his voice even more it was as though he were pushing her heels into the floor beneath her and she had no choice but to dig them in further.

'What if it is me? What would you do if I said I wanted to move out here for good and I wanted you to come with me?'

He tugged a hand through his hair. 'You're being ridiculous now. My job is in the city.'

'I work at a hospital here, you could transfer.' She knew it made no sense whatsoever. She was goading him, possibly to the point of no return, almost as though subconsciously she just wanted him to go.

'I'm not transferring, Carrie. What happened to you? All this country air is clouding your judgement.' His look of disdain made her angry. 'Maybe we'll talk when you see sense. I've got a job to get back to, a real job that I won't be quitting any time soon.'

'Not even for me?' she challenged, as he started to walk away.

He stopped beside her. 'Carrie, if I thought for one moment you meant what you were saying, I'd take you

155

seriously, but I don't think you do mean it. You wouldn't turn your back on the career you took so long to build and worked so hard for. Serena did me a favour giving you the part-time position at the hospital here, but it's not a permanent solution to whatever's going on in your head.'

'I doubt I'm the first person to take time away from a stressful career.'

'Probably not, but you're talking like you've been working for thirty years when really you're just getting started. You're letting patient outcomes affect you too much. You're a fledgling in a career that could be a promising one if you let it. But you've run away at the first sign of trouble. I figured you'd pick yourself up and get on with things.'

'You make it sound so simple.'

Exasperated, he said, 'Carrie, it is simple. You're the one who's making it complicated.'

There was a time when he'd understood, he'd been attentive and stood by her. Maybe he was right, maybe she needed to pull herself together. But she hadn't managed to yet and all the hounding her in the world wasn't going to make a difference.

'What I don't understand, Carrie, is how you seem to be coping at the hospital here, yet you can't entertain the idea of returning to a job in the city.'

How could she explain that it had little to do with the hospital and more to do with this town, the change of pace, the friendships she was making that were so far removed from her normal life?

'You're too involved.' He pulled his car keys from his pocket. 'Maybe you're right. Maybe this is where you should stay. Maybe you're not the girl I thought you were. Maybe you're too weak for the job.'

Her mouth fell open and tears welled in her eyes. She hadn't expected him to lay it quite on the line like that. 'I don't want it to be the end of my career,' she said simply.

'Well you're going the right way about it.' His jaw clenched. 'And I don't think many men would appreciate their girl practically living with two men, one of whom she used to sleep with, the other who has seen her naked.'

'You're being childish now.'

'Am I?'

'Yes!'

'You always did attract a man easily, Carrie. You could've had your pick at the hospital. Who knows, maybe you have. Maybe I'm just one of many.'

'I've been with you and only you for a long time, Lachlan. Stop being so damn insecure.'

'Funny, you've been with me for a long time, yet whenever I suggest taking the next step and buying a place together, you're not interested. You wave away the issue much like you do nowadays when I try to ask you about your career. You shut me out, you always do. Yet here you are with your own place, talking about how you don't want anyone else to live in it. It feels to me like another step farther away from me and our relationship.'

She couldn't deny it. It hadn't been the intention, but maybe part of what he was saying was right. Perhaps on paper she and Lachlan were pretty much perfect for each other, yet in real life they were starting to pull in opposite directions.

'I just want to get my head straight again. A year ago I never would've thought I would be in this situation, but here I am. Life threw something at me and I dealt with it the only way I could. Can't you try to understand that?' She swiped at a tear that dared to try and escape.

'I have tried to understand.' And with that he turned, went upstairs, grabbed his things and muttered a goodbye.

She heard the gravel crunch beneath his tyres as he reversed out of the driveway and left. Leaning against the kitchen sink, her back to the window, goose pimples crept over her arms and she went to shut the back door. But she came face to face with Noah.

'Everything OK?' he asked. He had a streak of mud up his cheek and Carrie wanted to reach out and wipe it away.

She ducked her head, not wanting him to see she was upset. He'd have to be very hard of hearing not to have heard the exchange between her and Lachlan. 'I'm fine. How's the garden going? Let me grab my sunglasses and I can come and see for myself.' She turned and trotted upstairs, washed her face and patted it dry with a towel, grabbed some shoes and returned downstairs, where she found Noah outside planting creepers at the base of the pergola.

'What colour will the flowers be?' Making conversation would be easier if she chose a favourable subject matter. 'I can't remember what you said.'

'These are the bougainvilleas.' He kept on with what he was doing, his fingers pushing firmly into the soil. 'They'll flower pink like the ones you remember from your holiday.'

'I fell in love with those flowers.' She hadn't meant to say it out loud, but he was concentrating too hard to make any cutting comments.

'I'm sure you'll love these just as much.'

'How do I look after it?'

He stood up and squinted as he turned towards the sun, beaming down across the roof of the house directly onto the pergola. 'It will thrive on full sunlight, which is why I wanted the pergola here. It'll need watering frequently and pruning to remove any obstructive branches or take away dead parts.' She must've looked lost because he said, 'I'll write it all down for you. Or, if you don't intend to be here full time, you could hire a gardener. Once the garden is established it should be reasonably low-maintenance.'

He moved around to the opposite corner of the pergola, taking a small trowel with him, presumably to dig the soil over there. 'How often do you think you'll be up here once you finish your jobs here and move back to the city?'

She shrugged, turning to face the sun now and let it warm her skin. Autumn sunshine wasn't as brutal as it could be in the summer. It was a gentler form of heat and along with the smell of the fresh outdoors it was an instant mood lifter. 'I'm not sure yet.' She sat down on the base of the pergola.

'How much longer will both jobs last?'

'The position at the hospital will be for a couple more months, I assume, and the nannying is ongoing until a nursery confirms they have a place for Maria.' She turned to face him. 'According to the parents, it could happen this week, next month or it may take a year. Childcare is in high demand.'

'Thinking of it as a full-time career?' There was no mistaking his grin.

'No chance.' She turned back and relished the sun's rays on her face again. 'Maria is lovely, don't get me wrong, but I think she's enough to convince me that looking after little ones could never be my full-time job. I need the adult company too much.'

'And how's it going up at the hospital?

'Really well. I've coordinated a few volunteer groups who have had their training. The first group, the Magnolia Girls, starts tomorrow.' When he laughed, she added, 'I guess your amusement means Owen told you.'

'That you guys are the Magnolia Girls?' He finished what he was doing for now and walked over to her side of the pergola. 'Yes, he told me. It's cool. They're a nice bunch of girls.' He sat down beside her, brushing his hands together to rid them of the soil.

She patted the base of the structure. 'I love this. I gave you free rein with the garden but that was because I had no idea what I wanted. I just wanted it to look nice and to enjoy relaxing in it when it was finished.'

'So you're happy with how it's turning out?'

She smiled. 'You've done a brilliant job.'

They looked over to the flowerbeds – the fresh beds he'd cut with curved edges, the existing flowerbeds that had been cleared of all debris and dead shrubs, ready for the new.

'When will the grass be ready?'

'The turf should arrive at the end of next week.'

'I can't wait to see it finished.' Looking around, she asked, 'Where's Norma?'

'Behaving herself in the car, I hope. She's in the front this time with the window open. She's too old to climb out of it. I go and check on her every so often, I've taken her for a couple of walks and given her plenty of water. She's well looked after, total princess.'

A look passed between them as Carrie remembered he'd used that term for her too. 'Can I get you something to drink? You must be parched.'

160

'I'd like that, thanks. I'll just finish planting these climbers.' He put his hands on his knees about to stand up but Carrie put a hand across his.

'You can take a break; I'm not that bad a boss.' Relieved they were being civil to one another and, more than that, they were talking as friends, she nipped into the kitchen and came back with two cans. 'Lemonade, it's all I've got, is it OK?'

'More than OK.'

She withheld the cans when he reached out for one. 'You can have the drink on one condition.'

'What's that?'

'Go and let Norma out the car – I can't bear the thought of her stuck in there.'

'Are you sure? She likes to wander, remember. Given half the chance she'd make herself right at home in your place.'

She thought of Norma walking in on her and Lachlan and the shock on her boyfriend's face almost made her laugh now. 'I know she does, but it's only me here – she can wander all she likes.'

'She might walk dirt into the house.'

'I'll live with it.' Carrie handed him both cans. 'You wait there, I'll get her.'

She was back with a very chirpy Norma, her tail wagging in delight, and before long the dog settled at their feet as they opened their drinks and sat on the pergola chatting about life in a country town, this house that had been sold to her after being with one owner for more than fifty years.

'Do you know what I really like about it?' Carrie began. 'I love that it's up the top of a hill, tucked around the corner, and people probably don't realise it's here.

Tourists can't be bothered to scale the hill, especially in the heat of the day, and that'll suit me just fine.'

'Antisocial.'

His comment earned him a nudge with her knee against his but the feel of his skin on hers left her wondering whether she should've really done it or not. 'I prefer to think of it as liking my privacy,' she said. 'In my apartment it was very different. I kept myself to myself but there was noise all around from the city outside the windows, the comings and goings in the corridor. It was as though you could never really think, at least not clearly. What I also like about this house is that it's hidden so in many ways feels far away from anything, but I know it's only a fifteen-minute walk down to Main Street.'

'I love living where I do too, for much the same reasons.' When he tipped his chin towards the sky as he took another swig from the can Carrie noticed the tendons at the sides of his neck, his tanned skin that stood up to the Australian sun.

'This is my first place with a garden.' She looked all around her. 'It's quite something having a space to call your own. I've lived in apartments for years. The closest I got to developing any kind of green fingers was looking after a basil plant on my windowsill. It died about two weeks after I got it, but it was about as intimate as I ever got with horticulture.'

'I think you'll like having the outside space. I spend a lot of time outside in my own garden.'

'Do you have many neighbours nearby?'

'No, Laurel Drive only has my place and three others, all separated by at least fifty metres.'

Carrie fussed Norma when the dog crawled forward on its front legs and put her chin on Carrie's foot.

'She's making sure you don't neglect her.'

'She sure is.' She ran her hand from the top of Norma's head, along her back, all the way to her tail. 'Is it true what they say?'

'And what's that?'

'A dog is a man's best friend?'

'I can't speak for all men, but for me it's true. She's been in my life for almost fifteen years and it's hard to imagine it any other way.' His voice wavered. 'I think if something good comes into your life you grab it with both hands and treasure it, even in the bad times, but if that something isn't what you really thought it was, then it might be time to let it go.'

Carrie put her hands in her lap as Norma sprawled out in the sun, her nose twitching when a fly buzzed unwelcomingly around her nostril. 'You're not talking about dogs now, are you?'

'He shouldn't talk to you like that.'

She knew he would've overheard. 'It was an argument – nothing more, nothing less. All couples argue.'

'Yeah, they do.'

'They do.'

'I know, I'm not saying they don't.'

'Then what are you saying?'

Still fussing over Norma, he said, 'He didn't sound very supportive. It sounded as though you're not doing what he wants so he's throwing his toys out of the pram.'

Carrie finished her drink and stood up, held out her hand for his empty can. 'I'm the one who walked away from him, not the other way round.'

'So it appears, but from where I'm standing he doesn't seem too interested in why you walked away, only that you come back.' He shrugged and Carrie turned to take the cans inside.

It probably wasn't the end of the conversation but Carrie was uncomfortable and she didn't want to talk about or even think about the argument with Lachlan. 'I'll let you get on, make the most of the sunshine.'

'No worries.' He patted Norma and returned to what he'd been doing before Carrie had persuaded him to take a break.

Inside, Carrie followed up with Owen on the progress indoors as he put the final shelf in the bottom of the pantry. She took out some washing from the machine and carried it upstairs to hang on the airer in the front bedroom, then decided to get out to the shopping centre a short drive away. Retail therapy could fix a lot, she decided, and today she'd choose fabric for the window seat plus cushions to complement the colour.

Back at the house, she braved the garden when she saw Norma lying in the same spot she'd been in earlier. 'Mind if I take her for a walk?' she asked before Noah could say anything else. The radio was perched on the edge of the pergola and, as hits from the eighties swarmed into the air, Noah was by the back fence planting a shrub he'd assured her would flower and cover the wood.

'Be my guest. Her lead is in the glovebox in my truck. You may not need it, she won't walk all that far, but just in case.'

'We'll walk down to town and back.'

'It may be a bit far, but give it a go.'

Carrie went to the car to retrieve the lead but no sooner had she shut the door than Norma appeared at her side. The tinkling of the chain on the lead must have alerted her to a possible adventure.

'Come on, you.' Carrie tapped her leg so Norma obediently followed her. 'Town's not too far, is it? And it's a lovely day.' Norma waddled next to her, slower than Carrie had thought she'd walk, but she didn't mind the easy pace as they crunched across the gravel driveway and continued down the hill.

Norma wagged her tail when they walked past the school as she drew plenty of admiring calls from kids behind the fence and on Main Street the dog veered into the pub garden as soon as they crossed the road and lapped water from the large bowl placed there for the purpose. Carrie bought a mint-choc-chip ice-cream from the chocolaterie and after Andrew had come outside and fussed the dog enough, they sauntered along Main Street past the gift shop, looking in the window at a delightful wooden doll's house Carrie bet Maria would have her eye on in a few years.

'Noah was right,' she said to Norma as she popped the remaining tip of the ice-cream cone in her mouth. 'You don't like to go far.' The dog was clearly tiring so Carrie turned and went back the way they'd come, crossing over to go up the hill.

'Come on, girl, let's go.' Carrie started up the hill assuming Norma would follow, but when she turned back to check, Norma had sat down and slowly lowered herself onto her front paws.

'I'm not going to carry you,' she laughed. 'I'm not that fit!' She fussed Norma for a while, then encouraged the dog, who followed for a few steps. But then she stopped again. 'What is it, eh? The sun too much? Too long a walk?'

She stroked Norma from head to toe, but after twenty minutes she admitted defeat and called Noah to drive down the hill and get them.

And Carrie didn't need to be a vet to know this wasn't good. It wasn't good at all.

Chapter Twelve

The camaraderie of a group of women was something Carrie was still getting used to. In the last few days she'd had coffee and cake with Gemma, she'd had a few glasses of wine with Bella one night at the café after closing and she'd had dinner with Owen and Rosie at their house.

Today was the first baby-cuddling session for the Magnolia Girls and Bella, Rosie and Gemma were in high spirits as they waited for Serena to get them going. But Carrie's spirits were low because all she could think about was Noah and Norma.

Noah had driven straight down to Main Street yesterday after Carrie called. But rather than return to the house he'd picked Norma up and taken her into the vet's surgery with Carrie following close behind. He'd disappeared out the back and when he returned Carrie asked whether the dog was going to be OK. Noah had lifted Norma into the back of the truck out on the street. He didn't answer her question. 'If you don't mind, I'll leave the garden for the next couple of days. I'll take you home now if you like.'

Carrie put a hand on his arm before he jumped into the driver's side. 'I don't need a lift up the hill, but I do need to know what's happening. Why aren't you telling me?'

He pinched the top of his nose. 'No, she's not going to be OK. She's old, Carrie. It's life, unfortunately. Life sucks some of the time and that time is right now.' He climbed into the truck, offered her a lift again, but she insisted it wasn't necessary and off he went. Carrie had walked home with a lump in her throat that still hadn't shifted by the time she woke up this morning.

With the session at the hospital about to start, Carrie needed to focus. Noah hadn't replied to her texts but her mind had to be on these babies now and she mustered up as much enthusiasm as Bella, Gemma and Rosie.

They followed procedures before going into the NICU, washing their hands, applying anti-bacterial gel, and Carrie reiterated what to expect. Today they would be cuddling four babies. Three boys, born to one mother, had come into the world premature at thirty-one weeks. The triplets were all doing well but the mum had an older child at home already and was desperate to give her some attention too, which was why baby cuddlers were a godsend for her right now.

Carrie kept a particular eye on Gemma, who didn't look quite as nervous now as Carrie settled her with the first baby. She moved tubes and wires aside and placed the little one in Gemma's arms, all the while talking in hushed tones, keeping calm in case Gemma felt like she was going to panic. But even as the baby grizzled and its balled-up fists looked about to do battle, Gemma kept her focus on his little face, let the fingers grip hers, and Carrie knew her friend could handle this.

'These babies were born too early,' she said softly to Gemma. 'The mum took a lot of persuasion to go home and be with her other child. Up until now the child has come here to see her, but she realised it's best to stick with normality wherever she can.'

'It'll give the mum a break.'

Carrie smiled. 'It will. Most mums don't want to admit they need one, but I'll bet she comes back to the hospital smiling. Desperate to see her other babies, yes, but glad she'd taken time out. And we're here to hold the fort. All these babies need from us are cuddles. The nurses will look after them from a medical standpoint, but human touch is the key.'

'It really is.' Gemma didn't look at Carrie, she was mesmerised by this new life, and Carrie left her to it.

Rosie and Bella were content enough with the other two of the triplets and so Carrie made her way to the baby she'd been assigned.

The little girl's arms flailed and she whimpered, whether in pain or loneliness Carrie didn't know. Negotiating more wires, Carrie lifted her up into her arms. 'Hello, Megan, I'm Carrie,' she whispered. Serena was on hand to help Carrie settle into the chair beside the bed but then she was off on rounds and Carrie was happy to be left alone.

Megan let out a few cries that seemed far too big compared to her size. At only two days old, this baby was going through the worst time of its life already. Born to a drug-addicted mother, the narcotics had been passed through the placenta and as soon as the baby was born and the food source had been cut off, the baby had begun to go through withdrawal. This was one of the worst cases and Carrie had spoken with Serena to ensure the other girls didn't get this as their first experience of baby cuddling.

Carrie stroked Megan's forehead gently with one hand as she held the baby firmly against her body. As with any addict, coming off the drugs with immediate effect meant going cold turkey so this baby was in distress. She wasn't sleeping, had difficulty feeding, she had muscle tension and was irritable and jittery.

Carrie rocked back and forth gently in the chair. Serena came in after a while and they tried feeding the baby again. She took more than at the last feed, so it was progress, but she had a long way to go.

Carrie's bum went numb from sitting for so long, she began to feel dizzy from shushing Megan softly over and over, but eventually Megan's body began to relax, her eyelids fluttered and she was coaxed into a gentle slumber. Carrie continued to rock back and forth, thinking about Noah and Norma, about Lachlan and how he'd spoken to her. She hadn't texted him and he hadn't messaged her either. Perhaps they both needed time to cool off, to think about what they really wanted.

Carrie stayed with Megan until the end of the shift, her heart breaking to think that if this little girl woke she'd most probably go through the same kind of hell the next day, and the one after that, until her little body had rid itself of all the poison her mother had ingested. And when Serena came to tell her it was time to go and helped put Megan back in her little bed, Carrie felt drained.

This was a bond she'd never known and could never know, because this – this pain of having something so precious that could be taken away at any second – was something she couldn't bear to put herself through.

*

The rest of the Magnolia Girls were already in the cafeteria by the time Carrie emerged and already they were chattering away at high speed.

'Those babies were so tiny.' Rosie couldn't get over it.

'I think my wedding ring would fit over Rupert's wrist,' said Bella, who had cuddled the smallest of the triplets.

'I can't wait to come and do it all over again.' Gemma's eyes lit up. 'How did you get on, Carrie?'

170

'Good. I'm cuddling a little girl called Megan.' She didn't elaborate on the details and hoped they all assumed Megan was born too early as well. She didn't want anyone to be overcome with sadness today, their first time as baby cuddlers.

By the time Carrie arrived home there was no sign of Noah's truck and still no text from him to update her on the whole Norma situation so, taking matters into her own hands, she made her way to Laurel Drive.

It wasn't hard to find the house. As he'd said, there weren't many neighbours and they were spaced out on a quiet road that allowed her to slow right down and peer at the numbers. His truck was outside too, so an instant giveaway.

'Hey, what are you doing here?' After she'd knocked it had taken Noah a while to answer the door. He stood there now in a spotless white T-shirt with jeans that frayed at the bottom over his bare, tanned feet. He looked tired, and if Carrie didn't know better she'd have mistaken him for a man who'd had too many beers the night before.

'That's not a very nice welcome.'

He managed a smile and stood back for her to come in. 'Sorry, that was rude. Come in. You took me by surprise, that's all.'

Inside, Carrie could see Norma at the end of the hallway in what looked like the kitchen and when Noah gestured to go right in, she took the lead.

'Hello, you.' She crouched down beside the dog, curled up in her basket. 'She looks thinner.' It was a shock to see her so lacklustre, so different to before, and the way it affected Carrie was more than she knew how to handle.

171

Noah cleared his throat. 'She isn't eating. Her appetite is all but gone, and yesterday she vomited up what she'd managed to get down.'

It was Carrie's turn to find her voice wobbling now. 'Was it my fault? Did I make her walk too far?'

'What?' Instantly he must've realised the conclusions she'd drawn. 'No, it wasn't you.'

She felt on autopilot. 'You said town might be too far for her. I should've stopped for longer on Main Street, got her to drink more. Perhaps given her food.'

'Carrie, it's not your fault.'

'I should've got the vet straight away rather than call you. They could've caught whatever it was and dealt with it.' Tears fell down her cheeks unbidden. She didn't even attempt to hide them, because after Megan at the hospital and now Norma, she could no longer bury her emotions.

Noah put his hand on top of hers as she fussed Norma around the ears, one of her favourite spots. 'Carrie, you're not listening to me. This is old age playing out. She's had a good life. I chose to bring her home. She's only got a couple of days at most, but she's not in too much pain. She's sleeping most of the time and at some point she'll fall asleep and won't wake up.'

Tears blurred her vision. She barely heard a word he said. 'It's my fault, all my fault, I should've known sooner. What have I done?' She couldn't see anything but she felt Noah pull her against him and she leaned into his chest, uncaring whether her sobs filled the kitchen, unconcerned whether the whole of Magnolia Creek could hear her and know about her mistake.

Noah held her that way until she calmed down and then he reached out to fuss over his dog again. 'Did you hear the story of how I came to have Norma?' He

172

stretched up to the benchtop, grabbed a tissue and passed it to Carrie. 'I was doing some work over at Magnolia House when the owner, Julie, found a sack in the lake. She pulled it out, yelled for me, and when we opened it up we found four pups. Someone had tied it at the top and left them to die.'

Carrie put a hand against her chest. 'How could someone do that?'

He shook his head. 'I have a few choice words when I think about the person who did it, not that we ever found out who it was. It still baffles me to this day. There are plenty of people out there to turn to; there's a veterinarian in town. All I knew was that when I found Norma, she was coming home with me.' He laughed. 'Sounds like I'm out on the pull and have picked up a girl, doesn't it?'

Carrie managed a laugh, thankful her tears had stopped. 'What happened to the other puppies?'

'Two were already dead. The third puppy was in a bad way and died before I could wrap it in my fleece and take it over to the vet's, and Norma was lucky number four.'

Norma made no moves to get up and Noah sat on the other side of her basket. 'She was a naughty pup.' He grinned.

'Really? What did she do?'

'She had a shoe fetish, typical woman. She chewed my brand-new runners – not the old ones, only the new. I wouldn't mind but I'd given her an old one as a distraction and hidden the others away, but she'd found the box, somehow got the lid off.'

'Maybe she's trying to tell you your feet are too smelly, even for a dog.'

'Maybe she was,' he laughed. 'But she's one smelly dog herself. I'm surprised she never treated you to a display of just how much she could fart.'

'I'm glad she didn't, she's a proper lady.'

'Ha! No, she's not. She farts so loudly at night that it's been known to wake me up from two rooms away.'

'I don't believe you. You wouldn't do that would you, beautiful girl?' Norma's mouth twitched every now and then as her eyes stayed firmly shut and she dreamed about something they would never know.

'She ate an entire giant Easter egg once,' Noah recounted. 'An Easter egg my niece saved up for and bought from the chocolaterie especially for her favourite uncle.'

'I'm no dog expert, but isn't chocolate bad for dogs?'

'It's very bad for them. It was an immediate and very expensive trip to the vet, where they induced vomiting. I never told my niece; I bought a replacement egg as I knew she'd check how much of it I'd eaten.'

Carrie stroked Norma some more. She didn't want to stop. 'How many nieces do you have?'

'Just the one, and four nephews. They're my sister's kids. She wanted a whole brood and she got them. I think she'd have liked another girl, an ally perhaps, but nature had other plans.'

'My sister Kristy and her husband Mitch would love to have a family, and I'm sure it's only a matter of time before they get started.'

'I've always wanted a house full,' he admitted. 'I want a home filled with noise, laughter, kids, pets…everything that makes a house a home. Or at least it would for me.'

It sounded idyllic, but everyone knew life didn't always work out the way you wanted.

'How about you?' he asked. 'Think you'll have kids?'

'Who knows?' She rarely told people that no, having a family was one of those things she never intended to do.

'Does Lachlan want a family?'

'Lachlan and I were always career-driven. It was what first attracted us to each other. We've never seen babies in our future and I'm pretty sure he still feels that way.'

'And how about you? Do you still feel that way?'

She wasn't used to such a personal grilling. 'I don't think it's for me,' she felt forced to admit.

'Because of your career.' It wasn't a question.

'At one time, yes. But even without that, I see so much heartache in my job – I'm not sure I ever want to open myself up to that.' She felt her cheeks warm as she realised how honest she was being without intending it. 'You know that most men don't really talk about this stuff, don't you?'

'Maybe I'm not most men.'

Suddenly awkward, she asked, 'Do you mind if I use your bathroom?'

'First on the left as you go up the stairs.'

In the bathroom she peered into the mirror wondering how Noah had this uncanny ability to wheedle the finest details out of her.

When she returned downstairs Norma had stirred in her basket and Noah was trying to coax her into taking a drink from the bowl he'd filled with water. 'Do you think you'll ever change your mind?' He gave up and placed the bowl on the floor beside the basket.

'About what?'

'Having a family.'

'I doubt it.' Back on a subject she didn't really feel comfortable talking about, she found herself asking, 'Have you ever come close? To settling down, I mean.'

'Once.'

Her phone rang and when Noah picked it up from where it lay next to the sink alongside her keys, he passed it to her. 'It's Lachlan. Sorry, caller display told me.'

She tapped the screen to decline the call. 'I'll talk to him later.'

'I appreciate you coming today, Carrie.' His eyes held hers.

'Keep me updated, won't you?' She didn't look away either.

When Norma shifted in her basket and tried to move, he comforted her and picked up the bowl of water to try again.

'I'll leave you to it,' she said, his attention now, quite rightly, elsewhere.

'Thanks, Carrie.'

*

'That's not good,' said Owen the next morning when Carrie explained why the garden progress was on pause.

'It'll hit him hard when she dies.' Carrie swallowed a gulp. 'Can I go up and see the bathroom wall tiles?'

He accepted the change of subject and continued sanding the mantelpiece in the lounge. 'Sure, I think you'll be very happy with them.'

Upstairs, Carrie beamed. She reached out a hand and ran it across the mosaic tiles that came halfway up the wall. 'They look amazing!' she called out. The bigger tiles had gone in just after the bathroom was refitted, but she'd waited for this more stylish wall to be finished and it was definitely worth the wait.

176

Owen came upstairs moments later. 'I'm glad you're impressed.'

'They're gorgeous.' She smiled. 'Oh, before I forget, I've arranged for a guy to come over this morning to measure up for shutters. He won't be in your way, will he?'

'Not at all. What time are you expecting him?'

'He'll be here before I leave for work so I'll let him in. If you could see him out and remind him to email me the quote, that would be great.'

'Are you having more than one quote?' He rolled his eyes when she looked sheepish. 'OK, well let me know what quote he comes back with and I'll tell you if it's reasonable or not.'

'Useless, aren't I?' She slumped down on top of the toilet seat.

Owen put down the piece of sandpaper still in his hand. 'Whatever makes you think that?' He crouched down on his haunches so he was level with her.

'Everything is such a mess.' She couldn't stop the tears falling, again.

'You're renovating, of course it's a mess.' His joke at least got a giggle between sniffs. When he pulled away he handed her some tissue from the toilet roll that had yet to be slotted onto the shiny new silver holder. 'I never once saw you cry; I didn't think you had it in you.'

'I'll take that as a compliment.' She smiled as she clasped the tissue in her hand.

'Would I be right in thinking there's something you're not telling me or anyone else in this town?'

'Did Noah say something?'

'He hasn't said a word.'

'He overheard Lachlan and me having an enormous row.'

177

'A row about what?'

She should tell him. He was a friend after all. But somehow she couldn't do it. 'Thank you for being here, to talk to.'

'If you need to talk more, I'm a good listener.' He picked up the sandpaper again. 'And Rosie's a good listener too. You've got some real friends in this town, don't forget it.'

She managed a genuine smile. 'I won't.'

After Noah returned downstairs she pulled herself together, took a deep breath and braved calling Lachlan, knowing it was far better to get it over and done with than to sit stewing about the situation. He was friendlier than she'd expected and rather than rehash the argument that had taken place the other day, they talked about the baby-cuddling program and his upcoming medical conference in Perth.

'I'll miss you,' she told him. 'Love you,' she said at the end of the call when the shutter man knocked at the door to announce his arrival.

But right now they felt like just words, things Lachlan wanted and needed to hear, feelings she was beginning to question nearly every day.

*

Carrie took Maria to baby music classes, their regular Wednesday activity, and when they returned to the house Maria had a nap while Carrie happily prepared a beef casserole for the slow cooker as a favour to Tess and Stuart. When Maria woke up, Carrie gave her fresh sandwiches with the crusts removed and mashed-up banana for her lunch, and with the sun gracing Magnolia Creek yet again, they headed into town, the well-rested ten-month-old getting into her stroller without any protest this time.

Carrie pushed Maria around the lake and Maria squealed with delight as they took it in turns to toss pieces of bread to the ducks. Maria's bread didn't go far but it still made her giggle as the ducks raced to get to each morsel first, creating splashes and wide waves in the water in their quest. Next it was on to Magnolia Gifts, where Carrie chose to leave the stroller outside and hold Maria. It was much safer that way, with more control over a child who liked to reach out and touch things purely for the sake of it.

She hadn't intended to buy anything but when she saw the perfect sign for the new shed Noah had talked about putting up in the garden, she wrestled to get her purse from her handbag as Maria tried to thwart any attempt to hand over anything bright, shiny or colourful to Mal. Carrie eventually won the struggle, pocketed the change and stowed the package beneath the stroller outside. She used all her leg strength to bend down with a child in her arms, then extricated Maria's hands from her hair so she could do up the harness.

When she stood up she felt a head rush and realised that between thinking about Lachlan, organising Maria, cooking the meal and worrying about Norma, she hadn't eaten since breakfast. Her stomach growled in protest.

'There's only one thing for it,' she told Maria, who giggled away over nothing, showing a nap could do wonders for the temperament. 'I'm just going to have to have one of Bella's famous scones.'

The bell in Finnegan's Café tinkled to announce their arrival. Carrie tipped the stroller a little and bumped it up the step to go inside. She was still smiling when she realised Noah was sitting at the table against the wall and his face said it all.

'Hello, Maria!' Bella was first over to make a fuss of the baby and Carrie forced her attention away from Noah. 'Lovely to see you both in here. Now, what can we get you?'

'Well, I've come in for the famous scones, plenty of jam and cream, but I think for this little one maybe a babycino and a small muffin if you have one. She's had lunch so I don't think she's overly hungry but we've been by the lake for a little while.'

'A babycino!' Bella's enthusiasm rubbed off on Maria immediately. Eyes wide with delight, she clapped her hands together exposing the two bottom front teeth that were yet to be surrounded by more.

Bella busied herself filling the order and when Carrie leaned over the counter Bella pre-empted her question. 'Norma died this morning. He's been at that table for an hour, just sitting watching the world go by. He didn't even want a scone – he must be bad.' Bella made the babycino, poured a fresh apple juice for Carrie and prepared the food. When Rodney took charge of the next customer, she said, 'Why don't I mind Maria for a bit and you go and talk to Noah? I think he needs a friend.'

Carrie looked over at him. He was still staring out the window, eyes glazed over. 'Are you sure?'

'Of course. What do you say, Maria?' She was already unclipping the baby. 'I'll pop her in a high chair and supervise her with the muffin and babycino.'

Carrie gingerly made her way over to Noah, who looked up and smiled.

'I'm sorry.' It was all she could say as she took a seat opposite. 'Have you been up all night? You look exhausted.' When he nodded she reached out and touched a hand to his.

He looked at their hands until Carrie took hers away. 'If you'd rather not have the company, I can leave you alone.'

'Don't be silly.' The same smile that had greeted her more than once was back for a moment. 'How are the renovations coming along?'

'It's all going well.' She thanked Rodney for the scone and spread some jam and cream on top. 'I'm going to put shutters throughout, give it a fresh look.' She was rambling but he didn't seem to mind the distraction. 'The bathroom tiles look even better than I'd imagined, the window seat in the bedroom is painted, the carpet goes down in there this afternoon. The upstairs is finished apart from another coat on the banisters for the staircase, and Owen has sanded all the floors. I'll need to move out again while they're polished.'

'Wow, that's progress.' He grinned and pointed to her mouth. 'You have a little bit of jam…'

'Where?' She wiped one corner but he was still grinning. 'Where?' She was grinning herself by now.

He reached out and wiped just below her lip and showed her his finger with the telltale raspberry jam. When he licked it she knew she was blushing.

'Will you go back to the city while the floors are done?'

His question brought her back to earth. 'I'm going to stay with Kristy.'

'I'll be back to your garden today if it suits.'

She let the cream dissolve on her tongue and finished her mouthful. 'You don't have to. Take all the time you need.'

'I'll be all right, Carrie.'

'Well, if you're sure.'

'I am. I want to stain the pergola as it's due to be dry for the next few days so I don't want to waste the opportunity. And you need to choose a shed so I can put it up at the back of the garden.'

'Can't you just use your initiative? I mean, it's a shed. I don't know what I want.'

He shook his head but not in a mean way. 'If you give me the go-ahead, I'll choose you something.'

'Consider it done. I'm giving you the nod.'

'Will you want it painted a colour, or stained natural like the pergola?'

She finished her scone and smiled.

'Don't tell me – use my initiative?'

'Exactly. Oh, I just remembered something.' She licked her fingers of cream and jam, went over to the stroller, took out the package and unwrapped the purchase from its tissue paper. 'What do you think?' She lay the sign on the table.

He read it out loud: '*Woman Cave*. And you're going to fix this on the shed?'

'Sure, why not?'

'It's just that I can't see you ever hanging out in the shed.' He grinned. 'Man Cave is a good phrase because men generally go into their sheds, garages, anywhere we can have a bit of space. You don't do outside, dirt, spiders or insects.'

'I think I'll survive. I'll have you know there was a spider in the bath this morning.' OK, so it was tiny, but he didn't need to know that. 'I covered it with an empty jar, then slid cardboard beneath it so I could throw it outside.'

He nodded, impressed. 'And there I was thinking you'd kill them if they dared to come within a fifty-metre radius of you. Not such a princess after all.' His cheeky remark earned a winning smile from Carrie.

He also didn't need to know that she would've killed it if she'd had a can of bug spray – but she couldn't find it, and she refused to squish it in her nice new bathtub, so the old-fashioned spider-removal method had been the one she used. She'd then taken the spider part way down the hill, jar and cardboard outstretched in front of her, and thrown the eight-legged terror into the bush.

Carrie noticed Maria beginning to get fractious and Bella looking unsure how to resolve the matter. 'I'd better rescue Bella. Maria can be a handful sometimes. It was great to see you, and I'm so sorry about Norma. I'm also sorry that all we've really talked about is my house – you must be sick of it.'

'On the contrary, it was a nice relief to think about something else.'

'I'll see you soon.'

His voice stopped her. 'You haven't finished your drink yet.'

She picked it up.

'Now where are you going?'

'You don't want to share your quiet time with a grumpy child,' she stated matter-of-factly. 'Maria was so serene when we first walked into town. I get the feeling I may have pushed it a bit now though.'

'Carrie, bring her over. I'd like the company.'

'Are you sure?'

'I'm sure.'

She rescued Bella, or Maria – she wasn't sure which of the pair looked more fraught. 'What's all the fuss?' she asked Maria, scooping her out of the high chair and into her arms.

'She was happy one minute and the next…' Bella puffed out her cheeks.

'Thanks, Bella. You get back to work and Maria can come and terrorise Noah instead.'

Bella and Rodney ran the café around them and with Maria refusing to sit on any type of chair, or sit full stop, Noah and Carrie eventually gave up and took her over to the lake instead. They sat on the low wall surrounding the water and watched the ducks, and Maria didn't seem to notice that they had no bread to throw this time.

'What do you two get up to most days?' Noah enquired.

'Oh, we get up to all sorts, don't we?' Carrie pulled on her cardigan and then took Maria back from Noah's arms. With the child on her lap she could smell the freshly laundered knitted jumper Maria was wearing, her angel-soft hair and the scent of baby lotion they'd applied after her bath. 'This morning it was music classes.'

'Bit young for that, isn't she?' He squinted in the sunshine and pulled his sunglasses down over his eyes, only for Maria to have other ideas and reach out to tug them off. He rescued them, returned them to his face and she did the same again, fascinated by this new game.

'I guess it's more what you'd call music appreciation,' Carrie explained. 'But it's loud.'

'I can imagine.'

'Picture this,' Carrie giggled as Maria squirmed in amusement on her lap, still playing the sunglasses game. 'Ten kids in a room, each with a percussion instrument.'

'I hope you took some headache tablets with you.'

'Always.' She joined in with his amusement. 'But Maria loves it and it's nice to have a planned activity for her.'

Noah let Maria grip his fingers as she sat on Carrie's lap.

'She likes you,' Carrie observed.

'Most women do.' He cleared his throat. 'I can't carry off comments like that at all, can I?'

Carrie didn't answer but being bashful was an endearing quality, unexpected of this rugged gardener who seemed confident in every other way. She reached beneath the stroller. 'Do you want the rest of the muffin?' she asked Maria, who took the proffered piece once it was unwrapped, grinned and squished it in her hand.

'How can you not want one of these?' Noah asked, and Carrie realised he was referring to Maria rather than the muffin. There's no way he could know how deep his comment ran, and it terrified her. *Because one of these could be taken away and the pain would be unbearable*, she wanted to tell him. *Because every time I see a parent break down in front of me it wears me down that little bit more.*

Noah did the honours and prised what was left of the muffin out of Maria's scrunched-up fist, flinging the scraps to the bird pecking by the wall to find what the ducks might have missed.

'I'd better get going,' said Carrie, looking at her watch.

She attempted to put Maria back into the stroller, much to the baby's disgust. For a girl so young, she sure knew how to dig her heels in. She arched her back, kicked her little legs, went rigid, making it next to impossible to get the harness in position and clipped up.

'I'm sorry, Carrie.' Noah waited until Maria was finally secured in the stroller. He must've known he'd hit a nerve and he was too sensitive to ignore his faux pas. 'I shouldn't have mentioned the B word.'

'The word is baby and no,' said Carrie, 'you shouldn't. It's none of your business. Everyone feels differently.'

'Carrie —' But his words fell short as she turned to go. 'Carrie, wait.' He followed close behind.

'I'm sorry.' She stopped, shook her head and then, not knowing what else to say, carried on walking. As he caught up with her, she added, 'I shouldn't have snapped at you, you didn't deserve it.' They passed the curved veranda at the front of Magnolia House and Rosie waved over to them.

'It was deserved, and for what it's worth, I'm sorry.'

They both waved back at their friend before continuing on their way and at the top of the path, Noah hovered uneasily. 'It was good to see you today.'

'You see me most days,' she smiled.

'You know what I mean.'

She really did. 'I'll see you again soon.'

When he tore his eyes away from hers he bent down and gently squeezed Maria's hand. 'Bye, Maria.'

Maria was too busy rubbing her eyes to make a grab for his sunglasses this time. Her head tilted to the side of the stroller as they said goodbye to Noah and Carrie wondered if she'd be asleep by the time they got back to the house.

If only she could close her eyes too, and turn back time to when she was confident, knew what she wanted out of life.

Chapter Thirteen

The girls gathered in the beer garden at the Magnolia Tavern after another stint at the hospital. The evening air was still warm enough to be outside, with the help of outdoor heaters, and they chatted about the babies they'd held, the new babies they'd met.

'I've got a little something for us,' Gemma admitted, with a raise of her eyebrows that told them they'd all love it.

'Oh, I like surprises!' Bella enthused as Gemma produced a carrier bag from beneath the table.

Gemma pulled out what looked like a bundle of T-shirts and when she unfolded the first and held it up to reveal *The Magnolia Girls* emblazoned on the front of each black T-shirt in pink writing, Carrie was more than impressed. 'They're brilliant! What a fab idea!'

'Oh, I hope mine will fit.' Rosie took one and peered at the label.

'They come up big but I think there's one in here that'll fit over your pregnancy tummy, plus another for once you're back to your normal size.'

'You're a star. I'm going to try it on now.'

Rosie marched off towards the pub and presumably the bathroom and Bella yelled, 'Wait for me!' and followed her.

When they returned, Carrie and Gemma took their turn and within minutes they were all seated at the table in their matching T-shirts.

'Are we allowed to wear these on the ward?' Bella asked.

Carrie nodded. 'Of course. We'll have the plastic gowns over the top, but these are great. What a lovely idea, Gemma.'

'Actually it was Andrew's idea. He found the website and made the suggestion.'

A collective sound of approval swept around the group.

'You know Molly will want one when she and Ben next visit, don't you?' said Rosie.

'Andrew already ordered her one.' Gemma grinned.

When they drew the attention of a couple of the regulars and explained why they were called the Magnolia Girls and what they did, they posed for a photograph that Carrie said she'd use in the hospital's next media release. 'Look out, girls, you're going to be famous!'

As they laughed into the evening air and chatted with people curious about what these T-shirts were and why they were wearing them, Carrie caught sight of Noah with Owen over the other side of the beer garden. If they'd spotted the girls they'd obviously decided to leave them to it, and with neither of them looking over Carrie watched Noah and thought back to how he'd been with Maria beside the lake. He was, she supposed, what you might call a natural. People used to say that about her and she knew she was good with the kids at work, but work was totally different.

'The triplets are doing well,' said Gemma.

'They really are,' Rosie agreed.

Bella had been cuddling Peter, the smallest of the babies, that afternoon. 'Peter's operation went well and he's fighting his way back. He was unsettled when I first arrived but couldn't fight sleep forever.' She smiled. 'I never realised how special baby cuddling would be, how much it would give to us as well as to them.'

'I'm glad it's all working out.' Carrie looked around at this group of women, this group of girls with whom she had bonded so easily in such a short space of time.

Bella tutted when her phone rang. 'I do apologise, I thought I'd switched it off.' She moved away from the table to take the call.

'How's Noah?' Rosie asked when Gemma went to buy a few packets of nuts for them all to share.

Carrie had wondered whether Rosie would remember seeing them together by the lake. 'He's upset, of course, but he's accepting too. Norma was old and it was her time.'

Rosie swirled the orange juice around in the bottom of her glass and finished the dregs. 'Is everything OK with you? You seem a bit away with the fairies.'

Rosie had become a friend – an unlikely one given Carrie's history with Owen, but this girl seemed to understand and see through Carrie more than anyone had in a long time. Maybe it was time she confided in a friend and told her why she'd really walked away from her big job in the city.

But the opportunity of saying anything disappeared when Rosie asked, 'What's wrong?' as Bella came back over to the table.

Flustered, Bella garbled, 'It's Rodney…he's had a heart attack.'

*

Over the next couple of weeks Carrie witnessed the true meaning of friendship. The girls had taken Bella to the hospital straight after she received the phone call, and the second they returned to Magnolia Creek it was all systems go.

Carrie, Gemma and Rosie had pulled together other residents to help out one of their own. Bella gave everyone a brief rundown of how the café worked and Rosie collated all the information into easy-to-follow charts, diagrams and explanations so they could produce a workable rota for the time being while Rodney was still in hospital. Bella had suggested the café simply close, but it hadn't been reopened that long and Owen had hinted to the girls that Bella wouldn't be able to afford to lose the income. Chris worked the early shifts in the café since his pub hours didn't start until later, Andrew helped at lunchtime while Gemma managed the chocolaterie, Carrie took over the final shift on the days when she had Maria but wasn't needed at the hospital, and Rosie and Owen slotted in wherever they could.

Bella hugged each of them as they herded into the café the morning Rodney came home. 'I couldn't have managed without your help. I owe you all so much.' Her eyes pooled with tears of gratitude because the girls had banded together and not only looked after the café, but had also filled Bella's freezer with enough home-cooked meals to last a few weeks.

'Nonsense,' Rosie insisted. 'We know you'd do the same for any one of us.'

Bella enveloped them all in another group hug. 'Too right I would.'

'The Magnolia Girls stick together.' Gemma hoisted Abby up onto her hip. 'But now I have to get this one organised for swimming lessons. Are you still OK for us to stop off at your place, Carrie? I can't wait to see the progress.'

'Sure, it's even clean inside now. Owen has a few bits to do but mostly we're there. I'll see you in twenty minutes or so?'

'Sounds good to me.' Gemma waved her goodbyes before crossing over Main Street to head for home.

Carrie and Rosie left Bella to it and as soon as they were outside the café Carrie lowered her voice. 'I'd help any of you out in the same way as we've done for Bella, but I'm exhausted.' There were a few times when she'd been tempted to share her story with Rosie since the night at the pub when catastrophe for Bella had meant she didn't get to say anything after all, but she'd never managed to come out with the words. And today didn't look like being any different.

'You and me both,' Rosie confessed. 'I'm going home to put my feet up, sit and read a book on my window seat. Which reminds me, how's your window seat looking? She pulled her sunglasses down from the top of her head.

'I love it. And I never would've thought to have one but after seeing yours…'

Rosie's eyes sparkled. 'What colours did you go for?'

'It's painted white and I've put a very light grey base on top with white scatter cushions.'

'Did you go for pull-out drawers below?'

'No, I went for a lift-up seat so I'll stash blankets in there for the colder months.'

'You'll love Magnolia Creek in the winter. We get frost sometimes and when the sun comes out it looks beautiful.'

Carrie didn't doubt it, and it was early May already so she wouldn't have long to wait. Slowly she was realising that, for a self-confessed city girl, she was falling head over heels for the country. Over the years Carrie had usually wanted the best of everything. Not in a selfish way, but she liked to have the designer shoes, the posh frocks, a fashionable apartment, exotic holidays and a nice car. But then there was nothing like a traumatic life-altering event to give you some perspective.

The girls parted ways at the bottom of the hill and Carrie walked up to the house, where she found Noah in the garden watering the freshly laid turf. She watched him from the kitchen window, wondering if she should go out and say hello. Things had been so manic with Rodney in the hospital and everyone pitching in that they hadn't spoken much since Norma died.

But she'd missed her chance, because Gemma had just pulled up on the driveway and was calling through the front door.

'Come in!' Carrie waved at Abby, who toddled in first and flung her arms around Carrie's legs, but then Gemma handed her a wrapped-up box that immediately caught her interest instead.

'Something to keep her amused,' Gemma explained. 'Otherwise she'll be into everything.'

Carrie took them both into the lounge, which was now finished apart from a second coat that Owen needed to put on the architraves. 'Sorry I only have beanbags,' she said to Gemma but they both grinned when Abby reserved one by plonking her bum down straight away.

'It seems Abby doesn't mind your choice of furniture.' Gemma looked around. 'Wow, this place looks so different already. I haven't been up here in months. We came and had a nosy when it was put on the market and both Andrew and I could see the potential.'

The smell of fresh paint lingered. The fireplace surround had been scrubbed to within an inch of its life and now the white tiles gleamed, the pomegranate and olive-green foliage detailing stood out, the grate was filled with fresh logs ready for a winter fire and the brass fire front was polished so that it shone proudly. In the corner of the room was a collection of accessories waiting to be installed: chrome door handles; a lacquered chrome light fitting with incandescent bulbs and transparent petal shapes; a silver mirror with bevelled edges to put above the fireplace.

With Abby amused with her new jigsaw depicting a collection of colourful Disney characters, Carrie showed Gemma the other room at the front of the house.

'I love the wood burner,' Gemma enthused straight away. 'We're thinking of installing one at the house.'

'You'll have to come up here and test this one out,' said Carrie, completely at ease inviting her over. 'You and Andrew, and Abby of course.'

'That'd be great. Andrew has rejected the suggestion of doing anything more to the house for a while, but I think if he could see this it might be a whole different story.' She raised her eyebrows conspiratorially.

'It's a bit over the top having a fireplace and a wood burner,' Carrie admitted, 'but I was thinking this room could be a library, so it would need to be cosy.' With a set of shelves already replaced, all they needed was more on the rest of the walls along the same side. 'I've got a lot of books in storage. Some of them have been boxed up since I moved out of home: there was never enough room in my apartment to unpack them all. But here, they can stay.'

'I'll be visiting your library in the future,' Gemma grinned. 'I read most of mine on my Kindle now but it's always nice to browse a new collection. What will you put in the middle of the room? It's a huge space. How about a rug?'

'I'm going to have my baby grand transported up here.'

'You play the piano?'

'I'm a bit rusty. I don't really play it enough, but I might do more out here.' The truth was, Lachlan had bought it for her after she reminisced about the time she'd spent as a teen playing the piano. But she'd given it up along with a lot of things when career became her focus.

'A piano would fit well – there's certainly plenty of light coming in.'

Gemma peeked in on Abby, who had got all the large jigsaw pieces out of the box and had fitted two together already.

Carrie led the way to the kitchen. 'What do you think?'

'It's lovely.' She nudged Carrie. 'I'm glad you kept the sink by the window – you need that when you're washing up.' After a quick glance out the window she added, 'If I were you I'd stand here washing up all day.'

Carrie knew she was referring to the view of Noah, who was bending over tending to the grass by the decking. His physique stood out in a pair of shorts and it was an impressive sight. 'You sound exactly like Rosie,' she laughed. 'Come on, I'll show you the upstairs.'

Gemma did her best to coax Abby into coming with them but the girl had certainly learnt the word 'no' and they left her to try and fit another piece onto the jigsaw, although moments later they heard Abby on the stairs having decided she didn't want to miss out.

Once Gemma had supervised Abby's climb to the top, they looked at the spare room. 'Owen suggested adding an en suite in here,' Carrie explained, 'in case I ever want to rent the place out. The only bathroom is off the main bedroom.'

Gemma checked out the en suite that had been installed in the far corner, with built-in wardrobe and shelving completing the look and giving the appearance of it always having been there. 'It's amazing what he's done with the space. And you'll be able to get a double bed in here no problem. It'd be a great source of income come tourist season.'

'I'm not sure I want anyone else to be living here.'

Gemma grinned. 'Well, I can't say I'm disappointed – because it means we'll be seeing a lot more of you.'

Carrie took the compliment and passed Abby a piece of discarded bubble wrap. Abby made them both laugh at her giggles every time another piece of it went *Pop!*

In the main bedroom, as Abby carried on popping, Gemma admired the window seat. 'It's gorgeous. May I?' She sat down when Carrie gestured to go ahead and looked out of the window to see views of fields and trees beyond. 'I'll have to get onto Owen and have him make me one or I'll be left out.'

'Come see the bathroom.'

With Abby popping away, Gemma admired the room that had been completely transformed. The glass in the window pane was frosted now but didn't make the room any less impressive as the chrome taps gleamed in the light and the scent from the vase of lavender on the inset shelf lingered in the air.

When Noah's voice called up the stairs Carrie left Gemma admiring the bathroom and excused herself to join him. He was clearing up for the day and had said he'd be back to put a few more plants in the flowerbeds.

'Thank you, Noah. It's all looking really amazing.'

'My pleasure.' With silence between them he said, 'I've watered the grass and I'll do it again tomorrow. You'll have to do the watering yourself a few days when I'm not around.'

'I think I'll manage.' She shook her head but smiled at his lack of faith that she'd tackle the task.

'You can handle a hose?'

195

She rolled her eyes. 'Of course I can.'

When they heard Gemma yelling, both of them darted from the room to go upstairs.

'What's wrong?' Carrie looked for blood in the bedroom, an unconscious child, something that had made Gemma yell so loudly. But Abby, momentarily stunned by her mother's outburst, launched into a crying fit so loud Carrie thought she'd need noise-reduction headphones if she didn't stop soon. 'Is she hurt?' she asked above the din.

'That's very naughty, Abby. So naughty!' Gemma scolded.

Noah looked as though he wanted to run the other way. It was a complete contrast to a couple of weeks ago when he'd basked in Maria's company.

'I'm sorry, Carrie. I thought she was still playing with the bubble wrap and when I looked down…' Gemma's voice trailed off because Carrie could see exactly what Abby had been doing.

Carrie crouched down and picked up the discarded bits of photograph that had been torn into little pieces, the photograph she usually kept tucked away so safely.

She fell back onto her bottom, clasping the pieces together in her hands, against her chest. She didn't register Gemma's repetition of apology, she didn't acknowledge Abby screaming and kicking her legs as Gemma scooped her up against her will and took her downstairs when Noah said he'd stay here. Because all Carrie knew was that the tears had come, she was curled up in a ball on the floor, and she could barely breathe.

Chapter Fourteen

'Do you want to tell me what that was all about?' Noah asked when Carrie's breathing calmed enough and she looked up from the floor she'd been staring at since Abby and Gemma left.

'It's a special photo,' was the only explanation she offered.

'Gemma feels pretty bad about it.'

'Oh, God, I didn't mean to make her feel terrible.' Carrie realised how it must've looked when she hadn't been able to utter a word to her friend. It was a mistake, that was all, and Carrie was well aware she should've handled it better. 'I'll apologise. Poor Abby, she was only playing. She's three; she wasn't to know.'

'Gemma did give her a right telling off. For what it's worth, the kid looked genuinely sorry and pretty distraught. But she wouldn't know a scrappy piece of bubble wrap from a precious photograph.'

'I know.' She shut her eyes and breathed deeply before turning to Noah. 'I bet when you took on this gardening job you didn't realise it came with an emotional wreck of an owner.'

He blew out between his lips. 'I wouldn't have wanted the job if you'd told me, but I'm stuck here now. That's better,' he said when she smiled. He stood up, held out a hand and pulled her to her feet. 'What are your plans for the rest of the day?'

'I was going to laze around and read a book, right there.' She pointed to the window seat. 'I'm not sure I feel like doing that now – not after I was such a monster to Abby. Why do you ask? I thought you were done for the day?'

'I am. But I wouldn't mind your help, if you have a couple of hours to spare.'

'Wait, it's not more heavy lifting, is it?'

He shook his head, his smile in place. 'I promise you, it's not.'

'Then I'd be happy to help. I could use the distraction.'

He led the way downstairs as Carrie badgered him to tell her what he had planned. Carrie still had the pieces of photograph in her hand, and in the kitchen she made a snap decision. She pulled out the bin beneath the sink and dropped the pieces in, watching them scatter like ashes following a devastating loss. Which was exactly what it had been. Who knew? Maybe in some way this afternoon's disaster could be the trigger she needed to move forward.

Less than forty minutes later Noah and Carrie were three towns further north of Magnolia Creek, and they turned off the main road and passed through the gate of somewhere called Mill House. Cows dotted the nearby landscape and there was nothing but rolling hills and the smell of real country.

'What are we doing here?'

Noah pulled into the free space out front of an old farmhouse. 'You'll see.' He climbed out of the pick-up and when Carrie did the same she registered the sound of barking coming from somewhere, but she couldn't see any dogs in the vicinity.

Noah knocked on the door of the farmhouse and they were welcomed by a lady, who looked to be in her fifties, wearing riding boots, a wax jacket and a cowgirl hat that had seen better days. She said hello and Carrie deduced from their discussion that Noah had already talked with this woman and arranged today's visit.

When they reached what looked like a row of stables the woman told them to take their time and to ask any questions as they arose.

'Are we going for a riding lesson?' Carrie giggled as she walked behind Noah, who was following the woman into the stable block.

'Dear me, patience, girl,' Noah whispered, enjoying keeping the surprise hidden.

The barking crescendoed and Carrie grew impatient. 'What is this place?' What she'd thought to be stables housed large spacious cages and in each of them were dogs of all breeds, shapes, sizes and ages.

First up was a German shepherd called Mary, second was a small white fluffy dog called Penny, then Shep, Stanley and another, called Veronica. Patsy, the lady who'd welcomed them, explained that at the front of each stable, or section, was a placard with the dog's name, sex, age, description and a rundown of vaccination information.

'There are so many of them,' said Carrie.

Patsy smiled at her as Noah fussed over one dog and then another. 'Some of the circumstances they come to us under are quite grim, but all these dogs are thriving now.' She stopped at one of the sections, undid the grill and was greeted by an older dog, who, rather than jumping up as some of the younger ones did, immediately rolled over, exposing her tummy for Patsy to rub. 'Maggie here came to us when her elderly owned passed away. There was no family to take on the responsibility so it was down to us. She's old now and I don't think she has long left, but she's happy here.'

Carrie swallowed hard and wondered if Noah had heard, whether it made him think of Norma.

Carrie asked Patsy more about the other dogs and the circumstances in which they'd come to Mill House, and when they reached halfway down the cages she found Noah fussing over one of the dogs with the same look on his face that he'd once had for Norma. 'You brought me here to choose another dog for you,' she said, knowing now that this would be the dog that went home with him.

'Are you glad you came?'

'Actually, I am.' She read the dog's information on the placard. This was Hazel, a chocolate Labrador. She was four years old and when they asked Patsy more about the dog's history they discovered she was malnourished when she came to them, having been found on a neighbouring farm where she'd likely been wandering around for days.

'We never did find the owner,' Patsy explained as Hazel rested her chin on Noah's knees.

'Probably a good job,' he said.

Patsy nodded, and Carrie got it. She'd only ever met parents of children who wanted the top level of care, the very best for their loved ones, who fought their corner at every twist and turn along the way. These owners were people you could never understand, with their attitude towards a pet, their propensity to neglect.

'You don't want to say goodbye, I can tell.' Carrie smiled at Noah after Patsy took down all his necessary details. Hazel nuzzled her nose against Carrie's wrist, exploring this stranger but soon turning back to the man who was going to give her a home.

'It'll be a few weeks yet,' Noah explained to Hazel, 'but not too long, my girl. I've got a lovely house, Norma's old basket and some new cushions, even the odd chew toy or two. Everything is ready.'

Patsy confirmed she'd come to Noah's place to give his house the once-over, an important step, she explained, in rehoming an animal. She asked all kinds of questions, from whether Noah had children or anyone else living at the home to how many pets he'd owned previously and how many hours he spent away from the house.

'I think Hazel will be very happy with you,' said Patsy before they left the farm.

By the time they got back to Magnolia Creek, the pitter-patter of rain on the windscreen had stopped and the bruised clouds above parted to make way for the autumn sunshine.

'Maybe you should adopt two this time,' Carrie suggested as they pulled into her driveway.

'Steady on.' Noah unclipped his seat belt.

'They'd keep one another company when you weren't there.' She hesitated. 'Talking of company, would you like to come in? I can make us a cup of tea and we could sit outside and admire all your hard work, until we get rained on.' She looked above because there were still dark grey clouds lurking in the distance. She hoped he'd agree to her idea because she wanted to clear the air. He'd seen her be a monster to a three-year-old that afternoon, completely overreacting at something that had been a total accident, and if she knew anything about this town it was that people liked life to be straightforward and out in the open – and if it wasn't, they at least wanted a little harmony.

'I'd like that, thanks.'

Owen had already been and gone for the day so after Carrie made the tea, she took two mugs outside and sat down next to Noah on the base beneath the pergola. She passed one to Noah. 'I need to get one of those cast-iron table-and-chair sets for here.'

'That'd look good, and you wouldn't have to take them in when it rains either.'

'Have you seen any suitable sheds?' she asked.

'I haven't had a chance to look yet, but don't worry, you'll get your woman cave some way or another.'

'Thank you.' She looked around her, at the garden, up at the house. 'I can't believe this place is nearly finished. It's even better in reality than I imagined it to be.'

'That's a good thing, isn't it?' When she nodded he said, 'Sometimes the things in our heads are different from what they are for real.'

'Cryptic,' she grinned.

'Thank you for coming to Mill House with me today.'

'I enjoyed it. But you didn't really need my help, did you? Something tells me you already knew which dog you were going to choose.'

'Caught red-handed. I'd already looked online and it was just a matter of visiting in person and sorting the finer details.'

'Why didn't you tell me?'

'I took you out there because I wanted you to see Patsy, to see how she takes dogs in and cares for them and most of the time they get to go to good homes. But, as she explained, some come to her and are too old so they won't be rehomed, they'll live out their last days with her. Some things are beyond our control, but if we care enough we can use our emotions to give as much as we can.' He put down his mug. 'Sometimes, giving as much as we can still won't be enough though.'

'Why do I get the feeling we're not talking about dogs anymore?'

'Who was he, Carrie?'

Goose pimples travelled up her arms and her neck and she swallowed, hard.

Noah spoke when she couldn't. 'The boy in the photograph was a patient, wasn't he?' When her head snapped up he shrugged. 'I figured it out. And I'm guessing he was behind this sudden move away from the city, upping and leaving everything behind.'

She didn't have to confirm it, he already knew. She shivered some more when a dull grey cloud blocked the sun and she picked up the extra cardigan she'd brought outside with her. Wrapping it around her shoulders, she told him all about Lucas, the little boy who lived on forever in her heart and the one who had changed her for good.

'Lucas came to us when he was eight years old. He was a bright, bubbly boy but was plagued with stomach aches, tiredness, a rash on more than one occasion and acid reflux. I think I always bond with my patients because it's the job, but Lucas was different.'

'In what way?' His voice was soft, patient.

'Lucas came to us time and time again, and on one occasion he asked me why I was so quiet. He wanted to know what had happened to make me different. I was taken aback by how perceptive he was and I explained that my gran had died that morning – peacefully in her sleep, but I had been very close to her.

'You know, he put a hand on my arm, much in the same way as I probably did to him a million times, and it was in that moment I realised the power of such a small gesture. There were no big words accompanying it, but the skin on skin, the reassurance that other people cared, well, it almost took my breath away. We started to joke more at Lucas's appointments, he drew pictures for me that I pinned up in my office, and I looked forward to seeing him. He took everything in his stride: tests for allergies, scans, endoscopies, a colonoscopy. But we couldn't find anything to explain what was going on.'

When Carrie stalled, Noah offered her another cup of tea, and they moved inside when the sun gave up and hid behind a cloud.

With the warmth of the second cup clutched between her palms, sitting next to Noah on the beanbags in the lounge, Carrie went on. 'Lucas had seen a photograph of me on the office pinboard with another patient. I was dressed as Supergirl and Lucas told me I was going to use my superpowers to fix him too. The photograph you saw was of Lucas and me, and it was taken by his mum one day at the hospital. He asked for the photograph so he could pin it on his own pinboard at home and every time his tummy hurt or his body ached, or when he had a fever, he'd be able to look at our smiling faces and know it wouldn't always be this way. His mum gave me the identical photograph and I kept it in my office alongside others, but it was the one that always felt the most powerful in a way that scared me.

'I found myself following his case more than I would any other child. I didn't cross any professional boundaries but his case became one I couldn't bear the thought of not solving. I think that was why I became a bit obsessed. Most of the time a diagnosis was straightforward enough but this went on and on and it really got to me. Lucas was still plagued with tummy aches and started to suffer at school because of it. One day he drew me a picture of him sitting at a desk, next to a window. I asked him who the other person in the picture was – was it his teacher, and was his teacher nice? He told me he wasn't going to school for a while and his dad was teaching him at home until things settled down.'

Noah waited for her to carry on and it took a while but she managed to get out the rest of the story. 'One day, Lucas was rushed into emergency. His organs were failing and we finally found that the root cause of all his problems was his heart. He needed a transplant. But we'd found out too late.' Her voice wavered and she almost lost control. 'He was on the waiting list and died before he got his miracle cure.'

'I'm sorry, Carrie.' Noah reached out and put his hand over hers. 'But the circumstances were beyond your control.'

'Were they?' She pulled her hand away. 'He trusted me to fix him. If we'd looked at the heart straight away, we would've known what was going on: he could've been on the list sooner.'

'Hindsight is a wonderful thing.'

'I failed him.'

Noah took something out from the pocket in his shirt and handed it to her.

Tears clouded her eyes but not so much she couldn't see it was the photograph of her and Lucas. 'How did you...' The photo she'd thrown into the bin had been taped together and she clutched it against her chest.

'I fished the pieces out,' Noah explained and then couldn't help himself. 'Not a pleasant task, sifting through scraps of food.' It worked, because she managed a small smile. 'I know it's not great, all taped together, but I thought you'd regret getting rid of it.'

'Thank you.' She dared to look down at the photograph now. 'He was just another patient, that's what Lachlan could never understand. But for some reason he got to me more than anyone else. I'd lost patients before – not many, but some – and it's always unimaginable. But Lucas…' She looked at Noah. 'His parents blamed me.'

'Are you serious?'

'They hated me. They yelled, they screamed, his mum came at me and tugged at my clothes, pounded her balled-up fists against my chest. One of the other doctors had to get her off me, hold her back.' She put her head in her hands and felt Noah's hand rest reassuringly between her shoulder blades. Even now she could remember the shivering Melbourne day with the temperature fixed at nine degrees as the wind howled around the hospital corridors, mixed with the wails from distraught parents who should never have had to go through anything like this. 'They blamed me for not finding the problem sooner, told me I should've done more. And we should have. We were the medical professionals, we were responsible.

She gulped. 'I've never seen anyone look at me the way his mum did.'

'Carrie, deep down you must know it was grief. I suppose to his mum you'll always be the woman who told her Lucas had died. She probably couldn't see past that.'

'Maybe you're right.'

'You know, people trust me with their money, they trust me to work magic on spaces that are neglected, run-down and downright awful. They want beauty and something to impress, and I'm lucky – I'm told I have a natural talent for it.' She wondered where he was going with this conversation until he continued. 'Doctors study and train for years, even I know that. And the reason is because medicine is so damn complicated. I did a short course in gardening, set up my own business and was good to go, but doctors don't have that luxury. If I'm wrong about something and a plant dies, I can get rid of it and put something else in its place. Quite often I realise I shouldn't have planted it in that particular garden anyway, but mistakes are easily rectified in my line of work. They aren't in yours. Sometimes, doctors don't have the answers – not because they're lazy or not clever enough, but because sometimes a problem is next to impossible to solve, and you can't afford to make mistakes. Only when you have the solution can you look back at all the clues and ask yourself why you didn't work it out in the first place.'

'I appreciate what you're trying to say.'

'But you don't believe it.' When she pulled a face he said, 'I bet every doctor goes through what you're going through. Lachlan must doubt himself sometimes.'

The mention of her boyfriend in their conversation felt intrusive but she answered anyway. 'I think he's got a tougher skin than me. He sometimes gets upset but he is always confident he did everything he could to help a patient. Maybe that's the difference.'

'I don't know you all that well, Carrie, but caring kind of makes you the person you are. If that makes any sense.'

She accepted the compliment but then looked down at the photograph again. 'I see his mum's face all the time.' Tears fell freely down her cheeks; despair rained out of every pore. 'I used to dread bumping into her on the street, thinking she'd out me to everyone around, yell that I'd taken her boy from her.' Her voice broke and Noah moved from his beanbag to hers, squashing in the best he could to hold her as she cried.

'You need to remember that for every child you can't save, there will be hundreds of others you can.' He stroked her hair. 'Let the good override the bad.'

She looked up at him and for a moment their faces were so close she could feel the warmth from his skin, the feel of his breath, and she knew he felt something too. They moved closer still, and he looked about to kiss her, but he pulled away.

He took his keys from his pocket. 'I'd better go. Patsy's coming over to check the house.'

She looked at her watch. 'I need to get going too.' She had half an hour to get to the hospital and although she felt drained, she also felt better now she'd finally told just one person the truth. Funny – she'd thought it would be Rosie she confided in, or her sister. Never for one moment had she thought it would be Noah.

'I'll let myself out,' he said.

'Good luck with Patsy.' It was all she could manage because she knew she hadn't misinterpreted the chemistry between them, but it seemed they'd both chosen to ignore it.

Chapter Fifteen

It was the middle of May and Carrie had had a hectic couple of days. Maria had turned one and Tess and Stuart had thrown her a big party, which Carrie went to, and although it had been great to celebrate with Maria, the post-party few days had seen the toddler either bouncing-off-the-walls excited or completely inconsolable as she failed to cope with her overtiredness.

At the hospital today, the Magnolia Girls were one woman down on their team, with Bella at home managing her business and caring for Rodney, but there was still no stopping them.

'Carrie, can I talk to you?' Gemma caught her before they went off in different directions to their assigned cases, each of them as enthusiastic as they had been back on their first day.

'Sure. Is everything OK?' She knew full well what Gemma was going to say because Gemma had texted her enough times over the last few days to say how sorry she was about the photograph being ruined.

'Of course it isn't. I feel terrible after what happened.'

'I completely overreacted, Gemma. And I'm so embarrassed. I should be apologising too. Abby's only a little girl.'

'Who was the boy in the photograph?' Gemma asked and immediately added, 'I know, none of my business. But, Carrie, if you ever need to talk, you have a lot of friends who would be willing to listen.'

'Thanks, I appreciate it.' Talking to Noah had been enough so she assured her friend that everything was fine between them and got on with the task in hand.

Carrie started her session by looking after Maisie, the three-year-old sibling of a baby girl in the NICU whose mum was having time with her newborn. Sometimes it wasn't possible to find a babysitter and so this was part of the role as a volunteer, and Carrie passed the time with puzzles and playing shops, where she rung up plastic loaves of bread and a pretend burger bun on the till so Maisie could pack everything into a little bag to take home with her.

After she'd played with Maisie, Carrie cuddled baby Megan again, greeting her with familiarity and a smile. She adjusted the tubes and wires, which was a puzzle in itself but with the baby cradled against her she could tell Megan was improving since the last time they'd been together. She was a fighter through and through, putting on weight and getting stronger each day. Megan calmed quickly in her arms, perhaps recognising Carrie's voice, maybe her smell, most likely realising how safe she was now. It was amazing the level of help you could give one of these children by such a small act of kindness.

Help was exactly what she'd wanted to give Lucas. But she hadn't been able to, and no matter how much she tried to remind herself of Noah's words and accept what had happened, all she kept thinking was that she'd failed the little boy.

'Your T-shirts are awesome.' Serena admired the motif of The Magnolia Girls when Carrie removed the plastic gown and gathered her things together after the session. 'The media release is fabulous too – thanks for organising.'

'No worries. The girls are glad to be famous.' Carrie had produced a short write-up about the baby-cuddling program that would appear in local newspapers next week, and the girls had all had their photograph taken together. It was good publicity for the hospital, letting people know where they were, the sort of work they did.

Earlier that day an elderly gentleman had cornered Carrie and wanted to know all about the Magnolia Girls: who they were, what they did. He'd told her it was a wonderful thing they were doing. His wife had twins more than fifty years ago and he'd worked full time, they had no family. 'What we would've done for a Magnolia Girl,' he'd grinned, progressing his way down the corridor with the aid of his walking frame. Carrie had walked away wondering what his story was now. Where were the twins? Where was his wife?

But maybe that had always been her downfall. Lachlan had told her she always got too involved, and perhaps he was right. Then again, Noah had told her it was what made her the Carrie he knew.

'Megan is much more settled,' she told Serena now. 'She fell asleep in my arms and much quicker than she usually does.'

'She's a tough one,' Serena confirmed without looking up from her paperwork.

Carrie picked up her bag. 'I'm off to the city tomorrow but I'll be back for next Wednesday's session.' The truth was she wished she wasn't going away for two nights. She wanted to be here to see Megan, satisfy herself with every bit of progress the baby made. She had a sudden, unwelcome thought of what it would be like to have her own baby. She couldn't imagine ever leaving his or her side, one day letting her child out in the big, bad world where so many terrible things happened. You saw it on the news every day: children having accidents, predators lurking around every corner.

211

Serena finished whatever she was writing and stacked the papers together before slotting them into a brown folder. 'Everything OK?' Her harried manner dropped back a notch.

'Sorry, yes.' She shook herself back to reality. 'I was just thinking about plans for the weekend,' she lied.

'Well, have a wonderful time.' Serena stood and picked up a clipboard and they left her office together. 'Are you staying with Lachlan? He'll be glad to have you back.'

'Unfortunately he's still away on a conference. And I have to be out of the house this weekend because the floors at the house are being polished.' She wasn't sure whether she was entirely disappointed he wouldn't be around. Since the day they'd fought and Noah had overheard, Lachlan had been nothing but nice on the phone and had backed off in his quest to get her back to full-time paediatrics, but since the moment between her and Noah and the kiss-that-never-was, work wasn't the only confusion she had right now.

*

The weekend with Kristy was probably one of the best Carrie had had in a long time with her sister. They had the place to themselves with Kristy's husband away, Kristy had swapped her Saturday morning shift with another medical receptionist, and they spent the afternoon trawling the Queen Victoria Market, buying up produce to make dinner ready for a girls' night in with a movie and plenty of wine.

'You seem different.' Kristy scraped the sliced peppers and onions into the pan as Carrie took charge of the steak and prawns in Kristy's kitchen. Two skillets were warming in the oven ready to set on the table in the centre where the tortillas were waiting, plus shredded lettuce, grated cheese and little pots containing sour cream and guacamole.

'In what way?' Carrie scooped the beef out with a slotted spoon and left it on kitchen towel while she cooked the prawns.

'You seem more relaxed. I'm telling you, it's Magnolia Creek. I might move up there myself one day. It's cheaper, it's beautiful and I expect it's a wonderful place to bring up kids.'

'Does this mean we're going to hear the pitter-patter of tiny feet soon? I thought you weren't quite ready for that step.' Carrie used oven gloves to take one skillet out of the oven. She took it over to the table and Kristy tipped on the cooked prawns at one end, the beef at the other.

'I'm not – not yet. But long-term, I think being out of the city would be good for us. It's certainly worked its charms on you.'

The sizzling, wafty smells of cooked meat snaked into the air and when Kristy declared the vegetables ready, Carrie took the other skillet to the table and Kristy did the honours again, putting the colourful selection on top of the piping-hot surface.

'Let's dig in.' Carrie pulled out a chair. 'I'm so hungry.'

Kristy joined her but not before she'd poured two glasses of crisp sauvignon blanc and they'd toasted to being sisters. 'I don't know how you survived with no kitchen for weeks, Carrie.'

'I think I've learnt I don't really like instant, microwavable meals, put it that way.' Carrie laid a tortilla on her plate and, using a spoon, smoothed across some sour cream. She sprinkled the surface with lettuce, grated cheese, a few prawns and some steak, and then rolled it up into a cigar shape.

Kristy lost a prawn out the end of her fajita but plucked it from the plate and ate it separately. 'How's the garden coming along?'

'I should send you photos; the grass is down and the pergola is looking good. I can't wait for the bougainvillea to grow and add some colour.'

'Listen to you. My sister the gardening expert.'

'Hardly. Although Rosie leant me a beginner's gardening book so I can learn some of the basics and hopefully manage to not kill anything off. And I've left the shed choices up to Noah – I've got no idea. What, why are you looking at me like that?'

'Noah. Such a dreamboat name for a guy who isn't far off the mark.'

Carrie picked up a second tortilla. 'He's a guy who's not my type.' Denial was the best way when she had no idea how she felt.

'Talking of your type, how's Lachlan?'

'He's on a conference at the moment but when he gets back he'll come up to the house again.'

'What I really mean is how is he, with this new arrangement? Not seeing you, not having you at the hospital.' When Carrie's face fell she said, 'Come on, sis, I know what he's like. He's a wonderful man but he likes to have you at his side.'

Carrie reached forward to add some steak to the fajita she was putting together. 'I think he's coping OK.'

'I always wondered what would happen when you left work eventually anyway, whether he'd be OK with it.'

'I'm not sure I follow.'

'When you have kids. You'll be an entirely different woman then; you may want to really pull back from your career. Would he be happy for you to do that?'

'Lachlan doesn't want kids.' She didn't miss the strong draw in of breath from the other side of the table. She'd never once mentioned this to Kristy. They'd talked about kids over the years but Lachlan was the first man Carrie had been remotely serious about. He'd been there when they lost Lucas, when Carrie's perception of the world altered. She'd gone from a confident woman riding the wave of a busy and rewarding career to one who'd begun to doubt herself. She'd seen kids in her future once upon a time but never spent much time thinking about it, until Lucas died under her care and everything caved in around her. It had been like pouring hot chocolate sauce onto an ice-cream dessert and watching on slowly as the sturdy, hard-packed lump of vanilla broke down and became liquid. The only way the vanilla could stand up in the future would be to not add the sauce in the first place.

'You never told me.' Kristy had stopped eating and was busy topping up both of their glasses of wine.

'It's no biggie.'

'What do you mean, no biggie? It's huge!' Her wine glass almost reached her lips but she stopped. 'Unless you're telling me you don't want kids either.'

'And what's wrong with that?'

'Nothing, nothing at all. It's just…well, you work with kids, you're fantastic with them, and I'm sure whenever we've mentioned it in the past you've always seen them in your future.'

'We're not in the back garden playing with our dolls now,' she quipped, thinking back to the games they'd played as little girls, pushing prams up and down the

215

garden path with their baby-like dolls bundled up inside. 'Things change.' Carrie finished the last of her fajita.

'I know they do. I'm just trying to figure out exactly *what* has changed, that's all.'

She could turn this into a conversation about every woman's right to choose, she could tell her sister the effect Lucas's death had had on her confidence, or she could move on to something else. Carrie chose the third option. 'When are you next coming over to Magnolia Creek?'

Kristy let her change of subject slide. 'I'll be there again soon enough, don't you worry. I can't wait to see what you've done with the place.'

Carrie had half of a third fajita before declaring herself too full to fit another thing in. 'How about I clear up while you take the wine into the lounge, put on some music and get the wood burner going?'

'Sounds good to me. Make sure you rinse the plates before they go in the dishwasher.' Kristy rolled her eyes. 'Mitch is completely anal about it. I keep telling him he's doing the dishwasher a disservice not letting it actually wash the plates.'

Carrie sniggered. The dishwasher had long been a gripe between her sister and brother-in-law.

She cleared the plates, rinsed and stacked them in the dishwasher, and when the wood burner was going, Kristy washed the skillets and the bigger pans while Carrie grabbed a tea towel and dried.

Relaxing in the lounge, talk turned, as Carrie had known it would, back to her career. But this time she didn't mind. What Noah had said to her made sense, and even though she still blamed herself for not getting to the root of Lucas's problems before it was too late, talking to someone about it had helped her move the pieces

216

around in her head so that rather than being an unsolvable mess, they were beginning, she felt, to fall in a more orderly fashion.

'I need to explain what happened.' The words were out of her mouth before she had a chance to reconsider. Maybe because of Noah's understanding, she was at last able to talk to someone else, someone who knew her so well.

'Only if you're ready,' said Kristy.

'I think I am.' Carrie smiled.

They talked, they hugged, and Carrie told her sister all about Lucas. She told Kristy the extent of the stress she'd been under, her need to escape everything and leave it behind.

'No wonder you've been in pieces.' Kristy hugged Carrie tight until they both giggled and she finally let her go. 'I'm glad you told me.'

'I'm glad too.'

'Have you made any moves to find out about a permanent job again?' Kristy asked. 'Or is it too soon?'

'I haven't yet, but I will.'

'Back in the city?'

'At first I would've always said yes, but since being in Magnolia Creek I'm more taken with the place than I thought. I bought my little house out there because I knew I had to jump onto the property ladder before prices went up even more, even out in the country, and I wouldn't be able to do it. And it gave me a different focus to throw all my energies into.'

'Kind of a retail therapy?' Kristy grinned from behind her glass.

'I suppose it was. I set myself a budget though, didn't go over the top, and it's better than I ever imagined.

Once upon a time I thought I'd rent it out, make some extra money.'

'And now?'

Carrie put down her wine glass. 'Now, I really don't know.'

'Why do I get the feeling you're talking about more than the house?'

Carrie closed her eyes and shook her head. 'You're far too clever, you know.' When she opened them she looked at Kristy. 'When I walked away from my job I was at the point where I had to. I thought I'd have the time away and I'd be able to get back to the old Carrie again – you know, the Carrie who was in control, who knew exactly what she wanted and went out and got it.'

'That Carrie is probably in there somewhere, she's just a bit lost right now.'

'That's the thing.' Carrie topped up both wine glasses. 'I'm not sure if I want to find my way back to where I was before.'

'But you worked so hard. Correction, you worked your arse off to get where you always wanted to be. I can't imagine you throwing that all away.'

'I won't throw it away. I'll get back to paediatrics, but I'm not too sure if I want to be in the big city hospital again, with the life I had before.'

'You mean the life you have, or is it had, with Lachlan?'

Carrie's brow furrowed as she made her admission. 'He's perfect in so many ways and I always thought we'd be together for good. It's not him who's changed, it's me. I don't know, being away from the daily grind, the conveyor belt I found myself on, I've had a chance to think more.'

'Do you still want to be with him?' When Carrie shrugged and didn't meet her gaze, she said, 'Oh, Carrie. I don't know what to say.'

'I really need to talk to him.'

'And where does Noah fit in with all of this?'

'Noah? What's he got to do with it?'

'You told me I was too clever, so I'm asking the obvious.'

'Noah and I are two very different people who want very different things.' This time she didn't deny anything. 'A physical attraction to someone only goes so far.'

Kristy jutted a finger into the air. 'Aha! So you admit there's an attraction.'

'Like I said, it only goes so far. And real life isn't like that.'

'I think you need to really consider what you want, long-term. Don't stay with Lachlan because you're too worried that leaving him will be the wrong thing. I'd hate to see you unhappy.'

'But you like Lachlan.' It was the first time she'd ever detected an ounce of doubt from her sister.

'I do like him. Look how he waited for you when you upped and left, how he's supported you during this move, how he's always waiting in the wings. He helped you pack all your things, he arranged the specialist removal firm to shift the baby grand piano to here – thank you, by the way, my rendition of 'Chopsticks' is coming on beautifully – and he treats you like a princess.'

Carrie jolted at the use of the word Noah had once applied to her. 'Why do I sense there's a "but"?'

'I like him,' Kristy began, 'but there are things I don't like. I've never interfered in your life, Carrie, never.

Even back when you were dating Owen and I could see it was no more than a fling and I was worried you'd get hurt, I knew you'd say "I can look after myself".'

'I can.'

'I know. But I'm going to be completely honest with you now, seeing as you've asked. I don't trust him.'

'You think he's cheating on me?'

Kristy pulled a face and shook her head. 'It's a different sort of distrust. I don't trust him not to hurt you. I don't think he'll break your heart, but I think he'll hurt you without intending to. He has your back in so many ways, but I know you've felt pressure from him to return to work when something clearly happened. You don't run away, Carrie, not unless you're forced to, and I guess I feel as if a boyfriend – anyone who is genuine husband material – should support you no matter what you decide. I'm not sure Lachlan would. Will he stand by you if you never return to paediatrics? Can you see him doing that?'

'Plenty of couples have different careers, go in different directions.'

Lachlan had come along with impeccable timing. Carrie had dated a couple of guys since Owen but then stopped being so flighty and gave everything to her career. Lachlan waltzed into her life and her plans with ease. Well-educated, attractive and attentive, Lachlan was a heart surgeon who just got her. He'd never question her own dedication to her job as previous boyfriends had sometimes done, and not having to explain yourself in a relationship was something Carrie found she appreciated. It made her feel settled, in control.

Lachlan had stood by her soon after Lucas died and he seemed to get where she was coming from, but the cracks were beginning to appear now as he was growing tired of her inability to put the past behind her. Kristy was right, he was unlikely to approve if she jacked in her job permanently, and even though she had no intention of doing that, surely the person you were with should support your choices if those were best for you in the long run.

'I know they do,' Kristy said in answer to her point. 'But for you two, you were always in sync at the start and now you're following different paths – not only in your careers. Could you ever see him taking to Magnolia Creek in the same way you have?'

'You think we're pulling apart as a couple.'

Kristy looked into her lap. 'I'm sorry to be so honest, sis.'

'No, don't apologise. I guess I have a lot of thinking to do.' She knew it was time. Time to think about what she really wanted, out of her career and her personal life, from the sort of man she saw herself being with long-term to the house and town she wanted to live in.

'How about we forget all your stresses and put a movie on?' Kristy picked up on Carrie's discomfort and, like any big sister, rallied round.

For the next couple of hours Carrie felt relaxed and managed to watch the movie without her mind drifting to any of the hassles that were evolving in her life, and by the time they'd finished and moved on to hot chocolates with extra marshmallows in the kitchen, Kristy wanted to know more about the house. 'I bet those floors will look amazing.'

Carrie grinned. 'I can't wait to see them. They'd already been sanded before I left.'

'I'll bet that was dusty.'

'It wasn't too bad…lots of plastic sheets everywhere and he'd work when I was looking after Maria or up at the hospital.'

'Are you ready to unpack all your books onto those shelves in the second lounge?'

'I sure am, and I'm more than ready to get the wood burner going as soon as it's winter.'

'Are you ready to take your piano back?'

Carrie laughed. 'I wondered how long you'd take to ask me that. I'm sorry it's been in your way for so long. I've already called the piano removalists and they can take it up mid-week so will be here at nine o'clock on Wednesday morning. I can be here to supervise the collection if you're not around.'

'I'm happy to do it. I'm not at work until midday Wednesday.'

'Thanks, Kristy. Not just for storing the piano, but for being here to talk to this weekend.'

'Took you long enough to confide in me,' she answered cheekily.

'Yeah, sometimes I forget I need my older sister.'

'Everyone needs someone, Carrie.'

She was fast beginning to realise how true that actually was.

Chapter Sixteen

Carrie's smile matched the brightness of the autumn sunshine outside her house that already felt like home. She stepped inside and the floors looked nothing short of amazing. The Baltic pine had been covered in a stain that lifted the boards from drab, dull and unnoticeable to glossy and eye-catching. She went into each room in turn, marvelling at how different the place looked.

'Not disturbing you, am I?' The back door opened when Carrie went through to the kitchen and Noah popped his head in.

'Noah, you gave me a scare.' Hand on her chest, Carrie smiled.

'Didn't mean to make you jump. Owen had to go down to the fire station so left the door unlocked. He's expecting the replacement extractor hood to be delivered and installed and he didn't want the fitters traipsing on too much of the nice new flooring so I said I'd let them in this way.'

Carrie looked at the perfectly fine glass extractor hood. 'Why did he order a replacement?'

'There's a scratch, apparently.'

Carrie peered closely from all angles and eventually found the tiniest of marks. 'He shouldn't have worried about it.'

'He's a perfectionist, remember.' His smile was highlighted by the sun streaming in the window and his left cheek dimpled beneath his stubble. He had on khaki shorts, work boots and a T-shirt that must've been black once upon a time but had now faded to a charcoal shade.

'When are you going to start your training at the fire station?' she asked. 'You were scheduled to go and then you hurt yourself.'

'Work has been full on but Owen won't let me off the hook that easily. He'll get me down there at some point.' He lifted the back of his arm to wipe his brow, already lined with sweat, and as he did so revealed enough of his stomach to send Carrie's thoughts spinning. As a distraction she looked around at the other finishing touches Owen had begun to add: the immaculate ceilings with aluminium light fittings, the sleek polished chrome handles on the kitchen cupboards and the taps at the sink that hadn't been used enough to take away their shine.

He was still watching her and, uncomfortable under his gaze, Carrie left him to it and headed to Maria's place.

Maria always welcomed her with a big grin on her face and by clapping her hands together over and over while mumbling incomprehensible words that probably meant something to her, yet didn't to anyone else. It was lovely to see her happy and even though she grizzled when Mummy left for work, she was easily distracted now she was used to Carrie.

After lunch, when she and Maria had done puzzles, made colourful shapes with playdough and danced to two episodes of *The Wiggles*, it was time to get out, and when Carrie got Noah's text and photo of the deep pink daisies she'd one day have along the far border of her garden, she couldn't resist taking Maria up to the house. It meant she could get some fresh air and a much-needed walk, and hopefully Maria would sleep. These days she was beginning to resist a daytime nap, which, as her mother had warned Carrie, made for a particularly difficult afternoon.

'I underestimated how heavy this would be.' Carrie huffed and puffed her way up the hill to her house, pushing the stroller, head down looking at the ground, arms outstretched in front of her. It was easy to push a child around Magnolia Creek, up and down Main Street, popping in and out of shops, but tackling this climb was another thing entirely. But she couldn't stop or Maria would start fretting, rubbing at her eyes. Why kids fought sleep so vehemently Carrie would never understand, but fight it they did.

'This is my place,' Carrie announced with a big exhalation when they reached the top and the stroller came to a standstill in front of the porch with its little step up and canopy top above to shelter from the rain. 'What do you think, Maria?' Hands on hips as she got her breath back, Carrie looked down into the stroller. She smiled. 'So now you fall asleep.'

Maria, head lolled to one side on the pale pink teddy bear she'd brought with her and dropped out of the stroller four or five times, had fallen into a blissful slumber and as the birds twittered around them Carrie wondered how she was going to keep her sleeping. She didn't really want the stroller on the new floors inside, so instead she parked Maria up in the shade beside a tree and went over to sit on the porch step armed with the ice-cold can of Diet Coke she'd stowed in her bag.

She cracked open the can and breathed in the country air, the Magnolia Creek that was undiscovered to many. Even tourists didn't take enough of a step back to fully appreciate what this town and surrounding countryside was like. Carrie knew she'd been guilty of the same thing and had never understood her sister's fascination, until now. It was almost winter but still mild, and Carrie wanted to savour the outdoors as much as she could today. She had enough layers on that it felt more like spring and the sunshine hovering tentatively above the house detracted from the season. Her house at the top of the hill had a view for miles around. Undulating fields rose and fell in the distance, trees swayed gently in the autumn breeze and wildlife went about its business as though Western civilisation wasn't even there. A bunny rabbit hopped in between two bushes and Carrie wished Maria had seen it. She took a photo with her phone to show Maria when she woke and as she tucked the phone back in her pocket, Noah came around from the back of the house.

'Hey there,' his voice greeted.

She put a finger to her lips and he got the hint. When he crept closer she whispered, 'She's asleep. Thank God.'

Noah peeked around the stroller and smiled before taking a seat next to Carrie on the porch step. 'She looks so peaceful. Oh, what it would be to fall asleep like that, outside with nothing but the sounds of the countryside around.'

'And great big lolloping men with loud voices.' Carrie grinned and when he nudged her, the hairs on his arm made her shiver.

He noted the absence of Carrie's car. 'Did you push her up the hill?'

'Yes, and believe me, I need this.' Carrie took a big gulp of drink, letting the coolness flood her body. She remembered his text. 'Thanks for the photo of the flowers.'

'I thought you'd like to know what they'll look like eventually. That's the thing with gardens, they're not as instantaneous as the house itself. You need to have a vision of what it'll be like eventually. The flowers I've chosen for you are hardy and will add a lot of colour. I've chosen deep pink for now but later you could always add some white or yellow too.'

'I'm sure it'll be perfect.'

'Come on.' He stood up. 'Why don't you wheel Maria round the back and we can chat while I work.'

Carrie looked over at the stroller and detected no movement. 'Do you think we can do it without waking her?'

'Sure we can. You take one end; I'll take the other.'

Noah lifted the front wheels off the ground as Carrie simultaneously lifted the rear wheels and they gently manoeuvred Maria in the stroller round to the back of the house, where they positioned her in a shady spot. Carrie gently laid another blanket over Maria's lap so she wouldn't get cold.

'The climbers up the pergola should be in abundance within a year.' Noah pointed to the plants. 'You'll need to keep an eye on them, not let them take over.' He pushed some kind of sapling into the ground and Carrie peered at the label, trying to visualise the garden as he'd advised.

'Have you had any luck finding me a shed?'

He looked up at her, squinted in the sun before he pulled his shades down so he didn't have to look away. 'As a matter of fact I have.'

'Come on, share. I want to know what it's like.'

'Don't spoil the surprise.' He was definitely amused by the secrecy and her yearning to know more.

'Will my sign look right on the door?'

'I think it'll look great.' He looked past her, to the stroller again. 'She's still asleep.'

Carrie looked at her charge. 'She's peaceful like that.'

'You're good with her.'

'That's because I get to go home and put my feet up after a day's work. I'd be drained if I had her 24/7. Apparently this skipping the daytime nap has become a habit and then she's a shocker to be with for the rest of the day. I might have to start making the hill walk part of my daily routine, for my mental well-being.'

'My sister was the same. She kept her sanity by doing a lot of walking when the boys were tiny. Even if it was pouring with rain she said she couldn't bear to be inside with them all day.'

Carrie smiled. She discreetly investigated some of the labels on the already planted shrubs as Noah continued on with the garden, and then she ducked inside for a brief chat with Owen, who was giving the mantelpiece in the lounge a final coat of varnish. She'd only been gone for a few minutes when the sounds of crying came from the back garden and she was back on duty.

'Hello, you.' Carrie unclipped the harness and scooped Maria up into her arms. 'I'll bet you were wondering where you were.'

Noah didn't miss a chance to grab this young lady's attention and came over to gently say hello. Maria looked as though she was about to burst into tears and with some quick thinking, he pointed at the ladybird crawling up his arm.

'Thank you.' Carrie mouthed the words as Maria's attentions turned to the red-and-black insect, the split down its back where wings twitched ready to take flight. And the ladybird did exactly that when Maria was awake enough to prod it. They watched the red dot fly away, up, up into the air.

'How did the visit from Patsy go?' she asked as Noah pointed out a caterpillar on a leaf and let it crawl onto his finger so he could show Maria.

'She was more than happy, so it won't be long before Hazel arrives.'

'There was never any doubt she'd approve you.' Carrie watched him with Maria, whose eyes still glistened with the tears that had been scared away by country creatures and this man's kindness. This man was meant to be a father, she was sure of it, and she doubted he'd ever compromise on that. Not that she wanted him to. Or maybe she did. The only thing Carrie was sure of right now was that she had no idea what she wanted anymore.

Carrie took Maria around the garden on the boards Noah had laid down for the purpose, and for a while let her crawl on the base of the pergola. Noah had said it was best to let the turf settle in and not walk on it, although Maria clearly had other ideas and put up a protest every time Carrie dragged her away from it.

By the time Carrie walked home – far more enjoyable going down the hill – Maria was content and smiling away, much to Tess's relief when they arrived at the house. She'd had a busy day at work and looked exhausted so Carrie was glad to be handing over a happy child.

Next up was the hospital, and Carrie was in a good mood when she pulled into the car park ready for the baby-cuddling shift. Holding Maria in the garden and talking with Noah, she'd briefly had a glimpse of what family life could be like. Instead of thinking she couldn't have that ideal, that it could be painful if the unthinkable happened and her child was taken away from her in an accident or because of a medical condition that couldn't be cured, she found herself asking what if she had a child who was happy, healthy and went on to lead a long and untroubled life?

She locked her car and made her way inside the hospital. Her role there had really turned into just an extra set of professional hands, a baby cuddler who had more experience than most. The admin side of her work took very little management now it was under way and she could see how Serena had most likely made this position for her as a favour to Lachlan – because it was something that could easily be tagged onto someone else's full-time job description.

The other girls were waiting in reception for Carrie to join them and Rosie was beginning to feel uncomfortable. 'It might be almost winter,' she said, 'but I constantly feel like I'm cooking as I grow this baby.' She drank from a bottle of water. 'It's like having a portable heater strapped to myself.'

'Rodney's sister used to say the same,' said Bella.

'How is Rodney?' Carrie hadn't been into the café for a few days but had texted to keep up with Bella's husband's progress.

'He's getting on my nerves,' Bella smiled. 'That's a good sign, right?'

'Sure is.' Gemma grinned. 'When Andrew had the flu last year I was really worried about him, thought I was going to have to take him to hospital, but as soon as he began irritating me I knew he was going to be just fine.'

The baby-cuddling shift got under way but when Bella, Rosie and Gemma went off in different directions, Carrie found Serena before she headed to the NICU herself. She poked her head around the office doorway. 'I wanted to ask how Megan was doing. Could I take a quick peek at her charts?'

Serena looked up from the mound of paperwork she was sifting through and Carrie knew what she was going to say before she even said it. The fact she was focusing her attention on Carrie, the subtle head tilt to the side as she was giving the bad news, the lack of multi-tasking while she did it. 'Megan didn't make it.' She stood and came towards Carrie. 'She didn't have the fight left in her and died on Sunday evening.'

When Carrie felt her legs wobble beneath her, Serena guided her to the spare chair in her office. She made mumblings of tea, coffee and goodness knows what else, but Carrie wasn't listening. Her brain was still trying to process what she'd been told. 'I thought she was getting better,' she said over and over, but no matter what medical terms Serena used to explain the outcome, Carrie couldn't bear to listen. This was the job, the highs and lows of paediatrics, but it was too much to bear.

Carrie shook her head when Serena tried to hand her a cup of tea. The look on Serena's face told Carrie that Lachlan had shared all the details of what had happened to Carrie, with Lucas, his death, the parents blaming her.

She ran – out of the office, through the corridors, out the front entrance and back to her car. She couldn't be here. She couldn't be in a place with so much despair and sadness.

It was what she'd run from once before, and here it was, happening all over again.

Chapter Seventeen

The next week passed in a daze for Carrie. She came down with a cold, she refused to see anyone, and the only visitors she accepted were the removalists with all her things from storage, delivery men with brand new items, the firm to finish installing the shutters, and the specialist removal firm with her baby grand piano. Owen had started work on another property and so it gave her most of the week to get herself sorted while he stayed out of the way. Noah had nipped back and forth to finish the garden, but they hadn't crossed paths.

Unpacking and arranging furniture kept Carrie busy. She barely ventured out apart from to the mailbox at the foot of the driveway. She had the week off nannying duties anyway, with Maria and her family going away to Lorne for the week, and so it was time to get everything shipshape. She hung clothes in the built-in wardrobe that had been repainted, she put other garments in the new chest of drawers she'd ordered, she put towels in the linen cupboard beneath the stairs, vases went on windowsills, the new sofas she'd ordered went in the lounge, crockery and kitchen accessories went into the brand-new units in the kitchen. She made up the bed with fresh light-blue linen with intricate little daisies, and put a lamp onto the bedside table next to it. She even played the piano for a couple of hours each day, which gave her more joy than she'd ever thought it would, and provided an escape she'd thought was impossible to find.

Lachlan had been up to see her in the week and she'd put on her makeup, dressed immaculately and not once let on what had happened at the hospital. He'd brought an enormous bouquet of flowers with him, which she divided between a white jug on the kitchen windowsill, a vase in the bedroom and another on the shelves in the alcove in what was now officially the library as it housed the books she'd finally dragged out of their box and put on the bookshelves.

Her cold hung around and she texted her excuses to the girls when they begged her to come over for a chat or wanted to visit, and by the end of the week, with the weather looking dismal outside and nothing else to be done inside the house for now, Carrie had little reason to want to get out of bed. Along with the dust she'd swept from the floor and away from the windowsills as she unpacked and made this place her own, she'd pushed away all thoughts of Megan. Until now.

From beneath her duvet this morning, instead of feeling satisfied at how hard she'd worked, she felt bereft, lacked energy and couldn't be bothered to move. Someone had been knocking at the front door for ages but she hoped they'd soon give up and leave her in peace. When they didn't, she pulled the duvet all the way over her head hoping it would muffle the sound until it stopped. It didn't. She pulled the covers around the top of her head to shut out any light at all, although the big clouds gathering over Magnolia Creek ready to unleash melancholy rain hadn't allowed much light into the house anyway.

When the knocking at the door stopped, Carrie thought she'd shut out the world and could forget anything else outside of this beautiful house, at least for today. She could pretend nothing else existed, nothing else mattered. But when she heard the front door open and a female voice call gently up the stairs, she knew she couldn't do anything of the sort.

Rosie poked her head around the bedroom door. 'Owen let me in. I hope you don't mind. He was coming to do the light fittings downstairs, but said he'll come back later. He said to give you some space but I've been doing that for days. And now I'm worried about you. How's the cold?'

'It cleared up after a couple of days.' Carrie forced a smile. Ordinarily someone coming into her place would send her into a complete spin but she guessed she'd got used to intrusions during renovations, and realising how much people cared for her made her take pause. 'I'm not contagious, you can come in. I've been busy getting this place sorted so that's why I haven't been in touch. My goodness, it's dark.' She reached out and turned on the lamp beside her bed.

'I know, there's a big storm coming by the looks of things.' Rosie wouldn't be distracted. 'I talked with Serena at the hospital.'

'How's the baby cuddling going?'

'That's not what I meant and you know it.'

Carrie didn't have an answer for her this time.

'I'm sorry about baby Megan. When you weren't there at the end of the shift I assumed you were doing something else. It was only when we were at the hospital the next day and you weren't there that I started to ask questions.'

Carrie leaned back against the bedhead. 'What's wrong with me? I used to take it all in my stride; now every loss, every setback gets to me.'

Rosie sat down at the end of the bed. 'I've got no idea how doctors and nurses do the job, to be honest. I have such admiration for anyone who can. My dad was the same – he saw devastation in his job as a fireman and it nearly broke him more than once. But he kept going because he knew he was making a difference. And so are you. We all are with the baby cuddling, and you will do again in your job.'

When Carrie's phone rang she saw it was Lachlan.

'Aren't you going to get that? I can make myself scarce.'

Carrie let the call go to voicemail. 'I'll call him back later.'

'Listen, why don't you have a shower, I'll make us both a cup of tea, and we can sit in your nice new lounge and have a chat? That's what friends do, after all. Why are you smiling?'

'I never thought you and I would be friends.'

'Because we're different?'

Carrie shook her head. 'No, because of Owen. I don't know, I thought it would be too awkward at the start but you've made me feel such a part of the friendship group here.'

'Well, you deserve to be a part of it. And be warned, Gemma is so worried about you that she's been putting together a chocolate surprise package with Andrew's help. So you'd better get down to see her unless you want so much chocolate you'll be the same size as me, except without a baby in your tummy.'

Carrie grinned. 'I'll take the warning, thanks.'

'Right, I'll go and get the cups and tea bags sorted and I'll see you downstairs when you're ready.'

'Thanks, Rosie.'

Rosie turned in the doorway. 'It's my pleasure.'

Carrie savoured the feel of the rainfall shower, washed her hair, dried it and already felt better for the first time in days. She called Lachlan and then ventured downstairs, where Rosie handed her a cup of tea. She took it, glad the warmth immediately calmed her down after Lachlan's news.

'It's nice seeing a sofa in here,' said Rosie as they made their way into the lounge. 'The floors are great and I love the mirror above the fireplace. No lighting the fire yet though.'

'Still feeling like a furnace?' Carrie sipped her tea.

'Furnace, fat, fed up…so many adjectives beginning with F that I could mention.'

'It'll soon be over and it'll all be worth it.'

'The storms are coming,' Rosie continued as the room darkened some more. 'Watching a storm from inside is kind of nice.'

'I might watch it from the window seat upstairs later, with a big glass of wine.'

'That sounds good.' Rosie checked her watch. 'I hope Owen gets back to collect me before it really buckets down.'

'I could run you home if you like.'

'Oh no you don't – you're trying to get rid of me!'

'As if.' Carrie smiled. She genuinely felt better than she had since hearing about Megan and she would rather Rosie stayed, so didn't push the offer of a lift.

'I want to be cosied up at Rosie Cottage later,' Rosie continued, one hand rubbing her belly. 'Me and Owen, a plate each of beef hotpot, followed by hot chocolates and marshmallows.'

'That sounds very romantic. I mean it,' she added when Rosie looked doubtful. 'Sometimes it's the simple things.'

'I bet your Lachlan is romantic.'

'He can be.'

'I bet you go to the fanciest restaurants, wine and dine eating food far finer than a beef hotpot.'

'Romance isn't always having the best things in life, sometimes it's taking the most basic of things and turning them into something wonderful.' Was Lachlan romantic? Carrie wasn't sure. He'd showered her with gifts, no expense spared, he took her out to places, but she'd never really stepped back and wondered whether those things were romantic or not.

'You know,' Carrie continued, 'the most romantic thing a boy ever did for me was at school. I'd had a very bad day, a tough science exam and was really upset. I'd had two awkward dates with Max, a boy in my class, and when I couldn't find him after school I headed home pretty dejected, and there he was, waiting at my front gate with a posy of daisies he'd picked from his mum's garden. They lived all the way across the other side of the suburb and he'd biked the journey in the scorching heat, as well as stopping to buy me a big bar of Dairy Milk, which was all mushy when he took it out of his pocket. But you know what, I didn't care, because it was the thought behind it that was romantic rather than the gesture itself.'

'You're right. Men must hate women expecting big gestures. I bet they feel under all kinds of pressure.'

'What about Owen? Is he a romantic?'

'I didn't think so at first, but I think he can be without even trying. When I was ten weeks pregnant I couldn't eat chillies. I love chillies but they started giving me really bad indigestion. Thanks to my pregnant brain, I'd forgotten and ordered a pizza with the works, plus extra chillies, and when it arrived and I realised what I'd done, I stood there and cried. I mean, really cried. I was so hungry, so tired. Owen stood there and picked off every single chilli and ate it himself – he was sweating by the end – and then he announced the pizza was clear and I could go ahead and help myself.'

'Wasn't the pizza still hot from the chilli seeds?'

Rosie shrugged. 'It had a bit of a kick but my stomach coped with that; it was the chillies themselves that really didn't agree with me. Owen downed a few glasses of water before he could eat anything else, and seeing him do it I realised he didn't have to do anything big to impress me. He only had to keep doing the little things.'

Carrie started to laugh. 'Poor Owen. I bet he ran a mile today at the thought of an emotional woman hiding upstairs. I'll be lucky if the last couple of light fittings go up at all.'

'Rubbish, he'll do it. But he knows I'll handle emotions better than him.' Rosie smiled from behind her mug of tea. 'May I?' she asked when she saw Carrie put her feet up on the sofa.

'Of course, sofas are meant for relaxing.'

'I know, but they're new.'

'Rubbish, we'll wear them in.'

Rosie lifted her legs onto the upholstery and relaxed into the cushions. 'That's better. Oh, so much better.' She closed her eyes.

'You look exhausted.'

'I am, but not long now. I've finished work at least, and Owen runs around after me at home.' She opened her eyes and smiled. 'I hope that continues.'

'He'll make a great dad.'

'He's so excited. We haven't done much to the little room that will be the nursery but we've got the cot sorted, and he picked out one of those mobiles to hang over it when we were at Magnolia Gifts the other day. It has cute little grey and white elephants that go round and round and splashes of orange with an orange heart. We got the quilt cover for the cot to match, and it's gorgeous. And, more importantly, gender neutral.'

'I wonder what you're having.'

'I've no idea, but I love the element of surprise.' She grinned. 'I heard Owen and Noah talking the other day. It was weird hearing men talking about babies – I hadn't thought about them doing it, not like us women.'

'What were they saying?'

'They were speculating about the sex, possible names, big families, siblings, sibling rivalry.'

'It sounds like they were really getting into it.'

'They were.' She grinned. 'So did you get a chance to call Lachlan back while I made the tea?'

'I did.' She hesitated, unsure of how to feel about the latest development. 'He's set up a job interview for me.'

'Oh?'

'It's at the same hospital in the city where I was before.'

'Is that what you want?'

'I've said I'd go.'

'That's not what I asked.'

Carrie took a deep breath. 'I couldn't handle hearing about Megan, a baby I've only held a few times and whom I have no real connection with. The fact I couldn't handle that situation has made me doubt myself all the more. I worked my butt off to get the career I always wanted, and now it's all falling apart.' She didn't cry. She'd cried too many times since Lucas died so, instead, the tears balled up inside her like a big globule of fear. Fear of the unknown.

'Maybe go to the interview, see how you feel,' Rosie suggested.

'I guess.'

A big clap of thunder from the heavens above made both girls jump. 'Crikey!' Carrie looked out of the window. 'No rain yet but it's so dark. You wouldn't think we had such beautiful weather yesterday, would you?'

'I'll send Owen a text.' Rosie went to the hallway to get her phone. 'See where he's got to.'

When Noah pulled up Carrie opened the shutters and waved at him. She opened the window. 'You're mad, it's going to pour down soon.'

He dismissed her concerns. 'Just wanted to check the proportions for your woman shed, make sure I've got them right.' A spot of rain fell on his nose and made Carrie laugh. He looked like a startled cartoon character as he swiped it away.

She shivered. 'It's cold outside. I might light a fire, although it'll have to wait until Rosie has gone – she's overheating as it is, being a human incubator.'

'Hi, Noah.' Rosie came back into the room. 'Incubator is about right,' she said as both women kneeled on the sofa facing the window. 'Owen isn't answering his phone.' She rolled her eyes.

'Do you need a lift home?' Noah offered. 'I'm taking some measurements and then I'm done.'

'She doesn't want to leave,' Carrie laughed.

'I didn't, but actually I'm really tired now so I think I'll take Noah up on the offer.' When her phone rang Rosie darted out to the hallway to answer it.

'You'd better get on,' Carrie suggested, 'before you get soaked.'

Noah tipped his head and when he went round the back Carrie shut the window. 'Was that Owen?' she asked when Rosie came back.

'He's held up a few towns away, called in by the fire station. It's all hands on deck – the storm is wreaking havoc already. Electricity pylon down, strong winds.'

'That doesn't sound good.' Carrie looked out of the window again and she could see the tops of the trees moving far more than usual. 'It looks like Magnolia Creek is next on the storm's list.' She gazed outside a bit longer and when she turned back to Rosie her demeanour had changed. 'Are you OK?'

Rosie had a pained expression on her face, her hands either side of her tummy rubbing away the discomfort, and then she recovered. 'You know, that could have possibly been a contraction.' A huge grin spread across her face. 'I think I'll get home and rest up, perhaps get Owen to take me to the hospital when he's home, although they say not to come in too early.'

Carrie didn't know much about midwifery but it definitely looked like the very early stages of labour so Rosie more than likely had hours to go yet.

'I'm not sure you should be alone, Rosie.'

'Don't be daft. Owen's parents live around the corner from Rosie Cottage, remember, so they'll come over if I need them to. I just want to get some sleep, have a warm bath.

'Well, if you're sure.' She smiled. 'You scored well with your in-laws, they seem lovely.'

'They're really ni—' Rosie's words were replaced by a groan. Not a scream, but a low moan of pain as she put her hands on the mantelpiece, arms outstretched and head between them as she coped with whatever her body threw at her.

'We need to get you to the hospital.' Carrie didn't want Rosie to panic but the contractions looked to be coming hard and fast already and they had no time to waste. She wondered whether the pains had started hours ago and Rosie had dismissed them as mere discomfort or false labour.

The wind howled outside and rattled the window pane in the back door, making them both jump. The sky was completely overcast now and a light spattering of rain at the window signalled the heavens were about to open.

Carrie took control. 'I'm going to get Noah from the back garden and then we are both going to drive you to the hospital. OK?'

Rosie grunted in agreement, face pale, her mouth forming an 'o' shape as she tried to keep breathing through the pain. Before Carrie could move away, Rosie grabbed her arm. 'I'm scared, Carrie. This is too quick.'

She was right, it was, but Carrie couldn't tell her that and frighten her even more. 'I'll get Noah, we'll head to the hospital and call Owen on the way.' She ran outside but Noah couldn't hear her shouting. Thunder rumbled overhead and the rain teemed down all of a sudden, drenching her as she ran to the end of the garden.

'It's Rosie!' she yelled the second he looked up. 'The baby's coming – we need to get her to the hospital.'

Noah ran straight round to the front of the house. Carrie went back inside, helped Rosie up off the couch and, outside, Noah had started the engine and was ready to go. They helped Rosie into the back of the pick-up and Carrie sat with her because Rosie was so petrified she wouldn't let go of her hand.

Noah put the windscreen wipers on full pelt but it made little difference. 'I'll have to drive slowly, I can barely see.' He was almost shouting to be heard over the rain, a match for even the strongest of voices.

'Just get us there,' Carrie called from the back seat, consumed with worry at how close together Rosie's contractions were. 'I'll try Owen.' When Rosie told her the passcode to her phone Carrie tapped his name into the contacts but the phone rang and rang and rang.

'Owen, where are you?' she muttered under her breath, knowing it was futile.

'Did he answer?' Rosie begged, eyes closed, breathing hard.

'No answer yet, but I'll keep trying.' Carrie called four or five times, but still no luck, and all the while Noah drove on slowly, his vision impeded by treacherous Mother Nature unleashing her power in the skies.

'Damn it.' Noah smacked a hand down on the steering wheel as they got to the foot of the hill down from Carrie's house. Carrie could make out the corner where the vet's surgery was. Why weren't they moving any further?

'What is it? Noah, why aren't we moving?'

He turned to face both women. 'There are trees down all across the road.'

Carrie leaned through between the driver's seat and the passenger seat and as the windscreen wipers swished away another gallon of rain, she saw exactly what he meant. She swore in her head, knowing to do so out loud wasn't going to help Rosie, who was moaning in the background and shuffling around in her seat – a woman in labour, a woman who was terrified. And she wasn't the only one.

'Should we call an ambulance?' Carrie leaned as close as she could to Noah and when his face turned they were only centimetres apart.

His piercing blue eyes bore into hers. 'Do you think she has time for us to wait for them to clear the road and get an ambulance up here?'

She shook her head. What were they going to do? Rosie was having a baby. Two lives were in the hands of a paediatrician and a gardener, and it looked like they were on their own for the duration.

'Carrie, what are we going to do?' Noah's voice said more than once.

Carrie turned back to face Rosie, who was screaming in the back of the car. She'd gone to a place where she wasn't asking questions; all she could focus on was her pain. 'Turn the car around.'

'Go back to the house?'

'We don't have any choice. This baby is coming and it's not going to wait.'

Noah turned the car round in the narrow road, reversing, going forward, reversing again, until eventually they were heading uphill.

And now Carrie had a huge responsibility resting on her shoulders. And the fear of God ran through her veins.

Chapter Eighteen

Carrie tried calling Owen again but the more they knew he wasn't answering, the more it sent Rosie into a panic, and by the time they got back to the house Carrie knew she had to keep her friend calm.

'There's no way any vehicle can get through those trees,' Noah whispered the second they got through the front door and Carrie went to call the ambulance. She'd settled Rosie on the sofa, where she was now writhing around in an agony befitting any labouring woman.

He didn't need to tell her. She knew it already, but she dialled anyway. She was assured an ambulance would be sent on its way but the bottom of the hill wasn't the only place trees were down. The call handler took their address, but no sooner had she done so than the phone line went dead.

'What is it?' Noah's face mirrored Carrie's panic.

'The phone line, it's dead.'

'Are you sure?' He took the phone, pressed buttons – but nothing. A flash of lightning outside highlighted their faces, the terror that ran through their every limb.

Carrie found her mobile and dialled the emergency services but her heart sank when there was no answer and she checked the screen display to see there was no coverage. 'Don't panic, I'll try the alternative emergency number,' she rambled. 'That way the emergency services should get the call via any network that picks me up.' She wasn't sure who she was trying to convince right now.

'Well?' Noah was growing impatient and the groans from the lounge room were becoming more frequent, more urgent.

'Damn it.' Carrie put the phone down on the benchtop and stared at it. 'Still no coverage. I can't get hold of anyone – we're on our own.'

Noah ran through to Rosie but came back quickly enough. 'Carrie…'

Carrie was staring at her phone, frozen in panic.

'Carrie…come on!' He was behind her as she turned and looked outside into nothing but darkness. Magnolia Creek was bereft of light; their only company was the sound of the storms, the howling wind and the occasional bolt of lightning, evil in its delivery. Rain pounded the window panes to prove this storm had no intention of easing up.

'I'm not a midwife. I don't know how to handle this.' Carrie shook her head over and over.

'You know more than me, now come on!'

'I can't do it, I can't.' Rosie's yell from the other room planted Carrie's feet even more firmly on the spot.

'Carrie, I have no idea what to do.' Noah's voice softened but his breathing was hard. 'We can hope the ambulance crew get here on time but I'm worried they won't. Carrie, please, Rosie needs us.'

She slumped down against the cupboard, covered her ears at Rosie's wails asking where they were, shouting for help, begging to keep her safe.

She felt the warmth of Noah's hands as he tried to gently coax her palms away from her ears. She opened her eyes and looked into his. 'I can't do it, I can't.'

He kneeled down on the cool kitchen tiles. 'You can, Carrie. This isn't about Lucas, and it's not about Megan. It's not about either of them. This is about Rosie. This is about her baby. Owen's baby. I know you think you can't do this, but I'm telling you that you can.' He smiled at her and touched a hand to her face. 'I think if you had a choice between your baby being delivered by a paediatrician or a gardener, you'd most likely choose the first option.'

She closed her eyes, tipped her face so his hand was between her skin and her shoulder, but when Rosie yelled again she realised what she was doing. She jumped up.

'What do you need me to do?' Noah looked ever thankful she was finally getting a grip.

She froze, but only for a moment longer, and then it was all systems go. And as she called through to Rosie that she was on her way, she yelled out words to keep Rosie informed, words designed not to make her panic, anything she could to keep Rosie calm and herself mentally ready for what was about to happen. Because she had no doubt this baby was coming, fast.

'I'm getting my first-aid kit,' she called out. 'Noah is getting towels…the ambulance is on its way…don't worry.' The ambulance would never be there in time, but Rosie didn't need to know that. Carrie darted around her new home pulling together everything they needed. Noah kept Rosie calm but when Carrie was still upstairs he took the steps two at a time to find out what the delay was.

'What are you doing?'

'I can't find my first-aid kit.'

'I don't think it'll do much good, and we don't have time to worry about it. Carrie, come on!'

She followed him down the stairs and grabbed the rug from the library. It was still wrapped up in its cellophane waiting to be unrolled when the light fitting was finished in the lounge. She hadn't wanted it to have a stepladder placed on top, or drill dust caught up in its fibres. She unrolled the rug in the middle of the lounge room floor.

'I'll ruin it,' Rosie shrieked when she saw what Carrie was doing.

Her concern made Carrie smile. 'I'm not thinking about that right now, Rosie.' Carrie tore bin liners from a roll and laid them out flat, put clean towels on the top of those and helped Rosie up off the sofa and onto the floor. 'Rosie, I'll need to take your trousers off for you, and your undies. Is that OK? I need to see what's going on.'

Even Rosie managed the twitches of a smile. 'Hey, I know we're friends. But this is kind of personal.' She grimaced as her body reminded her of who was in charge.

Carrie removed the garments and propped Rosie's head and shoulders up with a couple of pillows. 'You're much better off on the floor. I can see what's going on without cushions and arms of the sofa getting in my way.' When she squeezed Rosie's arm reassuringly Rosie grabbed hold of her hand.

'Carrie, I'm scared.'

'Me too.' She looked at her friend, then at Noah, all three of them wrapped up in this together. But she was the one with the medical knowledge, the only one of the trio who could take control, and she had no choice in the matter.

Beside them she had placed towels. She told Noah to wash his hands, up to his elbows. She did the same, scrubbing them over the kitchen sink as the wind angrily rattled the window panes. She dried her skin with kitchen towel and used the small hand sanitiser from her handbag, liberally, paranoid about spreading germs in a less-than-ideal environment for a girl giving birth for the first time. But as she rubbed the hand sanitiser in the groaning changed to a scream and she darted back into

248

the lounge, where Rosie was no longer writhing side to side but was lying on her back very much ready to give birth here and now.

'Hold her hand, Noah,' Carrie instructed. 'It's OK, Rosie. We're both here for you.'

'I want Owen.' Tears streamed down her face.

'I know you do, and he'll be here when he can.' She'd sent him countless text messages. She was as anxious for him to arrive as Rosie was. 'Just breathe, you're doing really well.'

'Oh my God, I want to push!' Rosie yelled.

Carrie checked and told her, 'I can see the head.'

'Really?' A look of elation was superseded by the onslaught of further contractions.

'Not long now, Rosie. Your baby is coming.' Carrie didn't have the same knowledge or training as a midwife or obstetrician and she hoped she was doing and saying all the right things. She had no intention of letting Rosie know a single one of her doubts, though, because this woman and child were relying on her. She couldn't let them down, she just couldn't.

'Can you push, Rosie? Push for me.'

'I can't do this, I can't.' Rosie tilted her head to Noah's arm, her forehead against his skin, and Noah cradled her cheek with his strong hands, telling her that yes, she absolutely could.

'The baby is coming, Rosie.' Carrie urged again. 'It's not the way you planned, but your body is built for this, remember. You can do it. Come on, push.'

Rosie pushed and the head emerged further. 'That's it, you're doing brilliantly. Stop pushing, pant instead.' Carrie was aware she was shouting, but tried to dial down her panic. 'Pant for me, that's it,' she encouraged when Rosie did as she was asked.

Carrie checked around the baby's neck but felt no signs of the cord. She almost collapsed in relief, but the job wasn't over yet. 'Can you give me one more push, just a small one?'

Rosie looked defeated but with Noah's encouragement the baby emerged further and Carrie was able to ease the shoulders out one at a time. 'Almost there. Once more, Rosie. Come on, we've got this.'

Rosie shut her eyes and gave one more push and Carrie felt the baby slither into the towel already covering her arms.

Rosie's relief was short-lived when she didn't hear the baby's first cries. 'What's wrong? Why isn't my baby crying?' She looked to Carrie, to Noah, and back again.

Carrie couldn't speak. She'd wrapped the towel around the baby and she massaged its body with the material to stimulate its breathing. As though nobody else was there, she breathed close to the baby's face. 'Come on, little one.' She rubbed again, blocking out Rosie's panic. And in those few moments, when she and Rosie made eye contact as though this was a real-life nightmare, when she and Noah looked at one another in sheer terror, the baby took its first cries.

'Thank God, thank God, thank God,' Carrie said over and over.

Noah suddenly shot up off the floor and Carrie was aware of footsteps before the ambulance crew and a midwife filled the room. She handed the baby to its mother and Rosie took the first peek beneath the towel. 'It's a boy,' she said to Carrie, crying almost as much as her little baby was.

'It's a boy,' Carrie repeated, only happy tears filling her eyes now.

Paramedics busied around them but Carrie couldn't hear any of it. She gazed at mother, at baby, the bond immediate, the power of something that happened every day taking place in her own lounge room here in the quiet, unassuming town of Magnolia Creek.

And then Owen was there, but as soon as he saw Rosie, the smile on her face, the bundle of joy in her arms, he kneeled down beside them both: their little family. Safe and intact.

Carrie crept away to the bathroom vaguely aware of the ambulance crew talking about the storms, the trees that had rendered the roads impassable, the fire brigade that had cleared the roads. Owen was a member of that crew, completely unaware of why the ambulance needed to get right through. He hadn't answered his phone, his mind had been on the job.

When Carrie emerged from the bathroom upstairs, Noah was sitting on the bed. The lamp was on, a soft light glowed, and the rest of the house was quiet. Even the wind seemed to have died down and the rain left them alone for now.

'The ambulance has gone,' he said.

She sat down beside him. 'Are they going to be OK?'

Noah put his hand on hers. 'Thanks to you, they're both going to be just fine. Owen went with them, said he didn't want to be around when you saw the state of your new rug.'

Carrie grinned. 'Typical men, making jokes in a terrible situation.'

'Hey, it's not a terrible situation. It might have been, but because you were here it wasn't. You were amazing, Carrie. You took control while I sat there terrified.'

'You told me I could do it, you said I had to.'

'I was literally shaking. Remember what I'm like with blood?'

'I'd forgotten about that completely.' She covered her mouth to stop the laughter, the release giggling gave her. 'There was a lot of blood.'

'I know, but I wasn't going to leave either of you.' He raked a hand through his hair. 'And to think, I only came here to measure up for a shed.'

'Kind of got more than you bargained for.'

'I'll say.' He looked at her with a fondness that catapulted their friendship into new territory.

'You don't fancy training up in a new midwifery career then?' she teased.

His brow crinkled. 'Do they even have male midwives?'

'Actually, they do. Not many, but it's not unheard of.' She reached for a hairband on the bedside table and wound her hair up away from her face. It tickled her cheek when a tendril escaped.

Noah reached out and hooked it behind her ear. 'I think I'll stick to plants – they're much easier to deliver into the world.'

'I still can't believe what went on here today.' She shook her head.

'Me neither. But we did it. Or at least you did it. You saved two lives tonight. You were in control in the end and the fact you were scared only goes to show how much you care. And it's not a criticism, believe me.'

Carrie knew tonight could've gone very differently. 'You're dishing out a lot of compliments. Does that mean you admit you were wrong about me?'

'How so?'

'Well, you called me a princess, assumed I thought I was better than anyone else, was afraid to get my hands dirty.'

He laughed. 'I don't think I could ever accuse you of that after tonight. So much blood.' He shuddered. 'OK, I admit that perhaps I was wrong about you.'

'So come on, I've divulged a lot of secrets to you lately,' she said. 'I want to know what *your* story is.'

He looked at her, perplexed. 'I don't have a story.'

'Of course you do. Everyone does.'

But before he could share anything, Carrie's phone rang. 'That could be Rosie or Owen.' She leaned back and snatched it up from where it was lying on the bed but when she saw the display and the name she walked over to the window. 'Hi, Lachlan.' She turned and Noah nodded to her, stood up and made for the stairs.

She didn't want him to go but Lachlan was talking in her ear. He'd heard about the storms, wanted to check she was OK, and so she had to take the call.

'You're not going to believe what went on here tonight,' she began, resigned to the fact that Noah had already gone.

Chapter Nineteen

'He's a gorgeous baby.' Carrie was sitting with Bella in the café and Bella was itching to visit the new arrival now he was home safe and sound, with mum and dad.

The storm almost a week ago, when little Tyler Harrison was brought into the world in less-than-ideal circumstances, was a distant memory. The winter sunshine came out in full force now they were into June, the roads had been cleared and, apart from a few damaged fences and patches of debris at the fringes of the main roads, in Magnolia Creek it was business as usual.

Carrie's new floors at the house had miraculously been saved with the sheets, towels and bin liners, and Noah had cleaned up by the time she'd finished on the phone with Lachlan that evening. He'd left her a note in the kitchen to say she was to let him know if she needed anything, but he hadn't hung around. And over the last few days things had settled into a strange kind of normal. Carrie had seen Noah walking Hazel, she'd fussed over the dog, she'd been watering her new lawn to keep it as nice as it had been the first day it was laid, and her back garden had weathered the storm better than she'd have thought. The pergola was still standing strong, Noah had replaced a couple of shrubs decimated in the storm, but other than that it was all still there, just as it was before.

Carrie finished her scone and cappuccino just as Gemma came into the café with Abby clutching at her trousers and hiding behind her legs.

'Hi, Carrie.' Gemma tried to use her arm to bring Abby around to the table.

'Hello Abby, why are you hiding?' She smiled at the little girl when she popped her head around her mum's leg but Abby swiftly drew it back where it had come from.

'We've been to the gift shop, haven't we, Abby?' Gemma coaxed again.

Abby still clutched Gemma's trouser leg but stepped forward a little. She was holding on to two brown paper bags.

'May I take a peek?' Carrie asked.

Abby held out one bag and Carrie took out a sky blue Babygro with matching booties and gloves. 'It's gorgeous.'

'For Tyler,' said Abby, although she wouldn't make eye contact.

'Well, I think Tyler will love it. And the mittens are a great idea, do you know why?'

She'd piqued Abby's interest and the little girl shook her head.

'Tiny babies often touch their faces with their scrunched-up fists, like this.' Abby laughed when Carrie did her best impression of a newborn. 'When they get tired they put their hands to their faces, fuss about, but they don't realise their little nails can do so much damage. These mittens will protect Tyler, so it's a great choice for a gift. Are you going to see them today?'

Gemma sat down opposite Carrie and pulled Abby onto her lap. 'We are. Rosie declared open-house day today and said anyone could stop by so this little one' – she ruffled Abby's hair – 'couldn't wait to see the baby.'

'He's got Owen's dark hair, loads of it,' said Carrie.

'You're amazing, Carrie, you know that?'

Carrie coloured. 'I was just doing my job.'

Gemma guffawed. 'No, you weren't. You were in a terrifying situation and according to Noah, Owen, Rosie and everyone on this planet, you're a hero.'

'Oh, no, I'm really not.' Her mind went back to the days when Lucas had called her his superhero, the woman who would save him. 'Anyone else would've done the same.'

'You're being far too modest.'

Carrie popped the remainder of her scone topped with cream and jam into her mouth. She nodded to a second brown paper bag that Abby was still clutching. 'What's in that one? Something for yourself?' she asked the little girl, who leaned back against her mum.

Gemma pushed the bag towards Carrie. 'Abby knows she can't replace the photograph she tore up, but she hopes this goes some way to saying she's sorry.'

'I'm sorry,' said Abby as if on cue.

Carrie didn't open the bag, not yet. Instead she turned her chair and held out her arms. 'Come here and give me a hug.'

Abby obliged and after that cheered up immensely, wide-eyed when Bella brought over scones for her and Gemma.

Carrie opened the brown bag, reached in and took out something wrapped in tissue paper. She unwrapped it and found the prettiest white wood, carved-edged photo frame. 'Abby, did you choose this?'

With jam around her mouth, the child nodded.

'Well I love it, I really do. Thank you. Listen, I'd love to stay here and chat with you both, but I have an appointment.'

'Everything OK?' Gemma asked.

'Everything's fine. I have an interview to get to in the city. It's not for a while but I want to have a soak in the bath first, relax and get my head together.'

The corners of Gemma's mouth turned down and she shook her head, making Abby join in with the action.

'We don't want Carrie to move back to the city, do we? No, we want Carrie here.' When Gemma nodded, Abby mimicked her and collapsed into fits of laughter playing out their little skit.

'Let's just see what happens,' Carrie smiled.

'All joking aside, I really do wish you good luck with it – you deserve good things.' Gemma stood up and hugged Carrie. 'Let me know how it goes.'

'Of course I will.'

*

Carrie picked up the bottle of Jo Malone Pear and Freesia Bath Oil, undid the cap and inhaled the sensuous perfume. The bath oil was a gift from Owen and Rosie to say thank you. They'd also sent her an enormous bouquet filled with enough fragrant lilies, stunning pale pink gerberas and lush green foliage to fill three vases around the house now that the flowers Lachlan had brought were starting to wilt. She put the plug in the bath and was about to turn on the taps when there was a knock at the front door.

'Coming!' she called from upstairs, expecting it to be the postman or perhaps Noah come to finally deliver the shed he'd apparently chosen for her. The grass was already growing and she'd made up her mind to buy a small lawnmower and tackle it herself, or at least have all the equipment ready for a gardener to come along once a week and work some magic.

Still dressed but conscious of the time, as was the way when you had an impending interview, she trotted down the stairs, along the polished floorboards in the hallway and towards the main door that was propped open with a doorstop allowing air to circulate through the house via the locked fly-screen door.

As she approached she saw at once who her visitor was.

Her legs felt heavy with every step towards the front door but all too soon she was there, flipping the catch and opening it up.

'Hello.' The woman on the other side of the door, shorter than Carrie, dark-haired like her son and with the same soft green eyes, stood nervously waiting for Carrie to react. 'I know this must be a shock but might I come in for a moment or two? I have some things I need to say.'

Unsure, Carrie stood aside. She supposed this woman couldn't say worse to her than she already had the day Lucas died, when Carrie had been accused of not doing enough, told she'd never practise medicine again if this woman had her way.

As Lucas's mum, Brenda, stood in the hallway, her handbag looped over her wrist and hands clasped together, Carrie went into hostess mode. 'I'll make us some tea.' It would at least give her something to do. With her back to Brenda she waited for the onslaught, the accusations, words of blame, words of anger and regret, and claims of Carrie not acting fast enough to save her son. Carrie expected to hear Brenda tell her that months after the complaint was initially filed, then dropped, she was reopening it and Carrie should find herself a decent lawyer.

Carrie fully intended to lean up against the kitchen benchtop while Brenda said what she'd come here to say, but when Brenda's outstretched hand shook as she took her mug of tea, Carrie led them both through to the lounge.

'What can I do for you?' Carrie's words sounded so lame under the circumstances, but she wanted to get this over with. She wondered how on earth Brenda had known where to find her.

Brenda put her mug of tea onto the side table and fished in her bag for something. What she took out surprised Carrie so much she slopped her own tea on the knee of her jeans. She rubbed the liquid quickly, didn't care that it had soaked in; this was more important.

She took the photograph of her and Lucas, the same photograph that she had stashed away, held together with Sellotape. She looked down at Lucas's little face, grinning into the camera as though he couldn't squeeze out another ounce of excitement despite how sick he was.

'I don't understand.' Carrie's eyes filled with tears. 'Why bring this here? Why now? And how did you find me?'

Brenda pulled at the hem of her floral, knee-length dress, much too thin for the season, but it was a happy print, gave colour to a face that still showed the signs of grief months on and probably would forever more. 'It doesn't matter how I found you, but I'm glad that I did.' Her words took a while to come out. 'That photograph is one of my favourites. I know Lucas was very sick at the time, but somehow it captures who he was. It's been on my mantelpiece every day since it was taken.' She paused. 'I wanted to come here today to say how very sorry I am.'

'Sorry? I'm the one who is sorry. You trusted me – Lucas was my responsibility; I didn't spot the signs early enough.' She clutched her mug of tea and the photograph for support. 'You had every right to send me away from the funeral when I added to your pain by showing up.'

Brenda shook her head. 'No, no I didn't. It was rude, insensitive, and an action that came out of despair, not because I really blamed you. As a mother I will always blame myself, always think there was something I could've done. Should I have taken Lucas to the doctor sooner? Should I have insisted the doctors do more tests? Should I have had that one glass of wine when I was pregnant – was it that that gave him heart problems?' She noticed Carrie shake her head. 'I know, ridiculous trying to pinpoint exactly what could've been changed along the way, and not only that, but agonising. It adds to the pain, doesn't lessen it, and I've been beating myself up for a long time. I took it out on you, and I never ever thought for one moment it would've had a lasting effect.

'I feel so guilty,' she continued. 'I understand you took a lot of time away from your job because you were so affected by Lucas's death.'

Carrie instantly remembered this woman the first time she'd brought her son to see her. She'd been concerned, sure, but she'd also been full of positivity, her small mouth smiling so she didn't panic her son and her son putting a hand on his mum's arm as though to reassure her he was still OK.

Brenda reached for her tea and took a gulp as though she needed something to steady her nerves and her voice. 'I'm a florist, Carrie. I take payments for flowers over the counter, I chat with people on the telephone about how to make a magical order mean something to that special person in their lives. I have no concept of a job that stays with you day and night, where your mistakes make you accountable, where strangers can scream and yell at you that you are to blame, that they want to drag you through the courts and make you pay. I don't think people outside of the medical profession could ever understand what it is truly like.'

'I've been part of a baby-cuddling program, at a new hospital not far from here.' Carrie wasn't quite sure why she was telling Brenda this. 'We lost a baby the other day and it nearly finished me for the second time.'

'What happened?'

Carrie took a deep breath and explained as much as she knew. 'She was a fighter, we thought she was getting through, but her little body couldn't do it.'

'It must've been terrible.' Brenda didn't break eye contact.

'It brought back a lot of painful memories.' Carrie looked at the photograph and then at Brenda. 'I talked to a friend recently, I told him all about Lucas. I don't tell many people, but this person told me that for every loss there is, there are hundreds more children I would go on to save.'

'Your friend sounds very wise.'

'But I couldn't save Lucas.' Carrie nervously looked Brenda in the eye, something she hadn't done in a long time, and she realised what she needed from this woman was forgiveness, acceptance of what had happened. But Brenda had lost her child – how could she expect anything from her?

'No, you couldn't,' said Brenda.

Carrie waited for it. The storm to follow the calm. Brenda had been nice up until now but Carrie braced herself for news of a reinvestigation, another complaint, the blame landing firmly on her shoulders.

'Carrie, you couldn't save him,' Brenda continued. 'But nobody else could have either, not by the time anyone realised what was going on.'

Carrie's shoulders slumped. 'The body is complicated. We can be looking in one place and the problem is somewhere else entirely, it's like someone playing a mind game with you, and we don't always win.'

'You know, for Lucas, you did win.'

'How?'

'May I?' Brenda reached out for the photo Carrie was still holding. She looked fondly at it and, rather than sadness, Carrie saw joy ooze from every pore. 'This photo, that's how. He idolised you. You gained his trust, his respect. My little boy was beautiful inside and out and he never stopped shining in your company. You made the days he spent in hospital as special as some of those he spent out of it. You made him smile, you made him laugh, and I'm glad it was you and not someone who lacked your compassion, your empathy and your determination.'

Brenda wiped a tear from beneath her eye as Carrie did the same. 'Listen to me, I'm sounding all mushy now.' She took out a tissue and blew her nose. 'I suppose what I'm trying to say is that I'm sorry. I'm sorry I made you feel like you'd failed. You fought until the end and if Lucas had seen the way I spoke to you…well, he'd be ashamed of his mum.' She passed the photograph back to Carrie as they talked about the day it had been taken, some of the lame jokes Lucas had told them.

'He liked his joke books,' said Brenda. 'He decided when he got older he might like to be a stand-up comedian.' She grinned. 'I couldn't see it myself, but I wasn't going to crush his dreams, so we'd talked about the Melbourne Comedy Festival and how maybe one day he could perform there. We'd go and watch, you'd come along too, but we wouldn't eat or drink anything because we'd be laughing so hard.'

They let the memories settle, there in the lounge room on the soft furnishings and behind the brand new shutters.

'Will you return to work eventually?' Brenda asked.

Carrie gasped and looked at her watch. 'Damn!'

'What is it?'

'I have an interview…back at the hospital in the city. I have to get ready, stop on the way for petrol…'

Brenda stood up. 'Well then I must go.'

Carrie's heart melted. 'I'm sorry, it's rude, I know. I want to talk longer, I want to chat about Lucas.'

Brenda took both of Carrie's hands in hers as they stood in the lounge room. 'You get to that interview and get that job, because you're a good paediatrician, Carrie. Lucas said it himself and that boy…well, he never lied. I wish you all the luck in the world.'

Chapter Twenty

'Wow, look at you.' Noah whistled as Carrie climbed out of her car and onto the petrol station forecourt. Just outside Magnolia Creek she knew she didn't have enough fuel to make it all the way into the city. 'Not sure about the choice of footwear though.'

Her heart raced seeing him so unexpectedly. She looked down at her feet. Instead of a bath she'd had a speedy shower, then tugged on her clothes and flown out the door as quickly as she could, but she hadn't forgotten to grab some decent shoes. 'Don't worry, the thongs will be replaced by some fancy heels, but not for driving. I have my limits.' She smiled at him.

'I'm sure you do.'

His look sent shivers up her spine and she turned round to remove the petrol cap.

'Allow me.' Noah took the nozzle from the pump, inserted it and did the honours. 'Not because I think you're a princess and too good to fill up your car with fuel, but because you're immaculate and I'm assuming you're off somewhere important looking like that.'

'I have an interview, so thank you. I really appreciate it.' Dressed in a pinstripe trouser suit with a crisp white shirt, her hair pinned up in a chignon and makeup applied carefully, she was all ready to tackle whatever today threw at her. She felt unfazed now she'd seen Brenda and they'd talked. 'I don't want to fall at the first hurdle and turn up looking like a grease monkey.'

'I don't think that'll ever be possible.' Petrol glugged into the tank. 'How's the piano playing going? I heard you a while back,' he explained, 'and you're not bad.'

'You heard me?'

He nodded. 'I didn't knock; I didn't want to intrude.'

'I'm a bit rusty. I haven't played in a long time.' She wondered when he'd heard her, how long he'd listened for.

'It's a beautiful piano – it deserves to be played.'

'It was a gift, but I never really had much time for it, until now.'

Noah's grip changed when the pump clicked. He returned the nozzle and screwed on the petrol cap. 'That's the extent of my help; you'll have to take care of the payment.'

'Thanks, Noah.'

'No worries.' His gaze drifted up to hers.

'I had a visitor.' Her heart thumped at the revelation. 'Lucas's mum.'

He whistled through his teeth again and Carrie realised how familiar the gesture had become. 'How did it go?'

'It went well – better than I expected when I saw her at the door. And you were right: she didn't think those things she said, not really. She was angry, devastated. She still is, but she says she can see how it wasn't my fault.'

He smiled. 'What did I tell you?'

'OK, no need to look so smug.'

'Can I assume you'll go to your interview a bit more together than you might otherwise have been?'

'I feel like it's given me some closure. It was always hanging over me so now I feel I can tackle the interview as myself.' Whether *herself* was the same woman she used to be, Carrie wasn't so sure.

'So now you can move on, go back to where you were before.' He wasn't asking her. 'I'll bet Lachlan is made up you're going back. I never picked him out as much of a lover of the country.'

'No, he doesn't really appreciate it. I think he'll always belong in the city.'

'Good news for the hospital.'

'Yeah.' When their gazes locked again she looked past him to his pick-up. 'Is that Hazel I can see waiting for you?'

'She's my new recruit, goes everywhere with me. Although she's a lot livelier than Norma, given how much younger she is, and it's taking a bit of getting used to.' He seemed just as relieved at the turn in conversation as Carrie was.

'Is she behaving herself?'

He leaned against the bonnet of the Mercedes. 'She's not bad – needs a bit of training, but nothing I can't handle.'

'I went to see Tyler this morning.'

'I'm heading that way myself.'

'It doesn't seem real, what happened at the house.'

'No, it doesn't.'

She wondered if he was talking about the emergency that night or, like her, he was thinking about the connection between them both as they'd worked together.

'Let's hope that's the last of the storms and emergency baby deliveries in Magnolia Creek,' he agreed. 'So, you're really doing it?'

'What?'

'Going back to the city.'

She looked down at her feet, the red toe-nail polish that stood out against the white, sparkly thongs. They were the pair she'd been wearing when she first met Noah and the memory cascaded through her, making her jittery in his presence. 'It's just an interview; I don't know what I'll do yet. Do you think I'm ready to go back?'

His look softened.

'Sorry, I shouldn't be asking you. I should pull myself together and start making some decisions of my own.'

'You don't always have to do that.'

'What?'

'Operate as a one-woman band…people need people and I'm guessing you're no different.'

'I was brought up to be independent.'

'Let me guess. Top private school, all girls, all high achievers.'

'Well, yes, you're right.'

'Nothing wrong with that,' he said, 'but also nothing wrong with being anything outside of the norm. School shapes you but real life knocks out all the kinks and makes you into the person you are.'

Before she could saying anything else, some guy yelled from the truck behind. 'Get a room! Just give her one, mate – move it along and we can all get home! Today!'

Noah grinned and waved a hand to the man in the truck queuing up behind Carrie's car. 'You'd better go and pay. And good luck.'

'Thanks, Noah.'

*

'It's great to see you back!' Stella ran into Carrie in the corridor of the hospital. 'How was the interview, when do you start?'

'Slow down,' Carrie laughed. It was strangely settling to see so many familiar faces and comforting to have so many people ask her when she was returning to work permanently. 'The interview went well and they offered me the position.'

'That's fantastic – I'm really happy for you.' Stella tugged off her pager from where it was clipped on her belt and looked at the display. 'I've got to run. But keep in touch.' She was walking away already. 'We'll do lunch, the second you're back in the city.'

Carrie couldn't deny it. She'd actually missed the buzz, the busyness of the job. The interview had gone really well. It was for a year's contract in the same position she'd had before, so same job description with similar responsibilities. The blip in her career hadn't really taken anything away at all – in fact, Carrie felt as though it had strengthened her resolve. She'd even ended up telling the interviewer about Lucas, about how she'd coped, how she hadn't. She'd been forthcoming about Megan, too, and when she was offered the position on the spot, Carrie wondered if her honesty and tell-all approach was what had swayed it in her favour. She'd been completely open, not because she had to be but because she wanted to be. Acknowledging the past was the only way she would be able to move past it.

Carrie met Lachlan and they made their way from the hospital, through the buzz of the city, over to one of the restaurants they'd been to plenty of times before. Tucked away in a side street, they shared tapas and doctor-talk until it was almost time for him to get back to work.

'How's your friend and her baby?' He ate the last olive stuffed with goat cheese when Carrie declined.

'Rosie and Tyler.' She smiled. 'They're both doing really well. It was thankfully a straightforward birth.'

'I bet you're the talk of the town,' he beamed. He'd always held her in high esteem and seemed comfortable now she was in his life the way she'd been before.

'I think I might be, you know. I don't really like it though. I'm not good at being in the spotlight.'

'Well, you deserve to be. I bet Rosie is grateful she was with you rather than anyone else.'

Time to change the subject. She hadn't told him the extent of Noah's involvement that night and she didn't really want to. 'I had a visit from Brenda today.' A smile broke out across her face – she couldn't help it. She would be forever grateful she'd seen Lucas's mum again.

'Who's Brenda?'

'Lucas's mum.'

'Ah, yes.' He leaned forward, conscious to keep everything above board when it came to his career. 'I did get in touch with her, but only the once and she was under no obligation to contact you. I was breaking the rules and I wasn't entirely comfortable.'

'But you did it. You did it for me, and you've no idea how much it means to me. Seeing her helped me get through the interview today and I can see a way forward, at last. Why are you grinning so much?' He didn't seem all that interested in the details of Brenda's visit.

He dabbed his mouth with his napkin and reached across the table for her hands. 'I'm very proud of my girlfriend, that's all.'

'Lachlan…' In the moment, the way he was looking at her, everything seemed to fall into place; at least, everything apart from one thing. Noah. Because he was the man she'd confided in, who'd helped her work through her feelings. It hadn't been the grand gesture of making contact with Brenda, but he was there to talk to, to listen, to understand. Carrie knew Noah's words were what had helped her to even contemplate coming back to the city for the interview, even before she saw Brenda.

When she'd first passed through those corridors of the hospital, remembering her time here before, it had been Noah's voice saying she could do this, Noah who was in her head.

'I have something to show you.' Lachlan took out his phone and, oblivious to her confusion, passed it to Carrie.

She looked at a photo of a stunning house with a stone façade and imposing tall windows.

'Scroll through to the right,' Lachlan urged.

She did as he suggested. 'It's gorgeous. There's a pool!'

'Impressive, isn't it?'

She nodded, because she knew exactly what was coming. Or she thought she did.

'I bought it,' Lachlan announced.

OK, she hadn't been expecting that. Maybe a suggestion they look at it together, think about buying it when she started her new job. But he'd leapt in and gone ahead with the purchase without so much as a word.

Another grand gesture.

'It's for us,' he said excitedly. 'It's kind of a compromise. It's not apartment living, it's not country living, it's something in between. You're going to love it, Carrie. It's got a huge kitchen, all mod cons, even a built-in coffee machine. What do you think?'

Carrie was stunned. This grand gesture was working the wrong way. He was trying to win her heart over, but instead it was doing the opposite.

'I know it's sudden, but I feel like you've turned a corner in the last few weeks. It's like the old Carrie is back again, the one who knows what she wants. I'll rent my apartment out – I've got the finances to do so – and with your little holiday house up in Magnolia Creek we'll have quite the property portfolio.'

He seemed to have everything organised but the next part of his plan took her completely by surprise.

He reached down and put a hand into the pocket of his jacket, which was hanging on the back of his chair, and out came a small, black velvet box. All Carrie could think was grand gesture, grand gesture, grand gesture!

He opened the box. 'Carrie, will you marry me?' He took her left hand, pulled it towards him, so confident of her answer. 'We always said we didn't need to make it official, but I want to show you how committed I am.'

This was everything she'd ever wanted. The city life, the job she'd worked so hard for, the partner working his way along his own successful career path. She'd have a getaway cottage up in Magnolia Creek, a house in one of Melbourne's most prestigious suburbs. She'd have everything, except…

'Carrie, you're making me nervous.' Lachlan looked to the next table because people were beginning to notice the sparkling diamond still slotted into its soft cushioning, the outstretched hand that had yet to slip it on.

'I'm sorry, Lachlan.'

'Sorry for making me nervous, or sorry for not wanting to marry me?' Self-consciously, not a state she ever saw him in, he closed the box and covered it with his hand.

'I could marry you, Lachlan. But…you deserve more.'

'That's funny, because I thought you were what I deserved.'

Carrie had turned down dates before, she'd finished with guys when things weren't going all that well. She'd seen disappointment, she'd seen anger, but never before had she ended it with someone she'd thought was so right for her for such a long time.

'When I met you I couldn't have been happier,' she began. 'But when I lost Lucas —'

'Oh, for God's sake. Would you give that up already! We all lose patients, it doesn't go away, it's part of the job. I find it hard sometimes, but you have to carry on. It's what we all do in our profession. How can you not see that?'

She gritted her teeth and hoped his insensitivity was more to do with being hurt than being so callous as to brush the loss aside. In the whole time they'd been together she'd never known Lachlan to refer to a patient's family. He talked about people in medical terms, as though they were characters in a case study rather than real people. But then he was a great surgeon, he was top of his game. Maybe that's how he did it, how he got through the day, and you couldn't fault him for his professional performance.

'When I lost my patient, it knocked me sideways,' Carrie began, because she needed to be completely open with him. 'And, yes, I got too emotionally involved. But, you see, on the one hand the loss has hardened me to cope if…when it happens again, but on the other hand it's made me see that it's the type of person I am. I can't shut down my emotions; I can't just taper them off. I can't pretend I'm OK losing a patient, one whom I've spent many hours interacting with and getting to know. It would be a lie and disrespectful to the career I'm trying to build. I went into paediatrics because I had a passion for it, and I think that passion came from deep down in here.' She put her hand across her heart. 'I can't apologise for that. I thought it was wrong, I thought it was me and my inability to cope, but it was my individual way of preparing for the road ahead, sending me back to a career I love and enabling me to grow stronger.'

'And what does this have to do with why you won't marry me?' People in the restaurant were no longer staring, they were going about their business as usual, eating their meals and chatting away as though the man on the next table hadn't just proposed and wasn't in the process of being turned down.

'Getting away, up to Magnolia Creek, really let me take a good look at my life – where it is, where I want it to be.'

'So you don't want the big house in the suburbs now, or the career you've worked so hard at.'

'I still want the career, although I'm giving it a year here in the city and then I'll know how I feel, whether I still want that pace of life or whether I want to rethink and perhaps head out to a country hospital.'

'Has Serena offered you work?'

She shook her head vehemently. 'Absolutely not, she knows you wanted me back here and I don't think she'd ever try to poach me.'

He smiled at her then. 'You're too good for a small hospital. You need to be in amongst it, use your talents.'

'I'm not rushing into anything.' She fiddled with the napkin still in her lap. 'I think a part of me went away from this life here in the city because my home life wasn't right either. Perhaps deep down I knew we wouldn't be good together long-term.'

'So you've turned all country now and want to have chickens, take up gardening and have a bunch of kids.'

'You're getting ahead of yourself. I'm not sure about the chickens.' When he grinned she remembered the easier times, when they'd had a good laugh together and their relationship was uncomplicated, until life threw something into the mix that only highlighted their incompatibilities. 'I never wanted to hurt you, Lachlan, please know that.'

The waiter delivered their bill and Carrie wondered how much he'd heard of their conversation. Had he appeared by coincidence or did he sense that their meal as well as their time together had just come to an end?

Outside the restaurant Lachlan pulled her to him. 'Maybe when you're back in the city you might see things a little differently.' He planted a kiss on her lips that all of a sudden felt completely wrong. His confidence irked her. It was as though everything she'd just said had meant nothing. He was hurting, she knew, and he did love her. Who else would put their career on the line and contact a patient's mother to help their girlfriend through one of the most difficult times in her life, to ensure she didn't throw everything away?

'Lachlan, there's no going back.' She put a hand to his face and for some reason, feeling she had no other choice, she told him, 'I've found a happiness that I never thought I'd find. I was never looking for it before and it took me by surprise.'

'Carrie…' Exasperated, he shook his head, shoved his hands in his pockets. He pulled out the box containing the ring, confident again, as though every time he had a wave of superiority and she made it crash down, he could just build it right up again, knowing that at some point it would be epic in its proportions and he would win. 'You, me, a ring, a house…it's simple.'

He went one step further and took out the ring, lifted her hand and slipped it on her finger. 'Marry me, Carrie. I'd do anything for you – you must realise that by now.'

274

She did, but she kept picturing Noah's face every time she saw the glint of the diamond against the winter sunshine. She wiggled the ring off her finger. It was a surprisingly good fit and she wondered how he'd managed to do it. He was nothing but prepared.

When she passed him the ring he pushed it into the gap in the velvet cushion and snapped the box shut. 'Is this about him?'

'Who?'

'Noah.'

She couldn't deny she had feelings for Noah, but this was about so much more. 'It's not about Noah. It's about us, about our differences that we can't ignore. I know you bent the rules to get in touch with Brenda for me and I'll be forever grateful, but you deserve more than my gratitude.'

He seemed to mellow but not for long. 'Be honest with me. Do you have feelings for Noah? It's a simple yes or no question.'

Her hesitation confirmed it.

'The bastard.'

'There's no need for that. He's a good friend; nothing more has ever happened, I swear.'

'But you want it to.' It wasn't a question. 'He swore he'd back off.'

'What are you talking about?'

'Him, Noah! He came to see me, desperate he was. He begged – not a pretty sight for a grown man – for me to *pull some strings*, as he put it, and sort this mess out with Lucas's mum. He was so sure of himself – that he knew the woman had been so full of grief she would've said things she didn't mean. Should've heard him, Carrie, it was pitiful.'

275

'Pitiful he was trying to help me?' She tried to swallow the realisation that all along it hadn't been Lachlan but Noah who had instigated the whole thing.

'Quite frankly, yes. He's following you round like a love-sick puppy. He wanted me to help, and in return I made him swear he'd back off, leave you alone.'

'So I can't make my own friends now?'

'Friends, yes; friends who you want to turn into more, no.'

'You make it sound so calculated. I never planned on getting close to him.' She reached out to touch his arm but he swiped it away before she would make contact, as though she were a poison that could burn through his skin. 'Lachlan…'

He looked her straight in the eye. 'Goodbye, Carrie.'

Chapter Twenty-One

Even when ending a relationship is your decision, it still hurts. Deep down you know it's for the best, but all the history, the memories, the direction you thought you were heading in have changed and it isn't simply a matter of clicking your fingers for everything to fall into place.

Carrie had driven home from the city in a daze, pulling over just outside of Melbourne at a café where she spent a couple of hours drinking coffee, looking out at passers-by, thinking about the time she'd had with Lachlan, thinking about Noah and the lengths to which he'd gone to help her. Noah was completely different from any man she'd ever been interested in. The men in her life were usually high-flyers, confident and brooding, but Noah wore his heart on his sleeve, was down to earth and seemed content with what life gave him.

A place came up at nursery for Maria and after a busy few days baby cuddling and planning her housewarming party now the renovations were finished, today was Carrie's last day in her nannying job. She decided they'd mark the occasion with a stroll into Magnolia Creek, so, bundled up in their winter coats, she and Maria headed for town. Winter was well and truly in the air. Some days were glorious and sunny; other days saw the leaves whipping around your feet, the gentle breeze replaced by a biting wind that hinted at the cooler temperatures yet to arrive.

At the chocolaterie Carrie bought Maria a small packet of buttons and herself a steaming hot chocolate, which she intended to drink as she walked along Main Street. Maria had given up her daytime nap altogether now, but even if she sat in her stroller and didn't sleep, the trundling along the pavements with nothing but the fresh air and lulling sounds all around helped calm her.

Carrie left the chocolaterie, but with one hand steering the stroller, her other holding the takeaway cup, her driving skills were questionable and she collided with Noah, her hot chocolate sloshing out the spout of the plastic lid enough to spill down the front of his shirt.

'I'm so sorry!' With her free hand she bent down for the wipes stowed beneath the stroller. 'I should look where I'm going.' She hadn't seen him since that day at the petrol station, and her failure to deny her feelings for him when Lachlan asked had almost been an admission to herself too.

'Carrie, don't worry about it, it's fine.'

'No, no it's not.' Where were those wipes? She could've sworn they were in here a second ago.

'Carrie, leave it. I'm on my way to the fire station anyway; I'll be getting filthy dirty and, hey, I'm a gardener – I'm not supposed to look smart.'

'You've got a point.' She stood up and faced him. 'So you're doing the training today?'

'I told you Owen wouldn't let me forget about it. How did the interview go?'

She wondered what his reaction would be as she told him, 'I got the job.'

'That's fantastic news. I'm really pleased for you.' He held her gaze for a moment longer. 'I'd better get going or I'll be late.'

'Noah…' Her voice stopped him before he could escape. 'Will I see you at my housewarming tonight?' She'd dropped an invite through his door, in the middle of the afternoon a few days ago, knowing full well he'd be out at work.

'You betcha.' He smiled at her and went on his way.

She'd almost mentioned Brenda and his role in arranging for her to come up to Magnolia Creek and lay the past to rest, but she was scared. Scared that when she did, he'd tell her he couldn't help his feelings but there was no future for them as anything more than friends, they were too different, he wanted a family and she didn't. Truth was, she didn't really know what she wanted anymore. All she knew was that Noah was a man who didn't deserve to be messed around.

'Carrie...' Noah called out from way past the chocolaterie as Carrie had begun to push the stroller away in the opposite direction. Almost at the bend in the road, he'd waited for her to turn round before he hollered, 'When you get home later, there'll be a bit of a surprise for you.'

She clapped her hands together. 'My shed? Finally!' She put both thumbs up at him and Maria, chocolate squished all over her face, did the same.

*

Leaving Maria for the final time later that day was sad, but Carrie knew she was moving on to another stage now. She drove the short distance home, parked up outside, and rather than go in the front, excitedly let herself in through the new back gate to see her surprise. Noah had been there really early that morning getting everything ready.

She pushed open the gate and her mouth fell open. She walked slowly down the paved pathway at the edge of the garden towards the new shed. Which was actually a bit more than just a shed. The wooden structure was almost hexagonal and nestled neatly in the far left corner of the garden. It was painted with a sky blue colourwash and the trims on the half-glazed double doors that would open out onto the garden were finished in a rich cream.

Little boxes sat beneath the windows and already she could envisage putting colourful flowers in there. She almost wanted to run down to the florist's now and pick out something she'd like.

'Go inside.' She hadn't heard him come in the back gate, but Noah was suddenly there, right next to her.

'You gave me a fright.' She took in his clean-shaven jaw, the pale blue button-down shirt teamed with well-fitted jeans and a clean pair of leather Blundstones – not an outfit she usually saw him in, yet it was completely Noah.

He smiled back at her. 'Go inside.' He gestured towards the shed.

She turned the handles on the doors and pulled them open, stepped inside. The scent of the wood was intoxicating. 'It's nice and warm in here,' she said, marvelling at the structure, looking up at the ceiling, her hands tracing the walls as she thought about the home she'd created up here in Magnolia Creek, this cosy place being the finishing touch to her project. 'I can imagine sitting in here when the winter rain comes again, listening to it tapping on the roof —'

'Making a run for it to go back inside the house.' He laughed and she joined in.

'OK, mine was the romantic approach, you're being realistic.'

'Nothing wrong with that.' His gaze held hers until he beckoned her outside the shed. 'I took the liberty of adding a little touch.' He reached down beneath one of the window boxes, there was an almost imperceptible click, and the fairy lights he must've put up all around the doorway and beneath the roof line lit up like a million stars.

'Noah!' She grinned, she couldn't stop. 'It's beautiful. I don't know how to thank you.' She had plenty more to thank him for, but not just yet.

He looked away as though he didn't really want her thanks. He did all these things but never seemed to want to claim credit for any of them. It was as though they were all in a day's work for him. She was beginning to realise it was another quality that set him apart from the other men she'd known.

'Stay there, don't move,' she instructed, suddenly having a thought. He obeyed and she trotted across the garden, opened up the back door and when she came out she had the sign in her hand. She shut the doors to the summerhouse – it was way too fancy to call a shed – and hung the 'Woman Cave' sign across both handles. 'There, perfect. I can't wait to show the girls at tonight's party.'

'They'll all want one.' His smile reached his eyes.

'Speaking of the party, I'd better get organised or my guests will be here and I'll have nothing to give them to eat and drink.' She desperately wanted to talk about Brenda, about what she now knew, but it was a conversation she didn't want to rush. She needed to know exactly where each of them stood and where they went, if anywhere, from here.

*

'Carrie!' Gemma and Andrew arrived at the party first, bringing with them an enormous basket of chocolate samples. 'Happy housewarming!' Gemma held the basket over one arm and hugged her friend with the other. 'Andrew made far too many mini Easter eggs this year so these, believe it or not' – she nodded to the basket filled with a myriad of colour – 'are more leftovers.'

'Thank you, Andrew. I know how great they taste given how many I ate myself this year, and I doubt these will last five minutes once people spot them. Your chocolate is pretty legendary.' She took the basket through to the kitchen.

'This place is completely gorgeous.' Gemma was taking in all the finishing touches that had gone in since she'd last seen the place. She moved to the lounge and spotted the photo frame Abby had given Carrie. 'Isn't this…'

Carrie nodded. 'I managed to find a replacement,' she said, referring to the photo of her and Lucas.

'Andrew let her play with the coloured foil we wrap the eggs in, to make a big collage, and she was really concerned before she ripped it all up. I think she realises she can't destroy everything she finds. Or at least I hope she knows that now.'

'I'm so sorry. I overreacted, and she's just a kid.'

Gemma put a hand on Carrie's. 'I don't know anything about that photo. Maybe you'll tell me one day, but don't go apologising. Abby's young, she's resilient, she still loves you.'

'I'm glad.' Carrie smiled at Andrew, who had asked permission to have a nose around and had returned from checking out the upstairs. 'What do you think?' she asked him.

'You've done a wonderful job, you must be thrilled. I can't begin to imagine how much work it took to get the place looking like this.'

'Owen and Noah worked really hard; I'd recommend them to anyone.'

'Oh, no, don't go giving Gemma any ideas – at least not yet. Now, where should I put this?' He was still carrying the bottle of champagne he'd brought over.

'Wow, chocolates *and* champagne.' She nudged Gemma. 'No wonder you married him.' She smiled at Andrew and told him to pop it in the fridge.

'I'll love him more if he consents to us getting an adorable window seat in the bedroom, and a wood burner for the lounge.' She tried her luck with her husband and he laughed his way out towards the back garden, where everyone else was gathering.

The sun had given up a couple of hours ago but, thankful for the dry weather, Carrie had opened up the back door to let people mill in the beautiful garden. They'd come in if it got too cold but the Harrisons had lent Carrie two outdoor heaters so she had a feeling everyone would be just fine. Owen had helped put twinkly lights around the pergola too, and some were strung along the house beneath the guttering, and with the lights Noah had added, the garden came alive in the depths of the darkness surrounding the transformed little house at the top of the hill.

Rosie cradled Tyler in her arms when they arrived and sat in the lounge to feed him, and after everyone had oohed and aahed at the baby, Owen took over. He'd brought a BabyBjörn along with him, and watching him try to figure out how to put it on – let alone slot the baby in safely – kept many of the guests amused. 'I should have taken lessons from my brother Tom – he's a whiz with one of these things.'

Owen's parents, Jane and Michael, arrived with two enormous platters of all kinds of sushi, Mal from the gift shop brought a chicken salad as well as a guacamole dip, Bella had over-catered as usual and made two trips because she wasn't letting Rodney hold anything heavy for now. He'd shaken his head, clearly fed up with being mollycoddled, but Carrie suspected that, deep down, he was loving every minute of getting the attention and Bella was enjoying every second of giving it. Stephanie represented her family by coming along with her boyfriend, a German boy who seemed very pleasant and smiled a lot, and her parents sent their apologies but the Magnolia Tavern had to stay open for business. Julie from Magnolia House turned up, Carrie's sister and her husband came, and that evening it was a house full of fun, laughter and, above all, friendship.

The food was devoured, drinks were poured and savoured. Carrie did the tour of the house more times than she could remember, and everyone congratulated her on a stunning renovation, begging her to make it her proper home for good.

Part way through the night, as everyone congregated outside beneath the pergola, on the decking or inside the summerhouse, Carrie stood at the edge of the garden, climbed on top of a set of kitchen steps she usually had tucked away in the laundry, and clinked a spoon gently against her glass.

'Speech!' Bella hollered, as though Carrie was at a big wedding and people wouldn't know she was standing there unless they were told.

'Thank you, Bella,' Carrie grinned. 'Only a quick one. I just wanted to say a big thank you to all of you for coming along tonight.'

'Wouldn't miss a party for the world,' Gemma called across the garden from where she'd taken charge of baby Tyler and was sitting on the base of the pergola, cuddling him against her.

'Thank you for all the generosity: the food, the drinks, the gifts people brought me. I'm truly touched and I feel a real part of this town. It wasn't something I thought would ever happen. I was a city girl buying a house in the country, but you've all shown me that Magnolia Creek is something quite special, a place where people care about each other. Without being nosy parkers of course.' She raised a few laughs and even a round of applause. 'So if you'll charge your glasses, I won't run on any longer. Cheers. To Magnolia Creek and to all who live here.'

'To Magnolia Creek!' the crowd chorused.

Carrie stepped down off the stool but Bella was up next. 'You stay there,' she instructed before Carrie could walk away. Lucky for her, too, because when she wobbled, Carrie steadied her.

'How much have you had to drink?' Andrew called across the garden.

'Not enough!' Bella called back, steadier on her feet by now. 'Like Carrie, I won't drone on for ages with a long speech, but I felt I should say something. This girl…' She looked at Carrie with a fondness that took Carrie's breath away. '…is kind, thoughtful, generous and a real friend. And she's bloody beautiful and clever too. I'd hate her if she wasn't so damn nice!' The crowd roared with laughter this time. 'Here in Magnolia Creek we like to welcome strangers and treat them as our own. It doesn't always work with the tourists, but with Carrie, I feel like we've got a firm enough grip of her that she won't ever forget us. No matter whether she's here on and off and based in the city in that fancy job of hers, I know this girl is a keeper.'

Carrie felt tears form in her eyes. Nobody outside of her family had ever been so kind to her, given her such unconditional love. In the city, in her job, she was part of something amazing, but she was part of something incredible here, too. She'd never thought anything could be as big as her career, but it truly was.

'To Carrie!' the crowd chorused.

Gemma, Bella, Rosie and Carrie huddled together in a group hug and after she grabbed a big torch Carrie took them over to the summerhouse, where they chatted away making grand plans of popping the corks on bottles of champagne, being taste testers for Andrew's new chocolate recipes, gossiping late into the night the way old friends did.

'You girls have made Magnolia Creek the epitome of community life.' Carrie had positioned the torch on its end so it illuminated most of the summerhouse. She was sitting cross-legged on the floor, Bella was leaning against the doorway with one eye on Rodney outside to ensure he was OK, Rosie had shut her eyes, exhausted from sleepless nights but elated from new-mum euphoria, and Gemma sat down next to Carrie. 'I've had friends before, but they never went from friends to lifelong friends. Does that make any sense?'

'It does.' Gemma smiled at her. 'You've given your all to your career but you're only human, and I'm glad we found you.'

'Me too.'

'Me three,' Rosie muttered from where she was still lying.

Gemma giggled and tapped Rosie's foot with her own. 'You realise Owen's passing Tyler between the guests out there, don't you?'

'Fine by me,' she muttered, eyes still shut. 'The more the merrier.'

'You know we need to make another toast,' Bella announced. 'We haven't toasted the Magnolia Girls yet. And I think they deserve the biggest congratulations of all.'

All four of them raised whatever glass they had, whether champagne or water or in Gemma's case a white wine spritzer. 'To the Magnolia Girls,' they said in unison.

'I meant what I said out there, when I made my speech,' said Carrie, 'but I need to tell you…all of you…that without the Magnolia Girls, I'm not sure I would be quite so together right now. I would've hidden away up in this house, I wouldn't have realised how special friends could become. I could always rely on my family but it means so much to know I can count on any one of you, and in return I'd walk on hot coals for you guys.'

'Now I don't think that'll be necessary.' Bella, mouth with her trademark red lipstick, couldn't hide the wobble in her voice, the air of pride, the air of inclusion, a sense of belonging she seemed to want everyone in her presence to feel.

'Getting back to the workplace or anywhere near a hospital has been difficult for me.' Carrie looked down but then, head up again, she made eye contact with the others in turn. 'I never could've done it without your help. You made me realise I'm not less of a person for falling apart – I'm a much better person. In the city it was as though only part of me came to life, whereas here, you've got the whole Carrie.'

Gemma whistled through her teeth. 'That's a whole lot of Carrie.'

Carrie giggled. 'I won't ever forget you. Any of you.'

'Of course you won't.' Bella hugged her. 'We won't let you. Magnolia Creek is your home now, whenever you want or need it to be.'

'Thank you.' She'd tell them about Lachlan soon, but, for now, she wanted this to just be about her, about all of them. 'Did I hear someone mention Molly is on her way back to Australia in the next few weeks?'

Gemma grinned. 'She is. Andrew's overexcited already and Abby can't wait to see her. "Auntie Molly", she says over and over again each morning, and she's even got a calendar on her wall to mark off the days till she arrives. And I've already ordered her a T-shirt.'

Rosie piped up. 'Gemma here thinks she'll get Molly to come baby cuddling with us and it'll make her so clucky that she and Ben soon have one of their own.'

'It's true,' Gemma admitted. 'Although she's already a midwife so she gets her fair share of baby love. I think it's more that I want her to feel a part of things here.'

'I can relate to that,' said Carrie. 'You lot are like witches…good witches,' she added hastily, 'bringing people into your group, casting your spells so they don't ever want to say goodbye.'

Bella wiggled her fingers on both hands in the air. 'We have our ways. It worked on you after all.'

'I can't deny it.'

Rosie smiled. 'Molly had so many questions for me when she called after Tyler was born. Carrie, you can tell her all about delivering a baby on the lounge-room floor, and I shall tell her how amazing you were. Even Noah was impressive that night. I think he did well not to show me how terrified he must've been.'

Carrie smiled at the memory. 'He wasn't a bad support partner in my hour of need.'

Rosie sniggered. '*Your* hour of need. Really?'

'Don't underestimate how hard it was for me,' Carrie said, deadpan. 'While you were lolling about on the sofa there I was wondering how I was going to stop you from completely ruining my floors, my upholstery.'

'I don't know how you did it,' Rosie chided with good humour.

'Watch out – there's a man approaching the woman cave,' Bella warned.

Owen poked his head around the door. 'I hope I'm not interrupting.'

'You are.' Rosie had taken to lying down again, eyes shut as far as Carrie could see in the dim torchlight.

'Tyler's had enough,' Owen said, trying to see Rosie too, but they only heard her as she groaned and sat up.

'I guess that's me done,' said Rosie, hugging each of the Magnolia Girls in turn. 'These days, Tyler is the boss of me.'

'Don't you forget it,' Bella called after her. 'Actually, I'd better get going. Rodney should be taking it easy and we've been here for a while so I want to get him home. I'll tell him I have a headache.' She winked at Gemma and Carrie. 'Don't want him getting all uppity because he thinks I'm making a fuss.'

When the others left, Carrie brought the torch out of the summerhouse and she and Gemma shut the double doors. Some people had already left, Jane and Michael Harrison were calling it a night, Kristy had left to return to her own place, Mal said his goodbyes and Stephanie had already disappeared with her boyfriend.

Carrie dismissed all offers of help with the washing up as the crowd gradually peeled away and quietness fell around the house, but in the kitchen she surveyed the mess and almost wished she'd taken someone up on the offer. When she heard a noise behind her she turned to find Noah, the last remaining guest, leaning against the back door watching her.

'The summerhouse was a hit.' She scraped the remains of a winter salad into the bin. 'And the fairy lights all over the garden were spectacular.'

'You pulled off a brilliant party.' He shifted beneath her gaze. 'Come on, let me help clean up. You didn't let anyone else but I'd be happy to.'

She shut the back door. 'First, come with me.' She beckoned to him to follow her.

'Where are we going?'

She led him into the library. 'I don't want your help cleaning up, but you can get this wood burner going for me if you don't mind. I can fix us another drink. Tea? Coffee? Something stronger?'

'Tea sounds good.'

Carrie left the washing up and made the tea instead, and when she took both mugs into the library Noah was shutting the miniature door on the front of the wood burner. 'It shouldn't take long to heat the room up.'

Carrie passed him one of the mugs and they sat on the single sofa nestled in the bay window as the fire took hold and gentle flickering flames became more intense. The baby grand sat proudly in the middle of the room, offset enough that it didn't obscure the view of the wood burner from where they were.

'It'll get really hot in here.' Noah took a sip of tea and set his mug down on the coaster on the side table. 'Owen ran it a few times already, didn't he?'

'He said I'd appreciate him getting rid of the smell when I was out at work. It still has the faint chemical whiff of being new but it isn't too bad, is it?'

'Not at all.' He sniffed the air in case he'd missed something. 'Well done to Owen; he's a great guy – one of the best.'

'He is, and I'm glad I met him because I would never have come to Magnolia Creek otherwise. I never would've even thought to buy a property this far out of the city.'

'I never thought you could do country. From the day you turned up and I saw you with those immaculate white thongs on your feet, I gave you a couple of weeks at most before you hotfooted it back to the big smoke.'

'Is that so?' Her tone light, she asked, 'And now? What's your opinion of Princess Carrie these days?'

'I'd say the princess is reasonably down to earth. But she's going back to her kingdom, back to the city. All this will soon be a distant memory.'

'I'll be back, you know.'

'I think you will, but I think you'll base yourself in Melbourne. You took the job and I'm pleased for you. I guess I always knew you would.'

'Boy, you really know how to make assumptions, don't you?'

'It's true, you got the job.'

'I did, but it's a year's contract. I'll still be baby cuddling at the hospital near here, I still want to see the friends I've made, and I think the change of environment will help me know after a year how I feel, whether a quieter hospital or a city hospital is best for me.'

Noah lifted his mug and gulped back a few mouthfuls of tea.

'I need to talk about something with you.' The words were out before she could change her mind, because it was time they got everything out in the open.

'Go on.'

'I know it was you.'

'What was me?'

'You got in touch with Lachlan, pulled the strings that needed to be pulled to get in touch with Lucas's mum.'

'Ah, I did wonder how long it would take the boyfriend to blab.' He wasn't annoyed, more resigned to what must've happened.

'He didn't mean to let it slip.' Carrie remembered back to that day in the city after the restaurant, how hurt Lachlan must've been. 'But I'm glad he did. Why didn't you tell me?'

'I didn't do it to score points, Carrie; I'm not like that. I'm not university educated, rolling in qualifications with a job and a salary to startle the average person. I can't compete with that and I'd never try to.'

She was taken aback. 'Why would you ever want to?'

'It's obvious, isn't it?'

'You should never compete. Being yourself is the best thing you can do.'

'I agree.' He didn't break eye contact.

'I didn't like you much at first.' The upturned corners of her mouth gave away a fritter of amusement. 'But you've turned out to be a really good man.'

'I do my best.' His eyes twinkled with mirth.

'Don't joke, Noah. I'm trying to be serious and tell you how I feel. Because when I start my job I won't be around here much, and I feel like I need to get things clear before I go.'

'Do you have feelings for me?'

'Isn't it obvious?'

'It is, but I want to hear you say it, so I can get things clear in my own head.'

'I do have feelings for you, yes.'

What would Lachlan have to say about that?'

'Lachlan knows.' She felt him shift on the sofa next to her. 'The day of the job interview, he guessed.'

'So, a doctor and a mind-reader is he?'

She sighed because his comment was delivered without the usual undertones of amusement. 'You seem to have an enormous chip on your shoulder that gets in the way of letting normal conversation slip by you.'

'That's a little harsh, don't you think?' He knocked back the rest of his tea but Carrie wasn't going to let him escape yet.

She took off her cardigan. The heat in the room hadn't taken long to build from the wood burner. 'You used to call me Princess, you thought I was completely up myself, a snob, whatever…' She held up a hand to put a stop to any protest he might try. 'But even you admit that you were wrong. So I don't understand. Why do you still feel like you have to compete with men like Lachlan?'

He leaned forward, arms resting along his broad thighs. He clasped his hands together. 'Lachlan is one of your people. He gets what you're about and you do him. He can give you the big house in the suburbs, the wining and dining in the city, the life you've worked for and deserve.'

'Maybe it's not what I want anymore.'

He turned to face her. 'Can you honestly say you don't?' He mistook her hesitation for confirmation.

'Noah, don't go.' She put out an arm to stop him.

'I have to, Carrie. And you need to go back to the city, back to Lachlan.'

'Lachlan and I broke up.'

Her announcement took him by surprise but within seconds he'd gathered himself. 'I'll put this cup in the kitchen and walk home.'

Carrie followed him out and blocked the kitchen doorway once he'd deposited his cup in the sink. She really had changed, because the dirty bowls and glasses strewn across the benchtops didn't even faze her. 'What are you afraid of, Noah? You usually tell it how it is. Or at least you do when it's about someone else's life. But what about you? Why don't you see what's right in front of you? I've just told you I don't have a boyfriend anymore, I'm interested in *you*, and yet you still stand there and are prepared to walk away.'

He leaned against the sink and turned to face her, arms folded across his chest. 'I wanted to marry my childhood sweetheart,' he shrugged, as though the revelation was completely ridiculous. 'Crazy notion in this day and age but we met at sixteen, were still together at nineteen, and by the age of twenty-one, when most of my mates were sowing their wild oats, I wanted nothing more than to shack up with my girlfriend and stay that way. We were both from the country, our families lived nearby. It couldn't have been a more perfect picture in my mind.'

'What happened?'

'She found the city. She tried to encourage me to move there with her, while we were young. She insisted she still wanted me. Anyway, I stayed where I was while she went to university, moved closer to the city, and one night I turned up to surprise her thinking perhaps I'd closed my eyes to the possibilities of living somewhere else.' He took a deep breath. 'She was in bed with another guy. I yelled, I punched him, he ran off. My girlfriend and I fought, we screamed, and then we decided we'd give it another go. She lasted a week before she came to tell me she wanted to be with him, Phillip, and they were getting engaged.'

He harrumphed. 'I'd suggested marriage and she'd never been interested, yet here she was jumping into it with someone she barely knew. He was a hedge fund manager, whatever one of those is…the only hedges I know are out there.' He pointed into the blackness beyond the kitchen window and shared a smile with Carrie. 'Anyway, last I heard they were married, expecting a baby and settled in a suburb near the city. My parents stayed friends with her parents,' he said to explain how he knew all this. 'You know what it's like in a small town.'

'Has there been anyone for you since?'

His laughter bounced off the kitchen walls. 'Do you think I've been celibate for more than ten years?'

'Sorry, that was a ridiculous question.'

'I've had girlfriends but nobody has ever come close to being special. Not until I met you.'

Carrie's heart beat faster but plummeted when he spoke again.

'I know you say it's over with Lachlan, but I'm not sure it'll be over forever. You can't change so much, so quickly, Carrie, you just can't. I've been the same man for years. I live here, I do the same job each day, and I love my life. How do I know you won't get fed up and go back full time to the city?'

She couldn't answer that, because she didn't even know herself.

'When I saw Lachlan the other day, I was way out of my depth.' Noah's jaw tensed. 'I wasn't scared of him, but I knew he had the power, the upper hand, because of everything he is and everything he could offer you. That's why it wasn't so ridiculous for him to ask me to stay away, and I was willing to back off if you were going to be happy.'

'Noah, I spent a lot of time thinking I was really happy. I worked long hours, Lachlan and I were good together. We dined out, we had a group of friends, we holidayed in far-off places. But I think we were able to stay together because we barely saw one another.

'Do you know,' she said, watching Noah looking at the garden beyond, his back to her now as though it was the only way he could think of what to say next, 'I never spent as many hours alone with Lachlan as I have with you and Owen. Renovating this house, we were in one another's faces, climbing over each other – literally, on some days. If Lachlan and I had ever done that, we would've killed each other!'

She stepped forward and joined him at the sink, facing the opposite way with her back against it and her arm nearly touching his. 'Lachlan did love me in his own way, but he never saw me in the way you do.'

'Of course he did. He must've been worried to compromise his career by getting in touch with Brenda.'

Carrie shook her head. 'Lachlan has always been seen to be doing the right thing, but it doesn't necessarily come from the heart. I think it's how he came to be such a good surgeon. He does care but he has a drive that moves on past any of the other stuff, regardless of it sometimes, and that's what makes him great. But I think he needs a girlfriend who complements him, not one who stopped understanding what drove and motivated him a long time ago.'

Noah turned so he was leaning his back against the sink like Carrie. 'Did you buy a property because of what happened at work or because of what was going on in your personal life?'

'A bit of both. I was running away from everything. But what I didn't realise was that I was running towards something too, towards a different pace of life.'

In the gesture that had become familiar to her over time, Noah reached a hand up and rubbed the back of his neck.

She turned to look up at him. 'The truth is, I became scared of the unknown, frightened I couldn't do my job in the way I was supposed to. And it's you who made me see that my stress in my job, my feelings over Lucas…well, they aren't a weakness, they're a strength. I can't give you any guarantees Noah. I may decide in a year's time that I wholly want to return to the city, although being here now in my own home, I doubt that. But don't you see – you're the same as me in some ways?'

'What, I don't like to get my hands dirty?' He nudged her and it made her smile.

'You're happy here, you're content, but maybe you need to realise that not everything slots into neat little compartments in life; sometimes edges are fuzzy, shapes don't always fit, but it doesn't mean changes can't happen.'

'OK, you're speaking all clever now. I don't understand.'

'Don't joke.'

He hesitated but only for a moment. 'You and Lachlan looked right together. I'm worried I'll never be able to give you everything he could.'

'Appearances can be deceptive.' She let the silence hover between them. 'I always went for men who were either risky or top of their game and I was so busy building my career that I wasn't thinking about the future, at least not in my personal life. Leaving everything behind and running away, I was forced to take a step back, look at the bigger picture.' She allowed a glimmer of a smile to show through. 'I've always been confident, gone for what I wanted, and I guess that's what has made me finally tell you how I feel. But I'm not so sure of myself that I don't worry you'll always see me as different, you'll resent my commitment to my job if I work long hours, weekends, night shifts. It's not ideal for a good home life, and that's where I worry I won't be enough *for you.*'

'And what about a family?' Finally, he was being open with her and it was like a breath of fresh air. 'I've always been honest about what I wanted, perhaps too honest. It's one of my faults, so I'm told.' He allowed himself a tiny smile.

'I don't think anyone can say it's a fault.' She was still staring back at him. 'Right now, anything more than settling into a new job just isn't on my radar. But I'm not completely closed to the idea. Who knows what tomorrow will bring?' He'd gone silent again and she nudged him. 'It's not like you to worry about other men, be concerned about competition.' She grinned, hoping her humour would lift his spirits. 'You strike me as a take-me-or-leave-me type of Aussie bloke.'

'I am, usually. Except with you it kind of matters more. I guess it's the wanting what you don't think you can ever have.' He sighed. 'The man bought you a piano for fuck's sake. As soon as you said it was a gift, I knew it was from him. Do you know how much they cost? He took you on holidays, bought you anything you wanted.'

He'd bought her a house and a diamond ring too, but none of it mattered. 'There's more to life, Noah. Can't you see I'm scared too?'

'I could never offer the grand gestures that Lachlan can.'

'You kind of did.' When he looked at her quizzically she said, 'The shed. Kind of a very grand gesture, don't you think?'

He began to laugh. 'I suppose it is, but it's not exactly romantic.'

'I don't know about that.' She thought about her conversation with Kristy, how it was less about the gesture itself and more about the feelings behind it.

An owl hooted outside reminding them it was night-time. Carrie felt her mouth go dry. She'd laid her heart on the line but Noah didn't seem as though he wanted to make any move at all, now or ever. He didn't seem to be able to move past this assumption that he'd never be able to compete.

She heard him take a deep breath and braced herself for him to walk away, tell her that it was never going to happen.

But then, he was in front of her and he put his hands around the back of her neck, leaning down until their faces were inches apart. 'I guess it's time I told you exactly what I wanted.' He didn't look away. 'I've wanted you since the day I saw you half naked in your bathroom.'

She blushed at the memory but when she looked down he lifted her chin up again with his fingers beneath so she was forced to look at him and stay close.

'Do you think we can make a real go of this?' he asked.

She breathed in the heady smell of his aftershave and shampoo, not daring to say anything else out loud in case he was too afraid to do the same.

But when he lowered his lips to hers and kissed her, she had her answer. He was in this for keeps, just as much as she was.

Epilogue
Three months later

With winter enveloping Magnolia Creek and even hints of frost at the little house on top of the hill, Carrie had established a new routine. She worked longer hours in the city, where she'd rented a basic apartment near the hospital, and when she wasn't working she was in Magnolia Creek to spend her time at home.

Noah and Carrie had settled into coupledom nicely, with their time together shared between his place and hers, and Hazel even had a basket in the corner of Carrie's library where she could curl up beside the warmth of the wood burner, although a lot of the time she'd come and rest her head on Carrie's or Noah's knees wanting a fuss, making sure she wasn't missing out when they were together.

The Magnolia Girls were still a force to be reckoned with, although Rosie had her own baby demanding her attention so only made it to the hospital on occasion, but the team had an extra recruit now Molly had returned from the UK with Owen's brother Ben in tow. She'd been more than happy to don the Magnolia Girls T-shirt and become part of the crew.

Carrie, Rosie, Bella, Gemma and Molly were settled on a table by the window in the Magnolia Tavern.

'This is so good.' Rosie approved of her first glass of champagne in a long while.

'I take it Owen is on babysitting duty tonight,' said Bella.

'Not just Owen, but Ben and Noah too. They're having a boys' night apparently, Tyler included. All I can say is I'd love to be a fly on the wall if Tyler starts screaming like he's been doing for the last few nights.'

'I'll bet Owen doesn't waste any time sorting out a time when Ben can get down to the fire station and do his training,' said Carrie, aware of how much Noah was enjoying the camaraderie. He was yet to fight a real fire but the community spirit behind his involvement had pushed him this far.

'Fingers crossed,' said Bella. 'We can never have too many recruits.'

'Oh no, do not look at me!' said Carrie. 'I'm far too much of a princess to step into a burning building.'

Bella grunted. 'I might use one of my witchy spells, perhaps.'

'Don't you dare!'

'You sound like you're very capable,' said Molly. 'I still can't believe you delivered Tyler in such an emergency.'

'It's not something I want to repeat any time soon. I usually look after the babies *after* they're born.'

'Talking of which,' said Molly, 'I can't wait to get to the hospital for the baby-cuddling session tomorrow. I've got shifts at the hospital coming up, but this is something different.'

'It's really special,' Bella confirmed. 'They're such poor little mites, struggling away, and I know we're doing some good. Aren't you going to drink that?' She nodded to Molly's glass.

Molly shrugged the comment away, her fingers twiddling the stem of the vessel. 'I need to be introduced to Noah, Carrie. I met him once before, but it was a quick introduction on Main Street by the chocolaterie and that was it, he'd had to race off to a gardening job.'

'He's lovely,' Bella claimed before Carrie could say anything.

'He's very cute.' Gemma whispered this, in case anyone in the pub could overhear these women talking like a group of school girls.

'We'll have you over for dinner one night,' said Carrie. 'I'd like to meet Ben too. All I know about you both is that you're this jet-setting couple who share your time between Australia and England.'

Bella's brow furrowed. 'What *is* going to happen long-term? I assume you can't go on like it forever.'

Molly couldn't disguise her smile. 'Well, actually, we have come to a bit of a decision.'

'Oh, please say you've chosen Australia, please…' Rosie gripped Molly's arm.

'Actually, we have.'

Rosie squealed. 'I know you're not officially my sister-in-law, but you're as good as!'

Bella darted around the other side of the table and hugged Molly tight while Gemma stayed put, giving away the fact she must've already known.

'Abby is beside herself,' said Gemma with a smile that spoke of her excitement too. 'She can't wait to see more of Auntie Molly.'

'I have an idea!' Bella's eyes brightened. 'Noah could move in with Carrie, and he could sell his place to Ben and Molly.'

'Steady on!' Carrie giggled. 'We've only been together five minutes!'

Bella waved a hand to dismiss the claim. 'I know a good match when I see it.'

Molly nudged Carrie. 'Relax, Gemma and Andrew have kindly offered to redecorate the annexe for Ben and me while we look for our own place. You don't have to live with a boy just yet.'

'Thank goodness for that,' Carrie laughed.

'Oh, I almost forgot.' Gemma reached into her bag. 'I got these.' She passed a set of paint swatches to Molly.

'I only told you last night!'

Gemma shrugged. 'Abby and I went to the paint shop this morning – we couldn't wait.'

'I bet Andrew is thrilled.' Bella turned to Gemma.

'He is.' She put a hand on Molly's. 'But he's conscious of how Molly's parents will feel. He called them last night to talk as soon as she told us the news, and they're actually really positive.'

'Saying goodbye was hard,' said Molly, 'but I think they'll either do a lot more travelling or they'll move over here themselves at some point. My brother is in America,' she explained to Carrie, 'and they have no real ties to keep them in the UK.'

'I guess the deciding factor could be if one of you gives them a grandchild.' Bella lifted her champagne glass to her mouth but it didn't make it all the way. 'You still haven't touched your drink, Molly.'

Slowly, one by one, their faces turned – even Gemma's, though she clearly knew this already and was having trouble keeping a lid on it.

Molly beamed. 'We're having a baby!'

Excitement erupted and it didn't take long to filter round the entire pub, with glasses being raised from all directions both by those who recognised Molly and those who'd never met her, and Carrie felt goose pimples travel up her arms at this town and home she'd discovered quite by accident.

When the door to the pub creaked open, in came Noah and Ben, closely followed by Tyler all bundled up in a furry jacket with his face squished against Owen's chest as he hung in the BabyBjörn.

'What's going on?' Carrie stood and kissed Noah, the warmth of his lips never failing to feel good.

Ben grimaced and told the girls about the last nappy they'd watched Owen change. Apparently it had contained something that wouldn't be out of place in a horror film.

'He was really unsettled,' Owen added wearily. 'Bringing him out in this thing was the only way I could get him to sleep.' He looked strung out as he patted Tyler's bottom beneath the material of the BabyBjörn and Carrie found it as amusing as the rest of the girls did.

'Three men and a baby!' Gemma announced, gleeful at her summation.

Bella cupped her hand beside her mouth and whispered to Carrie, 'I think she's had Molly's share of the champagne. Don't let her have any more.'

Ben must've told the boys his and Molly's news because Noah smiled at Molly and offered his congratulations, and Owen made some joke about how his little brother was going to know what it was like 24/7 sooner rather than later.

'I can't believe Owen's a parent and soon to be an uncle all over again,' said Noah as he and Carrie went to the bar and ordered a round of drinks.

'Things certainly have changed for him. I remember him as being the man least likely to ever settle down.' She smiled at Noah. 'People used to say that about me.'

'That you were the man least likely to settle down? Must've been the moustache that gave it away.'

'Hey, enough of your cheek or you can sleep in Hazel's bed tonight.'

Noah handed over the money for the drinks as Stephanie put together their order, her German boyfriend working with her like love's young dream. He planted a kiss on Carrie's lips, hooked an arm around her shoulders and pulled her close.

Carrie wondered how he'd felt when Ben had announced that he was having a baby too, because when Molly had told the girls, Carrie, for once, hadn't thought thank goodness it's not me. She hadn't necessarily thought *I wish it was me*, but who knew what the future held?

As Noah took the tray of drinks over to the group, Carrie followed behind. All of the friends were laughing and chatting. Owen was jigging up and down as Tyler woke and expressed his disapproval at being stuck in a baby carrier in the pub, Rosie had her bag over her arm and was clambering over the multitude of stools, which had been squeezed in to make room for everyone, in a bid to escape and become mum again, Molly and Gemma were deep in conversation, most likely about babies, and Bella was sharing a joke with Noah as he approached the table.

Magnolia Creek had become a part of Carrie in a way she'd never foreseen and no matter what direction they took after this, the Magnolia Girls would forever be a big part of her life.

And she had a feeling that Noah always would be too.

THE END

Acknowledgements

Thank you to my editor, Katharine Walkden, and to my proofreader, Edward. Books go through many stages from the first draft to the final copy and the story is always so much stronger by the time you've both finished!

Thank you, Berni Stevens, for another gorgeous cover that fits so well with the Magnolia Creek Series. Looking at the books lined up in a row is always such a delight.

Thank you to each member of The Write Romantics, a group of writers who offer support and advice along the way. It just wouldn't be the same without our virtual office!

As always, I couldn't be an author without the unwavering support of my husband and children. It's a job I love and hope to do for many more years with you all by my side.

Helen J Rolfe.

Printed in Great Britain
by Amazon